SOUL CONNECTION

A DEADLY OBSESSION

Marla Brooks

First Edition:
First printing

PUBLISHED BY HAUNTED ROAD MEDIA, LLC
www.hauntedroadmedia.com

United States of America

To those souls who have shared my journey in this lifetime and in the past, be mindful of the fact that this was no accident. These spiritual homecomings are carefully planned long before our bodies meet because when souls are destined to reunite there is nothing that can keep them apart.

PROLOGUE

October 15, 1862

The brief funeral service was over. Finally. The heavy-hearted mourners, cloaked in black, their faces tense with grief, or just deadened with disbelief perhaps, left the gravesite in small little groups. Adam knew that now it was his time to say that final goodbye without the eyes of the world displaying the sorrowful pity that always happened at times like this. He needed this private time.

As he stared down at the coffin, all Adam wanted to do was scream but he had no voice. He needed to cry, but there were no tears left. In a stinging twist of fate, this was the day he was supposed to marry Rachel Warren, not bury her.

Rachel had planned the perfect wedding and relatives from all over the country had come to witness the happy event. Not so long ago, there weren't many folks who would have been willing to make the long, hard journey by stage—no matter how grand the occasion, but just three years earlier, the first train from the East had arrived, and St. Joseph, Missouri, was now the western-most point accessible by rail in the nation, so they were able to come and share the moment.

Situated on the banks of the Missouri river, St. Jo was founded by Joseph Robidoux, a smart, personable fur trader from St. Louis. The settlement, which was incorporated in 1843 and named after his patron saint, was established as an Indian trading post but quickly expanded into a major trade center when the discovery of gold in California in 1848 turned the area into a boom town. Hordes of prospectors flocked to St. Joseph by steamboat where the city's location on the westward bend of the Missouri River made it one of two choice "jumping-off" points (the other was Independence, about 60 miles southwest), a fact that city promoters enhanced with aggressive advertising in the eastern press.

Gold rushers bought supplies for their westward wagon trek and it was estimated that as many as 50,000 pioneers passed through the city in 1849 alone. 100,000 more would crowd the streets bound for California and other points west before trains shrank the distance and took most of the pain out of the trip. The little town basked in glory once again when on April 3, 1860, a lone rider left on horseback from the gates of St. Joseph's Pikes Peak Stables carrying saddlebags filled with our nations hopes and dreams. The rider traveled 2000 miles west to Sacramento, California in what was to be the first ride of the Pony Express.

The residents of St. Joseph were extremely proud of their heritage, but standing alone in the cemetery grieving over his tragic loss, Adam's home town meant nothing more to him than a place of heartache and painful memories.

Adam and Rachel Warren met as teenagers at a church social. The Warrens had just moved into town, and Adam's mother insisted he try and make the shy newcomer feel welcome by asking her to dance. After all, she explained, how would it look if the mayor's son didn't live up to his civic duties?

The two young strangers danced like wooden figures with straight backs and arms rigid, holding each other far apart, barely touching. Each glance at Adam brought a red tinge to Rachel's cheeks and Adam fought the trail of perspiration that ran down the side of his face making his cheek itch. When the music ended, they took off in opposite directions without a second glance, though, Adam, looking back on it now, remembered that he'd nearly tripped in his haste to get away—and that embarrassed him even further.

That first night over and done with, and with a little help from fate, Adam found that being the same age as the most beautiful girl he'd ever seen, and being forced to sit just two seats away from her in the one-room school house, had been the beginning of a clumsy friendship--one that, over time, blossomed into young love. By the time Adam had asked Rachel to marry him on the night of their graduation, neither could imagine spending even a single day apart.

Then, just two days before the wedding, Rachel went missing. She'd been on her way to the final fitting of her wedding gown and was bouncing with excitement!   Just like Adam, she could not wait for the upcoming wedding. Her new life would be a dream come true.

But Adam knew something was terribly wrong when she didn't return from the dressmaker in time for dinner. He watched the sun make its tracks across the sky, unable to move, knowing that nothing would keep her this long. Maybe she'd stopped for another errand? To see a friend? No. This was not like her. The minutes felt like hours and the waiting became unbearable. As the sun shot forth that final orange glow on the horizon, he could wait no longer. Adam went for help.

The sheriff sat with his feet up on the makeshift table he used for paperwork, dining, and sometimes polishing his boots. He didn't seem the least bit concerned with the plight of Rachel as he yawned and then blew his rather large nose. He even went as far as suggesting that perhaps Rachel was suffering from pre-wedding jitters. Adam, angry that anyone would think that of his Rachel in this way, grimaced as the Sheriff advised him to go back home, be patient, and wait for any news.

Adam, who had been nervously pacing the floor suddenly stopped dead and glared at the sheriff in disbelief.

"Go home?" he sputtered. "Why? So you can shirk your responsibilities and take a nap? My God! Rachel is missing and we need to be out there looking for her!"

"Calm down, boy. I intend to do just that," said the sheriff rather unconvincingly as he reached across the table and grabbed his pipe.   Then, realizing that the bowl was cold, he pulled a single wooden match from his shirt pocket, flicked the head of the match with his thumbnail and proceeded to relight his pipe.

The sheriff's casual manner brought Adam to his breaking point and he charged at the sheriff, nearly knocking him off his chair.

"Don't just sit there! Do something!" he demanded.

9

This sudden burst of anger was returned in kind as the sheriff jumped out of his chair and grabbed Adam's flailing fists, holding his wrists tight.

"You have a choice, Adam," he said, finally showing some emotion. "You can either turn around and walk out that door and go home or you can spend the night in jail."

In the time it took Adam to walk the short distance back to his house, he knew it would be impossible to sit around doing nothing so he turned back and searched the town from one end to the other on his own.

His obsession with finding Rachel was so strong that he was running through town like a madman, darting in and out of businesses and asking everyone on the street if they'd seen her. He was oblivious to the odd and sometimes frightened stares he was getting in return and the fact that nobody had seen Rachel infuriated him even more.

Finally, around midnight, with no place else to look, Adam reluctantly went home and made himself a strong cup of coffee to try and stay awake but fell asleep out of sheer exhaustion on the living room sofa before he had the chance to drink it. Just after sunrise, he was jarred awake by the sound of someone banging hard on his front door.

Sheriff Marsh was staring down at the ground as the groggy young man fumbled to unlock the door. When Adam finally managed to get the door open, he took one look at the sheriff's pale and drawn face and immediately knew the news was bad.

"I'm so sorry, Adam," said the sheriff, shifting uncomfortably from one foot to the other. Knowing there was no way to sugar-coat the information he needed to pass on, he took a deep breath and then blurted it out. "We just found Rachel's body in an abandoned barn five miles out of town on the old Sloan property. Looks like she was murdered."

The shock of hearing that Rachel was dead was almost more than Adam could bear. He broke out into a cold sweat, began to shake uncontrollably, then fell to the ground as if he'd been shot. Sheriff Marsh rushed in, helped him up off the floor and then guided him gently to the sofa. The two men sat in silence for a few agonizing moments until Adam was finally able to find his voice. Then the words began to fly out of his mouth so fast, he hardly made sense.

"Are you sure she's dead? Who could have done this to her? How did she die? Why would anyone want to hurt her? What am I going to do without her? What are you doing to find the person who did this to her?"

Rather than trying to interrupt, Sheriff Marsh wisely waited for Adam to run out of steam before even attempting to respond and when Adam's words eventually turned into heart wrenching sobs, he put his arm around the grief-stricken young man and said, "Nothing can bring Rachel back, but I will get to the bottom of this and by God, justice will be served."

The crowd of mourners were now long gone and although Adam was expected at Rachel's parent's house for the requisite after funeral gathering, he was reluctant to walk away from her casket. Finally, one of the cemetery workers, who was anxious to complete the sad chore of burying the coffin, pulled Reverend Henderson aside and asked him to lead Adam away.

The good reverend had presided over many an unhappy occasion but the sight of the young man literally laying on top of the coffin with tears streaming down his face was a picture that remained with him for the rest of his life.

Tokens of the ill-fated wedding were on display all around town. Rachel's parents' house was filled with gifts that now needed to be returned, a beautifully decorated wedding cake sat abandoned in the front window of Mrs. Wilkins' Bakery and the town florist had been forced to perform the unpleasant task of transforming the wedding bouquets into a funeral wreath; all ugly reminders of what might have been.

Hours turned into days and days to weeks. In time, the residents of St. Joseph managed to overcome their shock and grief but the case was never solved and Adam never got over the loss of his beloved Rachel. Each day without her seemed like an eternity and instead of being able to get on with his life, he merely went through the motions of living. He ate because he had to, not out of hunger, only spoke when spoken to, and spent his nights dreaming of the life he and Rachel would have had together.

The pain of losing a loved one never goes away entirely, but Adam soon realized that Rachel would not have wanted him to pine away for the rest of his life and slowly integrated himself back into the real world. He went to work for his father in the Mayor's office. Politics suited him well, and when his father's second term was over, Adam took over the post of town mayor and devoted himself to civic duties. Despite his many opportunities to marry, he remained a bachelor for the rest of his life and in the years that followed, the once vibrant young man was transformed into a brooding senior citizen whose only ambition was to die peacefully and spend eternity with Rachel.

Unfortunately, his prayers went unanswered because when the time came for Adam to finally meet his maker, he was dismayed to find that Rachel was not waiting for him on the other side as he had expected. She had, in fact, already returned to earth to begin a new life. This was a cycle that kept repeating itself. It was an ongoing game of celestial cat and mouse. You see, Adam and Rachel were very old souls who had spent several lifetimes together over the ages in different incarnations. It is the same with all of us. We've all walked the path with our friends and loved ones before in both good times and bad.

In the case of Adam and Rachel, they both spent those interim times between their lives on Earth searching the heavens for each other only to find out that they were never in the same place at the same time. On some level, they both always knew they were ultimately destined to be together again, but in the process, they had to endure many eternities never finding each other but forever searching.

CHAPTER 1

Kerrie heard the phone ring while she was fumbling for her keys at the front door, but she'd just been to the grocery store and her arms were overloaded, greatly limiting her dexterity. Once she finally managed to unlock the door and dump the bags on the kitchen counter, she and checked her messages. There was only one call, from her best friend, Meg.

"Hi, it's Me," said the cheerful voice. "I just wanted to let you know that Jerry and I are going up to the cabin for the long weekend and we want you to come with us. We're leaving tomorrow morning around nine and will pick you up on the way, so pack a bag and call me back as soon as you can, okay?"

"No, it's not okay," sighed Kerrie as she quickly erased the message. She hated the fact that all her close friends were either married or in committed relationships and felt the need to drag her along like someone's spinster aunt whenever they made plans. After playing the part of fifth wheel on one too many outings, Kerrie had finally made up her mind that she'd rather stay home alone than be a "pity guest."

She wasn't enjoying the single life, but all the men she dated lately seemed to have at least one irritating shortcoming that drove her away. Tom was a bit of a mama's boy, Bill was way too serious, and Hank had the most irritating laugh she'd ever heard. He actually snorted! Everyone said she should try to lower her impossibly high standards just a bit and not dwell on the minor flaws but Kerrie was stubbornly holding onto the belief that one day her prince would come, without compromise. Meanwhile, she was content to spend what little leisure time she had either catching up on her reading or renting movies.

Meg considered these solitary pursuits an enormous waste of time, but Kerrie always defended her actions by explaining that because she was a freelance writer, it was her job to keep current with the latest films and hottest celebrities, but in recent months she'd become less focused on the current batch of new releases and more in favor of British imports. In fact, all Kerrie watched these days were Brit flicks, with the exception of the few American films that happened to feature her favorite English actor, Andy Dickinson.

While he was now middle aged and his old nickname of Dandy Andy wasn't used quite as often, Dickinson enjoyed a prolific career, was always in the news and still quite popular with the ladies. It was more than good looks that drew them in. The characters he portrayed on-screen were usually of a brooding, sensitive nature which brought out the nurturing instinct in his myriad of female fans. The tabloids regularly featured stories about Andy and his many loves, but because he had never married, there was also simmering speculation that the actor might be gay. The rumors didn't bother Kerrie or lessen her interest because she enjoyed his body of work, not just his body; but it wasn't until she saw him play the part of an angst driven man searching for a lost love that she began to take particular notice. For some reason, he very much related to his heartfelt characterization.

At first, it was almost as if she was the one he was looking for in the movie and it seemed so surreal. And from then on, every time she saw Andy Dickinson, whether it was on the big screen, on a tv talk show, or even saw his name in the paper, she felt connected to him in a way that she couldn't understand. This had nothing to do with her merely being an adoring fan because it wasn't in her nature to swoon at movie stars. But the fact was, she could not keep Andy Dickinson out of her thoughts.

She bought all of his movies and watched them over and over again. Her friends began to worry about her 'Dickinson Obsession' as they called it, because it was so out of character for her. Although she wouldn't admit it to anyone, Kerrie was a bit worried herself, because she had recently developed an overpowering desire to actually meet the actor.

"I've read that Andy Dickinson is an egotistical womanizer, and I can't figure out why you've put him up on a pedestal," said Meg one recent afternoon when the friends met for coffee. It seemed like every conversation they had lately either began or ended with something to do with the actor and this afternoon was no exception. Kerrie had just told Meg about her plan to contact Andy Dickinson's manager and try to set up an interview. She had already pitched a story idea about him to one of the magazines she regularly wrote for, and since the actor was slated to soon be knighted by the Queen, her editor thought it was a timely idea.

"Don't you think you're setting yourself up for a big disappointment by trying to actually meet the guy?" asked Meg. "What if he turns out to be as big a jerk as they say he is?"

Rather than admitting that there was a real possibility of that happening, Kerrie went on the defensive. "You actually believe all that tabloid trash? You know as well as I do that lots of unscrupulous hacks make a terrific living writing fairy tales about famous people, but nobody in their right mind really believes them. Besides, I don't think Andy Dickinson will disappoint me at all."

Although Kerrie's editor gave her the go ahead to do the story, he had also warned her that Andy was notorious for turning down most interview requests. Kerrie found this to be true when she emailed a query to his manager the following day and got a speedy reply. "While Mr. Dickinson was flattered by your request, he is currently out of the country shooting his latest film and must regrettably decline. He thanks you for your interest and wishes you all the best in your endeavors."

Even though rejection was part of Kerrie's job description and she had been turned down many times before, she was usually able to take these refusals in stride. But being turned down by Andy Dickinson's people was truly devastating and she brooded for days, eating very little, ignoring the phone and marathon watching his movies. It wasn't that she was lovesick, exactly, it was more like frustration because she knew that somehow, some way, she needed to make a connection with him.

Kerrie was worried that she might be developing some sort of unhealthy attachment to the actor, so she called her longtime friend Ted Stephens, a noted psychic, and made an appointment to see

15

him. She hoped Ted might have a logical explanation as to why she was so captivated by the elusive Mr. Dickinson.

The following afternoon, Ted greeted Kerrie at the door with a big hug. "It's so good seeing you again." he said warmly. Then, standing back to get a better look at her, his joyful expression abruptly changed. "You look wonderful on the outside, Kerrie, but your aura concerns me. It's a bit murky today."

In psychic terms, a person's aura is a good indicator of their emotions, so Kerrie wasn't at all surprised that hers wasn't as bright and vibrant as it should have been. "I've had a lot on my mind lately, and was hoping you'd be able to help me figure a few things out." she explained. Then she went on to tell him about her recent concerns about Andy Dickinson.

"Ah yes, the mystifying Mr. Dickinson," said Ted, with a knowing look. "He's been a client of mine for many years and he usually stops by for a reading whenever he's in town, but come to think of it, I haven't seen him in quite a while."

"That's probably because Andy's been all over the world filming back to back movies, so I guess he hasn't had much of a need to find out whether or not he's going to be gainfully employed any time in the future," she laughed. "That is why he comes to see you, isn't it?"

Ted chose his words carefully before finally answering. "You know I can't breach client confidentiality, Kerrie, but without going into great detail, I can tell you that Andy first came to me because he's living with some very bad Karma. He's a very old soul who has lived many lives, and is dealing with a very traumatic experience from his last incarnation that he cannot seem to get over," said the psychic. "But then I suppose living with all that angst is what makes him such a wonderful actor. He truly is a tortured soul."

Kerrie was fascinated by Ted's revelation. "Well, he must be spreading some of that angst around because I'm feeling a little tortured myself these days, and it's all his fault."

She wished Ted could go into more detail, but she knew that he protected his client's privacy above all else and that code of ethics was what allowed the psychic to be a trusted advisor to some of the most famous and powerful people in the world.

"Maybe we should do a past life regression on you," he suddenly suggested. "They're quite helpful in learning a little more about who we are and why we act and react the way we do, and in many instances, being able to discover a problem from the past helps clear up issues we face in our current lives."

Kerrie was a little wary, but Ted assured her that the benefits of such a reading would far outweigh the risks and promised that if she began feeling uncomfortable or seemed to be experiencing any unpleasantness, he would end the session immediately.

A few minutes later while Kerrie stretched out on the comfortable leather recliner in the psychic's office, Ted, placed himself into a light trance. Then he suggested that she take a couple of cleansing breaths to relax and told her to allow her mind take her wherever it wanted to go.

Kerrie closed her eyes, and for a few seconds looked as though she was taking a peaceful nap, but suddenly her eyes popped open and she began to look around.

"I'm right here with you, Kerrie," said Ted in a soft but reassuring tone. "Can you tell me where you are?"

"I'm on my way to the dressmaker for the final fitting of my wedding gown," she boasted. "Adam and I are going to be married the day after tomorrow and I want everything to be perfect."

"And what year is it?" he asked, pleased to see that she seemed to be extremely happy.

"What a silly question," she giggled. "It's 1862, of course."

"Yes, I know that probably was ridiculous of me to ask, but I just wanted to make sure," he explained. "Can you tell me a little about yourself and where you are right now?"

"Well, my name is Rachel Warren and I'm nineteen years old. I was born in Kansas City, Missouri but we moved here to St. Jo when I was fourteen." She then began telling Ted about the tall trees and dense brush and the smell of pine needles that filled her senses. She sighed, thinking to herself how she loved the solitude here and told Ted about the new house Adam's parents were building for them in the country as a wedding present and how magnificent it was, surrounded by nature. They would be far enough away from the city that the hustle and bustle would not interfere, but close enough so that at a moment's notice, she and Adam could interact with their friends.

The name Adam sounded familiar to Ted, but he wasn't sure why.

He listened while Kerrie chatted on a bit longer, then, without warning, her cheerful demeanor was gone and a look of fear darkened her expression. The change was so abrupt that Ted worried she might be reliving something very traumatic and immediately decided to bring Kerrie back and end the session.

Normally, he would have let the regression continue a bit longer, but a warning deep inside him was so strong, he hastily cut the session short and brought her back as gently as he could.

"So, what did we find out?" she asked, after she was fully awake. "I'm not liking the look on your face, so please don't tell me I'm the reincarnation of Lizzie Borden or someone equally distasteful."

"Far from it." he assured her, trying very hard to mask his great concern. "You went back to the 1860s, your name was Rachel and you were on your way to try on your wedding gown."

"That's it?" she teased. She knew Ted well enough to know when he was covering something up, and this was one of these times, but she also knew better than to force the issue, so she played along. "No juicy details about the love of my life or our honeymoon plans?"

"We'll leave that for our next session, although I'm not sure I want to hear about the honeymoon," he joked, but not very successfully. He needed time to work all this out in his mind, so rather than having Kerrie come back immediately, he put her off for a few days. "How about next Tuesday at the same time?"

Over the next few days, Kerrie didn't give much thought to her regression other than being thankful in knowing that in 1862, at least, she had been in love. She couldn't wait to find out all about her husband and how their lives together played out, and in all the excitement, she'd all but forgotten about Andy Dickinson, the reason she went to see Ted in the first place.

"Okay, now close your eyes and relax," said Ted, as Kerrie settled down on the couch at their next session. "Let yourself go back in time, anywhere your spirit wants to take you." He watched with interest as she peacefully drifted off at first, then suddenly sat straight up and looked quite confrontational

"What are you doing here?" she demanded from the person she was now talking to.

Trying to ascertain which incarnation Kerrie was reliving, Ted gently interrupted. "Tell me your name and what year it is."

Kerrie looked agitated. "My name is Rachel and it's 1862."

"Are you alone?" asked Ted.

"I was until *he* showed up," she said, pointing an angry finger at someone only she could see.

"Who are you with, Rachel? Is it Adam?"

"No, it's that horrible Martin Smith, and it's a good thing Adam isn't here or he'd beat Martin to within an inch of his life."

"Why? What did Martin do wrong?" asked Ted.

"He insulted my honor, that's what," she said, sounding very self-righteous. "He was sitting next to me in church last Sunday and had the unmitigated nerve to reach over, take my hand and place it on his knee. And in God's house!"

Ted could hear the outrage in her voice, so he answered back calmly. "What did you do then?"

"What could I do? I pulled my hand away and slapped his face in front of the whole congregation," she shrieked. "He's been nothing but trouble since the day he found out Adam and I were engaged, following me around like a puppy dog and sending me love letters. Why can't he just leave me alone?"

"And he's there with you now? Where exactly are you?"

"I'm on a back road on my way to the dressmaker and he just popped out of the bushes along the path. He's trying to talk to me, but I have nothing to say to him and I must be on my way."

Kerrie's arm suddenly raised up off the sofa. It looked as though someone had taken hold of it and was trying to pull her away. She then began flailing her other arm so wildly that Ted had to back away. At the same time Kerrie looked down and her eyes widened as if she'd just seen something horrible. When she opened her mouth to scream, her voice was muffled. She struggled to get off the sofa but it appeared that she was being held down.

Seeing that she was in some kind of trouble, Ted's first instinct was to abruptly end the session, but he felt it was important to find out what was going on. "Rachel, what just happened?"

"H-He dragged me into the bushes and pushed me down on the ground!" She was having trouble continuing because she was now sobbing uncontrollably, but against his better judgment, Ted urged her to continue.

"He's torn my dress he's telling me that if he can't have me, nobody will!"

Ted could see by Kerrie's body language that Rachel was trying to fight Martin off, and he wasn't the least bit surprised to see angry marks developing on her arms from his grasp. Then her body looked as though it was being pushed into the couch by a heavy weight, as if someone actually was on top of her. Kerrie struggled to push this invisible force off of her and then her eyes opened wide and she let out a blood curdling scream before she fell suddenly silent.

Ted was horrified. He had never witnessed such a spectacle during a regression and he felt guilty for letting it go on so long, but he had to know the truth and broke the silence.

"Rachel, tell me what happened. Where are you right now and where is Martin?"

"He's just run off and I'm lying here in the bushes," she cried, "but then how can that be when I'm standing here looking down at myself at the same time?"

Knowing that Kerrie had just witnessed her own death, Ted brought her back as quickly and gently as possible. "Kerrie, listen to my voice. Slowly open your eyes and take a couple of deep cleansing breaths."

"My god," she said, gingerly trying to sit up with great difficulty. "I feel like I've been hit by a truck. My whole body aches, my neck is sore and I've got a terrible headache. What just happened?"

"You went back to 1862 again," he said softly. "and I'm afraid something happened to Rachel on her way to the seamstress."

Kerrie turned pale. She had a very fuzzy recollection that she had just gone through a terrible ordeal, and judging from the lingering feeling of fear and sadness she quickly figured it out. "I died, didn't I?"

Ted nodded and put his arms around her. He needed time to do a little digging through his files before coming to any firm conclusions but he was pretty much certain that he knew where he heard that story before.

"Don't give it another thought," he told her. "There are a couple of things I need to look into, and when I find what I'm looking for, we can talk more about it. Meanwhile, go home and take a nice long bath, and I'll call you later on."

As soon Kerrie had gone, Ted searched through his old files of client sessions. It didn't take long to find what he was looking for. As soon as he slipped the CD labeled "Andy Dickinson" into the player, he wasn't surprised to hear Adam Morgan finish the saga that Rachel had begun.

"I can't believe she's dead," sobbed Adam. "Who could have done such a terrible thing?"

After listening to the rest of the tape, Ted called Kerrie and carefully explained that her recent interest in Andy Dickinson now made sense because after to listening the tape of one of Andy's past life regressions, it was clear that Andy Dickinson was the reincarnation of her ex-fiancée Adam Morgan.

"Love is an emotion that bonds us through the ages," he explained, "but not everyone can recognize those who we have loved before. Something in your soul has allowed you to feel the deep love you had for Adam when you look at Andy.

"Then I definitely need to get in touch with him," she insisted. "Can you give me his address or phone number?"

"Any contact information I have on Andy is probably out of date by now, but even if it wasn't, you know I couldn't give it to you anyway. Besides," he warned, "you can't just call someone up and introduce yourself as their murdered bride-to-be back in 1862. They'd probably have you arrested."

"Then you need to try and get in touch with him for me."

"You know I'd do anything in the world for you if I could," said Ted with a sigh, "but in cases like this, destiny is what will bring you and Andy back together if it's meant to be, not a mutual friend. If the time comes for the two of you to meet, you will. Until then, you must be patient."

"That isn't one of my strongest virtues, you know," she sheepishly admitted. "Do you personally believe it will happen?"

"I honestly don't know," he said, trying to sound diplomatic. "There are always opportunities for two souls to reunite during subsequent lives, but it depends on a great many factors such as desire, necessity, or Karma. If you and Andy are fated to meet up with each other in this lifetime, it will happen when it's supposed to. Meanwhile, you must not attempt to alter destiny."

"I'm not trying to change it exactly, but couldn't we give it a little nudge? You could call Andy and tell him about my regression and remind him of the reading you gave him and maybe he'd remember who I am and want to meet me. I heard he's going to be in Los Angeles soon."

"I'm sorry, Kerrie, I can't interfere, and neither can you," he warned. "Now that you know why you're so drawn to Andy Dickinson, I suggest you put the whole thing out of your mind for the time being and get on with your life. What will be will be."

Later that evening, Kerrie made a decision to go against Ted's advice about not contacting Andy, but chose to go about it in a rather unorthodox manner. She remembered Ted once telling her that it was sometimes possible to communicate with people on a psychic level, but that information also came with a warning. "It is unspeakably bad Karma to try and interfere with another person's free will by attempting to draw them to you by any means," the psychic once told her, but at the moment, Kerrie didn't much care about collecting any negative Karma. All she knew was that she didn't want to risk losing the love of her life again, so disregarding Ted's warning, Kerrie attempted sending mental messages thru emotive telepathy or "emotional transfer" to Andy several times a day.

Kerrie would sit quietly and meditate for a few moments until her mind was clear and she was fully relaxed. Then, staring at a photograph of Andy, she would look deep into his eyes and express her desire for them to be brought together again. During these sessions she encouraged him to try and remember his life as Adam, to remember his love for Rachel and to please get in contact with Ted for another session when he got back to Los Angeles.

She had no idea whether or not she would be successful, but was diligent in her efforts nonetheless.

CHAPTER 2

"Okay everyone. That's a wrap!" shouted the director, and if Andy Dickinson hadn't been in such a foul mood, he might have been tempted to do cartwheels. After three months of filming on location in the scorching Las Vegas sun, he was anxious to get back to cool, rainy London. Ever since arriving in Sin City, the unnatural dry heat and high temperatures of the desert were affecting him both mentally and physically.

"Just walking out of the hotel and into the desert heat is like going from a freezer into a bloody blast furnace," he complained to one of his co-stars after the first day of filming, and that was before the record high temperatures kicked in a few days later. Las Vegas was experiencing a heat wave like no other and to say that Andy was hot under the collar would have been an understatement in more ways than one.

Two days into the shoot, he broke out with a horrible, itchy heat rash on his neck that drove him mad. The medic on the set gave him cortisone cream to quell the itch, but the necessity of having to wear makeup during filming all but negated the cream's healing effects and the itchy and then slightly oozy malady had turned Andy's usually calm, professional demeanor on set just the opposite. He became short tempered and uncooperative and wasn't the least bit friendly to cast or crew. By the end of filming each day, the on-set tension was so thick it was palpable.

To make matters worse, because he had already completed most of his key scenes back in London, there really wasn't a whole lot to do to keep Andy occupied when he wasn't needed on the set and while the rest of the cast and crew looked forward to partying every night, Andy felt that Vegas was a merely a caricature of a city with no real substance, and a complete waste of time. The bright lights, noisy casinos, and free flowing liquor weren't the least bit appealing, nor were the ongoing stream of beautiful women who paraded around attempting to lure him into spending the evening with them. In a town that centered on tempting vices, the only saving grace to Andy's "paying penance in this ungodly place" was the number of new, elegant, five-star restaurants that had recently changed the culinary landscape of Las Vegas from gluttonous All You Can Eat buffets and 50 cent shrimp cocktails to food that was actually fit for human consumption.

Andy was a professed gourmand and looked forward to his nightly fine dining experiences with great relish, but in the past couple of weeks, even that had lost its charm when he began having disturbing nightmares and thought that perhaps all the rich food was to blame.

He wasn't about to lower his standards and eat at lesser establishments, so Andy begrudgingly made a conscious effort to choose his menu options more carefully. Instead of the rich sauces and fatty meats that he considered to be his guilty pleasures, he compromised and added lighter fare to his menu but the dreams persisted despite the change of diet and his work began to suffer.

Andy had always prided himself in being a quick study and, like the consummate professional, he was known for getting out his scenes in just one take but lately, much to his chagrin and the frazzled nerves of his co-workers, "One Take Andy" was no more. Due to his lack of sleep he was either flubbing or forgetting his lines altogether on a regular basis, sometimes having to repeat the scenes three or four times before getting it right, and this turn of events only served to make him even more difficult to get along with as his frustration level was at an all-time high.

Each night Andy would wake up several times quite suddenly, and with a feeling of dread. Unlike most recurring nightmares where a person relives the same terrible dream over and over again, Andy's night terrors were more story telling in nature than repetitive. Each new dream picked up where the last one left off.

The first offering in the series been confusing. He was dreaming that he was asleep on a sofa in some strange house. A loud pounding on the door woke him up. He watched the door bow in like some horrible thing was on the other side. He didn't want to answer it but had to had to…didn't he? Wasn't that the way of dreams? One had to do it?

As he walked to the door, a calendar on the wall caught his eye. It seemed to jump out at him and for a brief second, it took away his fear of what was on the other side of the pounding door. He could see that it was October 13, 1862, and a big red heart was drawn around October 15, reminding him that it was just two days before his wedding. Inside the heart, "Rachel Loves Adam" was written in very feminine script. But the banging wouldn't stop and another voice inside his head screamed that something was very wrong! And then he remembered. Rachel was missing and bad news about her disappearance was right behind the door.

He had to find out and cautiously reached for the doorknob, steeling himself for news he knew he didn't want to hear.

The grim expression on Sheriff Henderson's face wordlessly telegraphed the young man's worst fears and Andy woke up in a cold sweat, screaming loud enough to wake the dead.

The story of Rachel's murder subsequently unfolded for him over the next four nights. The dreams were so upsetting, Andy tried staying up later and later each night in the hope he'd be too tired to dream once he did fall asleep, but the nightmares continued nonetheless. The fifth night's offering was the most horrifying of them all.

Andy found himself standing in the back room of what must have been a mortuary next to an older couple that he somehow recognized as Rachel's parents. A motionless human figure covered by a crisp white sheet was lying on an examining table just a few feet away.

Mr. Warren stood frozen, staring down at the table in disbelief. Mrs. Warren's head was buried in her husband's chest and she was sobbing uncontrollably.

When a somber-looking man wearing a black suit slowly approached the table and carefully uncovered the lifeless body, Mrs. Warren took one cautious look and then fell to the floor in a crumpled heap. She was hoping beyond hope that the mortician had made a mistake in identifying the young girl's remains and the horror of recognizing her own daughter was too much to bear. Both Mr. Warren and the mortician ran to her aid but ignoring the drama unfolding around him, Adam slowly approached the table and looked down at his lost love. He, like Mrs. Warren, had prayed that this was a case of mistaken identity, but it was not to be so and he had to grab hold of the table to steady himself when he saw her lying there and knew that his worst fear had come true.

Even though Rachel's expression was peaceful, the clearly visible contusions and abrasions on her face and neck told the tale of a needless, horrible death and Adam's heart broke in two thinking about what she must have gone thru in those last precious moments of fighting for her life.

Suddenly, the pain turned to rage at whoever committed this unspeakable act of brutality and Adam awoke to the sound of himself screaming at the top of his lungs like a wounded animal.

The nighttime horrors stopped after that terrifying revelation, but in their wake came the phantom voice.

"Andy, it's me, Rachel. Please come and find me. I need to see you."

At first, Andy tried to dismiss the unsettling phenomenon as an overactive imagination but over time, the familiar voice grew louder, bolder and more frequent, often popping into his head while he was on set and causing many delays in production when Andy, who seemed preoccupied most of the time would repeatedly flub his lines and then had to excuse himself in the middle of a scene to go "clear his head."

Finally, the director took him aside and asked what was wrong. There was one final scene to shoot and everyone was anxious to wrap the film without further delay. Not wanting to risk sounding like a raving lunatic, Andy explained that he was feeling a bit under the weather and promised to see a doctor as soon as he got back to London.

None of it made any sense and Andy questioned his sanity on more than one occasion, but the more he tried to convince himself that he was just experiencing nightmare remnants, the more certain he became that there was more to it.

Andy knew it wasn't a doctor he needed and got in touch with Phyllis Mead the day after he returned home. Andy had met Phyllis when she was the technical advisor on a movie he'd worked on several years ago. A psychic detective by trade, she had a sterling reputation in the field and was delighted to hear from the actor.

Upon being told about Andy's nightmares and the voice in his head, the psychic had no concrete answers, but did assure him he was not going insane.

"It's always the same," he told her. "This Rachel person is begging me to come and find her, but even if I wanted to, how does one go about tracking down a person they supposedly knew 150 years ago? Do I look like a ghost hunter, for God's sake?"

"What you're hearing may not be the cries of a disembodied spirit," said Phyllis. "Rachel could be very much alive."

That comment gave Andy cause to stop and think because Rachel had always called out to him as Andy, not Adam.

"But then if she is alive and believes that I am the reincarnation of Adam, why hasn't she tried to get in touch with me by normal methods? Surely her spirit has evolved enough to be able to use a mobile phone or the Internet."

"If someone managed to track you down and explain that you were the reincarnation of a lost love, you'd no doubt assume they were crazy," said the psychic. "My best advice is for you to do nothing. If you really are Adam, and you're meant to find each other in this lifetime, you will. Sometimes we have to just sit back and have faith in the old adage, *what will be, will be.*"

For the next several weeks, Andy continued hearing Rachel call out to him, but eventually these communications became less and less frequent. To say he was happy about the change in events would have been an understatement, but at the same time, he had a foreboding sense that Rachel wasn't done with him yet.

The reason for Rachel's sudden departure was because Kerrie was busy gearing up for the upcoming release of her new novel. All the last-minute edits and working with her publisher's publicity department to get the word out didn't leave Kerrie with much time for anything but work.

It had taken nearly two years to finish the book, but soon after it hit the bookstores, *What Have I Gotten Myself Into?*, her semi-autobiographical tale of a quirky and ambitious novice finding herself pitted against the Hollywood establishment quickly shot to the top of the New York Times best seller list; a rare occurrence for a first time author. Although Kerrie much preferring anonymity, she reluctantly agreed to the overwhelming task of getting out there and promoting her book.

It felt strange switching roles from interviewer to interviewee, and after spending weeks enduring one grueling Q and A session after the other, Kerrie came to understand Andy's strong aversion to the press. She even joked to Meg that she hoped never to make the best seller list again. When the hoopla finally began to wind down, all Kerrie wanted to do was hide out in her apartment and begin work on the sequel. A few months of peace and quiet was something she was really looking forward to, but all her plans were put on hold by a call from Stanley Kaplan, her publisher. He thought it was important that she do a short overseas tour to promote her book and wouldn't take no for an answer. He also mentioned that James Goldman, one of the firm's new publicists would be going to England with her, and promised that the trip would be quick and painless.

Other than a fun vacation in Mexico a few years before, Kerrie had never traveled anywhere outside the U.S. and had mixed feelings about traveling abroad. On the one hand, she was excited about visiting the country of her ancestors and hoped to have time for a side trip to Liverpool, where they came from, but she was dreading the business end of the trip because that meant more book signings, interviews and endless inane questions from reporters who hadn't even bothered to read her book in the first place. She also had reservations about traveling all over Europe with some still-wet-behind-the-ears publicist.

Kerrie's first contact with James was by phone when he called to make arrangements for them to meet outside the British Airways terminal on the day of the flight. He came across as charming, competent and made a good overall impression on the wary author. He assured her that he'd been on this sort of junket many times before, and promised that even though their short time in London would probably be quite hectic due to the many print interviews, television appearances and book signings he'd already lined up, she would still very much enjoy the experience. Unfortunately, her positive attitude about James changed dramatically when they finally met up at the airport.

Initially, he seemed to be one of those annoying types who clearly had to be the center of attention by standing too close, grabbing a person's arm during a conversation for no reason, began every sentence with "I," and wore an ingenuous wide smile that only served to remind Kerrie of a Cheshire Cat. *A typical Hollywood wannabe*, she thought to herself and made a mental note to try and ignore him as much as possible, but while they were waiting for their flight to be called, James showed another side of himself that she found even more annoying.

He began to gush on about how much he loved her book, said it was so good he'd read it four times, then proceeded to talk about all the things he knew about her, like her age, her marital status, what high school she went to, details about her Facebook Page and website and what type of computer she used. This was the type of behavior she'd expect from an overzealous fan, not a business associate, and it definitely put her off.

Once they finally boarded the plane and found their seats, Kerrie graciously took the pillow from the stewardess and slipped it behind her head. Sleep would make the irritation go away but the tiny pillow was of no use. She was tempted to bury her face in it and scream because he just wouldn't shut up. Her temples were throbbing and to make matters worse, James leaned over, adjusting her seat, offered her some headphones, and then attempted to clumsily cover her up with his jacket. She could take no more.

"James, you're smothering me!" she said, yanking the blanket down off her face. He began to apologize profusely, but she quickly turned towards the window in an effort to pretend he wasn't there.

She had been up half the night worrying about the trip to begin with and Kerrie was exhausted. James had finally stopped fussing over her and she managed to fall asleep. Pleasant dreams weren't in the cards, however. As if she wasn't comfortable to begin with, it wasn't long before she was roused awake by the sensation of another body pressing uncomfortably against hers.

She wanted to believe that James had fallen asleep himself and was accidentally leaning over the armrest, but when she tried to gently extricate herself from the situation, Kerrie realized that he was snuggled up as close as he could be without actually being on top of her. It was one thing to share an armrest with a fellow passenger, but being used as a pillow by a total stranger was going too far. She tried a little harder to pull herself away, but being in the window seat with the girth of a 200-pound man taking up a great deal of space, there was nowhere to go.

Kerrie decided that a sleeping James was preferable to a chatty, inquisitive one and twisted around as best she could to get as much of herself out from under him as possible, and eventually fell back to sleep. By the time they landed at Heathrow, she was ready to get as far away from James as possible.

She had requested a couple days off for sightseeing, and it was arranged well in advance that she do all the touristy things before the media blitz began, and she planned on doing them alone. There was no need for James to accompany her because this part of her trip had nothing to do with business.

After checking into their adjoining rooms at The Shaftesbury, a five story, 64 room hotel in the heart of Piccadilly, James knocked on her door to make sure she was happy with the accommodations. She was still a little put off by the snuggling incident on the airplane so she didn't ask him in.

"Everything is fine, thanks," she said, opening her door just wide enough to be polite. "Oh, and by the way, I won't be around much for the next day or two so you'll have some free time to yourself."

He knew about her sightseeing plans, of course, but was hoping she'd ask him to go along. "Um, yes, I did get a memo about that, but I naturally assumed I'd be going with you. I mean, I was hired to take care of you while we're here, and it really would be in your best interest if I came along. It's far too dangerous for you to be running around in a foreign country all by yourself."

The expression on James' face was far more worrisome than the notion of traveling around on her own. He looked like a petulant two-year old and Kerrie didn't know whether it was because he was afraid of losing his job if he actually did let her out of his sight, or because he really wanted to go with her and wasn't getting his way.

"Look, James, while I appreciate your concern, we're not exactly in a Third World nation, you know, and we all speak the same language, so I'll be fine. And besides, the hotel has arranged for a driver to take me around, and it was my old publicist, Gil, who set the whole thing up, so don't worry about getting into any trouble with the boss, okay?"

It had been a long time since Kerrie had seen a grown man pout, and because she didn't want to upset him any further, she came up with a quick compromise. "What if I save my tour of the Tower of London and a ride on the London Eye until the last day of my private excursion and we see them together?"

It looked as though James was trying to find a flaw in her suggestion, but not being able to come up with one, he reluctantly agreed. "Okay, but I would appreciate it if you would at least leave me your itinerary in case I need to get in touch with you."

"I don't have it totally planned out yet," she lied, because she didn't want him following her all over England, "but if something really important comes up, you can always call me. Meanwhile," she said, wanting very badly to end their conversation, "have some fun yourself and I'll see you in a few days. Cheers!"

James skulked back to his room in a rage. He felt that she had disrespected him by shutting the door in his face and when he tried to call her back to demand an apology, she didn't answer. When he tried to call the room, there was a Do Not Disturb message on the hotel line. This only added to his anger, but rather than going back down the hall and pounding on her door, he thought it would be a better idea to gather his wits for the time being and deal with it later. He had overwhelmingly strong feelings for Kerrie and wanted to make sure he stayed on her good side.

Having left a wake-up call and breakfast order for eight o'clock the next morning, Kerrie was just getting out of the shower when she heard a loud knock at the door. She quickly threw on a bathrobe and hurried to answer, but instead of being greeted by the room service porter, there stood James, looking as happy as if he had just won the lottery.

Without even giving her the chance to ask what he wanted, he pushed his way in. "I hate eating alone," he explained, maneuvering a breakfast cart though the narrow doorway and over to a small table next to the window. He seemed completely oblivious to Kerrie's unwelcoming glare or the fact that she was fussing with her bathrobe to make certain she was totally covered up.

"I thought we could enjoy a last meal together before you go traipsing off on your little journey so I took the liberty of calling downstairs to see what time you were having breakfast, then offered to bring the cart up myself."

31

His lighthearted manner did not completely mask an underlying note of contempt but Kerrie was so angry at him barging in on her that she didn't notice.

"I'm not fond of surprises, James, and I really don't like being forced to greet uninvited guests in my bathrobe."

She knew by the twitch of his upper lip that he was not the least bit repentant. In truth, he seemed to be glad she was annoyed. But he was hiding the pleasure of her discomfort by playing the pity card.

"I just thought since we won't be seeing each other for a few days, I could send you off with a smile on your face and a full stomach, but I guess I was wrong," he sighed, looking as though he was about to turn around and leave.

Kerrie didn't want to make any more waves and decided to go along with the charade. "No harm done, I guess," she said, trying to meet him half way. "And I guess it doesn't make a whole lot of sense to let a perfectly good breakfast go to waste, so why don't you set the table while I go get dressed?"

In the few minutes it took Kerrie to get ready, James set out the food and fussed with the table, making sure everything was perfect. They chatted about nothing in particular over breakfast, and were just finishing their meal when Kerrie got a phone call from the front desk saying that her driver was waiting downstairs.

"I'd better be going because I've got a long day ahead of me," she said, taking one last gulp of coffee. "I'm off to Liverpool to see if I can dig up any information on my ancestors and I don't know what time I'll be back, but if it's not too late, I'll ring your room and let you know that I returned safe and sound."

James made no move to get up, and because she was in a hurry, Kerrie simply grabbed her purse off the bed and headed to the door. "Would you mind letting yourself out? I don't want to keep the driver waiting."

"No problem." He said, watching her walk out the door. "I'll just stack the dishes on the cart, push it out into the hall and lock the door behind me when I'm done. Have a good time."

Kerrie's room faced the street and James waited a moment or two, then walked over to the window to make sure she got into the car before taking a quick look around Kerrie's room. Nosy by nature, he used to love sneaking into his mother's bedroom and rummage through her belongings, and was thrilled at having the opportunity to go through Kerrie's personal items as well. He wasn't looking for anything in particular, but the thrill of possibly unearthing any dirty little secrets was too tempting to pass up.

He meticulously went through her suitcase, which she had yet to unpack, even going as far as checking the pockets of her jeans and sticking his hand into the toe of her shoes to see if he could find something of interest, but other than a crumpled receipt from Victoria's Secret that was tucked away in a bag containing a couple of new bras and matching thongs, which he pulled out of the bag and inspected carefully, the suitcase yielded no treasure. Nor did the closet, which at the moment only housed a raincoat and a couple of warm sweaters.

On the way out, he took a peek into her nightstand table, where he thought she might have put the itinerary that she claimed not to have on. James noticed a DVD rental chart on top of the nightstand with several movies checked off. Curious to find out what sort of films she liked to watch, he was puzzled to see that all of the movies she chose starred Andy Dickinson.

He'd seen one or two of the British actor's films so James was familiar with his work, but couldn't figure out Kerrie's keen interest unless, of course, she had a penchant for older men with questionable sexual preferences. He hoped not, because although it was still early in their relationship, James felt an incredibly strong attachment to Kerrie and wanted her all to himself.

Mixing business with pleasure was strictly taboo, however, so he'd   have to wait until the tour was over before making any overtures, but that was okay because James was a firm believer in the theory that love affairs begin with friendship. That was a lesson he'd learned from his one and only serious relationship. Although his ex-girlfriend said the reason she eventually left him was because he was too smothering and possessive, he knew the real reason they failed together was because they just had gotten too close too fast and he wanted to make sure this didn't happen with Kerrie.

It was well past midnight when a tired yet exhilarated Kerrie finally got back to the hotel. It had been a four hour ride each way to Liverpool and back, and she did a lot of sightseeing in between. Her favorite part of the trip was the ride in The Yellow

Duckmarine, an authentic World War II landing vehicle. The hour-long trip began on dry land, taking in Liverpool's historic Waterfront, The Pier Head, The Three Graces, St. George's Hall, the Cathedrals and many other places of interest before making a dramatic "splashdown" in the Salthouse Dock. The tour then continued through the South Docks, via Wapping and Queens Docks to Coburg Dock. The Duck then traveled back to circle the Albert Dock before driving straight out of the water in front of the Albert Dock buildings.

Kerrie didn't have any luck digging up information on any of her ancestors, but it was just nice being able to walk down some of the same streets they used to frequent.

Still a bit wound up after her busy day, Kerrie stopped at the hotel bar for a Pimms Cup before going up to her room. She had heard about Pimms from a friend of hers who worked as a bartender in London and always wanted to try one, even though he referred to the beverage as an "old ladies' drink."

The bar was still quite lively given the late hour and the atmosphere very friendly. She ordered her drink then sat down at an empty table near the window. A couple of locals strolled by and struck up a conversation, and because the men seemed harmless enough, she asked them to sit down and join her. The fact that they were both about her age, good looking and weren't wearing wedding rings made them all the more interesting.

The threesome chatted for a few minutes until the combination of a long day and an alcoholic beverage suddenly caught up with her and Kerrie reluctantly left their company to go upstairs and crawl into bed.

She had barely gotten her key in the door when James burst out of his room next door looking extremely agitated. "Where have you been?" he demanded. "Do you know what time it is?"

Kerrie was surprised and at the same time annoyed by the unexpected confrontation, she glanced down at her watch. "Yes, it's three o'clock in the morning, and I asked you not to wait up." Then, not wanting to go into any long explanations, all she said was, "It's a very long way to Liverpool and back."

She could tell that James wasn't about to let things go at that but she didn't expect him to blow up in her face. "Right! It's a long way to Liverpool but it's only a short distance to the hotel bar, isn't it?" he asked in an accusing tone.

"For God's sake, James, you were hired on as my publicist, not my shadow, and I really don't like being spied on."

She could see her words had an effect on him. And it was all too plain that he hadn't wanted her to know that he was keeping such a close eye on her. He'd slipped, and that set the red flags waving.

"Don't be silly, I wasn't spying on you," he explained in an attempt to convince her that it was just a coincidence. "I just went down to buy a pack of cigarettes and happened to see you sitting in the bar having a drink. I'd hardly call that spying."

He wasn't a very good liar, but rather than risking any more unpleasantness, she took the diplomatic approach instead. "I appreciate your concern, but as you can see, I'm back safe and sound, so I'll say goodnight. Oh, and just so you know," she said, in a very businesslike tone, "I'll be out all day tomorrow and Wednesday, but I'll call you early Thursday morning to arrange our outing to the Tower of London, if you'd still like to go. Good night."

James stormed back to his room and slammed the door behind him. Kerrie's not so subtle way of telling him to bug off until Thursday was infuriating. *'How dare she treat me like that?'* he wondered aloud while pacing back and forth in his room. *'I was sent here to watch out for her, not be cooped up in some hotel room all alone while she goes gallivanting around the country on her own.'*

Then he stormed over to his suitcase and pulled out a framed 8x10 publicity picture of Kerrie and held it up to his face. "You don't know it yet, but you're all mine," he cooed. "And nobody will ever come between us."

Kerrie was just as annoyed as James, but with a decidedly different bent. She felt that James was taking his job way too seriously. He was hired to be with her while she carried out all her media obligations, not dog her every move. If they hadn't been out of the country, she would have called the publishing house to ask if James could be replaced with someone slightly less ambitious, but since that was impossible, the only solution for now was to act professionally and keep him at a safe distance because she had a

35

strong suspicion that he could be trouble if not handled with kid gloves.

CHAPTER 3

It had been several weeks since Andy had last heard that Rachel person calling to him in the middle of the night, but the respite wasn't to last long. And this time, she was more insistent than ever. It didn't matter where Andy was or what he was doing, she was always there, inside his head, and now she was relaying some rather cryptic messages. One night last week, she told him to try and remember the year 1862. The next day she suggested he go book shopping.

Because Andy was too busy to be an avid reader, he thought it was a rather strange request. What was he supposed to do, go into a bookshop and browse for no apparent reason? Or maybe she wanted him to go and buy a book about the year 1862. It just didn't make sense.

Kerrie's renewed interest in trying to contact Andy began the day after she returned from her trip to Liverpool. She'd gone out for a walk to see if the local bookstores had her novel in stock and was pleasantly surprised to find stacks of her books in several storefront windows, accompanied by large publicity posters. That's when she got the idea of trying to encourage Andy to go book shopping because even though she didn't know what she might have looked like as Rachel in her past life, he might recognize something in her face that would jar his memory. It was a long shot, but one worth pursuing.

Having skipped breakfast in favor of canvassing the shops, Kerrie was famished and hurried back to the hotel for an early lunch. She didn't mind eating alone, but picked up a local newspaper on her way to the restaurant because it made her feel less conspicuous if she had something to read.

As she was flipping through the entertainment section of the paper looking for some mention of her book, a small item on page 3 caught her eye. It said that Andy Dickinson was going to be appearing at a special charity performance for one night only at a theater in the West End that evening.

There was no way she was going to pass up the opportunity to see the actor in person, and as soon as she finished her lunch, she sought out the hotel concierge instead. Not only was he somehow able to secure a ticket to the already sold out charity event, he also managed an invitation to the after-theater party as well.

Rather than going back up to her room and run the risk of bumping into James, Kerrie opted to go out and do some shopping instead. Her plan was to buy a new outfit and wear it out of the store. She wasn't sure whether or not she'd actually get the chance to meet Andy at the party, but wanted to look her best just in case.

After finding the perfect little black dress and matching shoes in a small boutique just a few blocks away, Kerrie then went to a nearby hair salon for a new do, manicure, and to have her make up done. By the time she was all put together, it was time to head over to the West End, so she hailed a taxi.

Arriving at the venue along with a throng of other excited theatergoers, Kerrie pushed her way through the crowd. The lights began to dim as she frantically searched for Seat 12, Section C in the first balcony and then politely excused herself while squeezing past the already seated audience members. Her seat mates were two very dignified-looking men who acknowledged her late arrival with the briefest of polite nods.

Once settled in, Kerrie browsed the program she picked up in the lobby, and was excited to find out that not only was Andy starring in the play, he had also co-written and produced the original work.

Her mind was spinning in a thousand directions while waiting for the show to begin because she needed to figure out a way to wrangle an introduction to Andy at the after party, Kerrie was so deep in thought, she didn't pay any attention to the latecomer making his way to his seat directly behind hers, and nearly jumped out of her skin when she felt a hand on her shoulder and heard the person whisper in her ear, "Sorry I'm late."

Thinking she'd been mistaken for someone else, Kerrie turned around to let the stranger know he'd greeted the wrong person but was rendered speechless to see James grinning back at her instead.

"The concierge at the hotel rang my room this afternoon and told me he'd found you a ticket for this performance," he began, taking gleeful note of her stunned expression. "Knowing I was your publicist, he naturally assumed I'd be accompanying you and thought it was just an oversight that you neglected to pick up a ticket for me as well, so he took it upon himself to make sure I got one. Wasn't that thoughtful of him?" The dour expression on Kerrie's face just egged him on more.

"He apologized profusely for not being able to procure adjoining seats, but was hopeful that we'd be in close enough proximity to share the experience together."

The fact that James was even in the same building was too close for comfort, and Kerrie made a mental note to file a complaint with the hotel management. This was supposed to be her night to finally meet Andy face to face, and she had planned on doing it alone.

James continued to ramble on about how thoughtful the concierge had been, but Kerrie wasn't paying any attention. Instead, she was saying a silent prayer that James' ticket didn't include admittance to the after party, but soon found out that her prayers had not been answered.

"I told the guy that it didn't really matter where I sat for the show," she heard him say, "because we would be attending the after party together anyway."

Kerrie was clearly upset, but didn't have time to respond because the curtain was going up.

"Enjoy the show," he said, giving her shoulder a friendly squeeze before settling back into his seat.

As soon as the light romantic comedy began, Kerrie was so mesmerized by Andy's performance she was able to forget all about James. The actor was charming, witty, completely at ease, and had all the ladies in the audience wishing they could go home with him.

During intermission, Kerrie was so angry at James that she made a beeline for the ladies' room and remained there until the warning chime sounded for Act II, then took her time getting back to her seat. She knew it was the concierge who had inadvertently ruined her evening, but she didn't believe he had acted alone. No doubt James pumped the guy for information then insisted he had to go along.

The play's second act went by much too quickly and when it was over, the audience was up on their feet giving the performers a long-standing ovation. Finally, after several curtain calls, everyone began to file out of the theater, happily chatting about the show and hoping for an encore performance sometime in the near future.

Kerrie was so wrapped up in the moment, she nearly forgot all about James again until she saw him waiting for her at the end of the aisle, holding out his arm in grand style to usher her to the party. She half-heartedly accepted his gesture, but only because she was wearing new shoes with heels higher than she was used to and the stairs on the aisle were a bit steep with no railing to offer any other support.

"Personally, I thought the play was mediocre at best," he said as they made their way down to the lobby, "but what can you expect when an older gay man casts himself as a young heterosexual love interest? Who does he think he's kidding?"

"Andy Dickinson is not gay, and I think he did a wonderful job." she snipped, pulling herself away from James. She immediately regretted her sudden move because she pulled away from him so quickly that she was now off balance at the edge of another steep staircase going down.

He was genuinely surprised that she took his comment so personally. "Geez, Kerrie, don't be so defensive," he said, noticing her physical distress and taking her arm once again. "I was only offering my opinion. Who are you, the head of his fan club?"

It took every bit of strength she had not to turn around and slap his face. Was he purposely trying to make her angry or was he just a presumptuous idiot? "Think what you want," she said. "You have your opinion and I have mine, so let's just agree to disagree about the performance and leave it at that."

The party was being held at a nearby hotel ballroom and they walked the short distance in silence, both deep in thought. Kerrie was trying to figure out how she could break away from James long enough to approach Andy Dickinson on her own, and James was trying to decide the best way to keep Kerrie from meeting the actor.

When they entered the ballroom, James once again took hold of Kerrie's arm but she barely noticed. Andy Dickinson was standing not ten feet away, surrounded by a large group of admirers. The actor was graciously listening to what appeared to be a barrage of compliments, and smiling back at them attentively.

"I'll be right back." she said, struggling to pull her arm away from his tight grasp. "I just want to go over and tell Mr. Dickinson how much I enjoyed the performance."

"You actually want to talk to that ham?" he sniffed. "Look at him holding court in front of all those adoring fans. It's sickening."

Provoked by yet another insult, Kerrie was all the more determined to go meet Andy, but at the same time she was beginning to worry because James' surly tone had a tinge of jealousy attached. "Then I suggest you just stand over there and wait for me because I think Andy's a fine actor, a nice person, and I'm going to go meet him. Alone."

"I don't think so." he argued. "You can't just walk up to him all by yourself and start gushing about how wonderful you think he is. As your publicist, it's my job to make sure you don't embarrass yourself in public, so if you insist on meeting Mr. Wonderful, I'm the one who should be making the introductions."

"I had no intention of gushing," she said angrily, but before she could say any more, James grabbed her by the arm and dragged her towards the actor, who was now chatting politely with two older women who appeared to be clearly smitten and quite overbearing.

Thankful for an excuse to avert his attention elsewhere, Andy turned to Kerrie. He had barely gotten his mouth open to greet the newcomer when James stepped in between them, then placed a protective arm around Kerrie's shoulder and drew her close before making the cursory introduction. As he began to explain that Kerrie was a best-selling author who was in the UK to promote her

41

new book, the actor watched with mild curiosity as Kerrie extended her hand to him and at the same time tried to squirm away from James' vice-like grip.

"It's very nice to meet you, Mr. Dickinson, and I'm so glad I was in town to see the show. I enjoyed it very much."

Andy wasn't sure what to make of the tug of war between the writer and her publicist, but was pleased that she liked the performance. "Thank you, Miss Sherman. I read in the paper that you were here on tour and look forward to reading your book. It must be gratifying that your first novel was so well received."

"I'm not just gratified, I'm in shock." she laughed. "I hope my book does as well in England as it has back home."

"I'm quite sure it will, Kerrie," he said, giving her a warm smile. "I've read several glowing reviews."

Although he wasn't verbalizing his attraction to her, Andy seemed to be staring at Kerrie with great interest. And when he tightened his grip and gave her hand a squeeze, she felt as though he was trying to pull her in both mentally and physically.

James, being completely ignored and sensing some sort of connection between them, decided their brief encounter should come to an end.

"We've taken up quite enough of your time," he said firmly, and before either Andy or Kerrie had the chance to say another word, James forcefully yanked them apart, grabbed her by the wrist and began to drag her as far away from Andy as possible.

"How could you be so rude?" she hissed, turning back towards Andy to see if he was still watching them. He was.

"I can't stand that egotistical son of a bitch," said James, pulling her farther away from him and deeper into the crowd, "and maybe I was a little hasty in thinking that he was gay because it sure as hell looked like he was coming on to you. How dare he make a play for you in front of me!"

"What's it got to do with you?" she hissed, pulling her arm out of his tight grip and standing her ground. "You were hired as my publicist, not my chaperone so quit acting as though you own me!"

Although now involved in another conversation halfway across the room, Andy couldn't help but notice the heated exchange. He felt an inexplicable need to rush over and rescue

Kerrie from the unpleasantness, but before he could act on his impulse, he saw her storm off towards the exit, with her publicist trailing after her looking quite distressed. There was something about this woman that intrigued him so he was sorry to see her go, and hoped she'd be all right.

"Look, I'm sorry if I overstepped my bounds," said James, running after Kerrie onto to the busy sidewalk outside the venue. "I just didn't think he was acting in an appropriate manner."

Kerrie didn't stop to respond. Instead, she ran to the curb and tried to jump into a taxi. When James tried to reach for the car door she slapped his hand. "Where do you get off embarrassing me like that in public? The party was probably crawling with tabloid reporters and that's not the kind of publicity we're looking for on this tour, is it?"

With each word, her voice got louder and louder and the usually demure author now found herself yelling at James in the middle of the busy street and didn't care who heard her. "You can walk back to the hotel or go jump off the Tower Bridge for all I care, but you're not coming with me."

That being said, she jumped into the cab and slammed the door behind her.

James stood at the curb for a moment and watched the taxi pull away. It was a long walk back to the hotel, but he needed to be alone for a while and think about what had just transpired. He thought about going back to the ballroom and punching Andy Dickinson in the nose because after all, this whole ugly mess was the actor's fault, but he was afraid Kerrie might find out about it if the scuffle appeared on the front page of the morning paper and things were bad enough with her already.

Kerrie had the cabbie drop her off at a small neighborhood pub that was within walking distance of the hotel. Not much of a drinker by nature, James had pushed her to the limit and she really needed to calm down.

With drink in hand, she sat down at a vacant table near the bar. A television set blared in the background and when she looked up to see what was on, there was Andy Dickinson at the after party jovially talking to the reporter about the play. She wondered what he thought about James' disgusting display or if he'd even given their brief introduction any thought at all. This

43

had been her one chance to meet with the actor and while she hadn't planned on disregarding Ted's warning about bringing up the past, she felt it was important to make a connection. But now, thanks to James, any hope of getting to know the actor better was ruined.

Andy was both exhausted and exhilarated when he got back to his flat in the wee hours of the morning. The performance had gone better than he imagined and the after party offered him the opportunity to bask in the glory of a job well done. If it hadn't been for that unfortunate incident with the writer and her publicist, it would have been a perfect evening.

Not one to dwell on negativity, Andy tried to put the incident out of his mind but he was puzzled by his reaction to the argument between the two American strangers and tried to figure out why he felt an overpowering need to interfere. He didn't actually think the woman was in any real danger, but at the same time instinctively knew that she and her publicist needed to be as far away from each other as possible.

A good night's sleep did nothing to erase the events of the night before from his mind, and the next morning Andy decided to go out and purchase Kerrie's novel. After all, he told her he was looking forward to reading it, and besides, he was curious to see what the hoopla surrounding the book was really all about.

There were dozens of copies of Kerrie's book on display at his neighborhood bookseller, and one very large photo of the author with a sign underneath announcing an upcoming book signing. His first instinct was come back and purchase the book then, but fearing that her publicist would no doubt be with her, and not wanting to be witness to yet another public scene no matter how much he would have liked to see Kerrie again, he walked into the shop and purchased the novel with high hopes there would be another chance meeting between them in the near future.

As he exited the shop with book in hand, Andy nearly walked straight into a casually dressed man with a baseball cap pulled down low over his face. The man stared down at Andy's book and looked as though he was about to say something, but then just scowled and walked away without a word. Andy was used to having fans come up to him on the street and occasionally the shy ones would change their mind and run off before saying anything to him, so he didn't give much thought to the man's odd behavior.

After the short walk back to his apartment, Andy made himself a cup of tea then sat down on the couch and picked up the book. Looking at the photograph on the back cover he was reminded of Kerrie's warm smile from the night before. She seemed to radiate an attractiveness and familiarity he found irresistible. In the few brief moments they were together, he felt as though he'd known her all his life and wanted very much to get back in touch with her. In his mind, the only thing standing in his way was her publicist. The man's sudden hostility towards him was certainly uncalled for, but there was always the possibility that there was more than a business relationship between them and the man felt threatened.

When Kerrie woke up, she was still very angry and dreaded the day ahead. She was supposed to go sightseeing with James but he was the last person she wanted to see so she picked up the phone and called his room to cancel their little excursion, but there was no answer.

Hoping the unpleasantness between them was responsible for James' absence, she showered, got dressed and was looking forward to her James-free day. She called down to the desk to make sure her car was ready, then hurried out the door. She had just reached the elevator when James came rushing down the corridor.

"Hey, wait for me" he said cheerfully as though nothing was wrong. "I heard you come in at about two o'clock this morning and thought you might want to sleep in so I went for a short stroll to kill some time. Shall we be off to the Tower then?"

His Jekyll and Hyde attitude made her uncomfortable, but since he seemed to be in a good mood, she managed a weak smile. '*Best to get this day over with,*' she thought to herself, '*and then I'll only have to deal with him during the scheduled media events.*'

The tension between them lightened somewhat in the taxi when, in the middle of their conversation about the Tower of London, James suddenly broke into song. *"With her head tucked underneath her arm, she roams the bloody tower,"* causing both the cabbie and Kerrie to burst out laughing at his off-key reference to the headless ghost of Anne Boleyn who supposedly haunted London's most famous tourist attraction.

Their tour of the Tower was very interesting and even though there were no ghosts to be found, headless or otherwise, the costumed guides and Yeoman Warders made it an enjoyable and educational outing. Kerrie knew a little bit about the place, but was surprised to learn that the venerable Tower had served not only as a royal palace and fortress, but a prison, arsenal, royal mint, menagerie and jewel house as well. It was also where Henry VIII imprisoned, then beheaded, three of his queens on the Tower Green.

The small paved area between the Chapel and Tower Green, where the scaffold was erected for the beheadings, was of particular interest to James, and he stared at the inscribed names of the six tragic figures who died on the fateful spot for quite a long time.

"Anne Boleyn had it coming," he finally said, sounding extremely judgmental. "Anyone who commits adultery should suffer the same fate."

Not only was Kerrie shocked by his comment, she had recently read an article on the Queen that claimed the charges of adultery were false.

"Anne Boleyn was said to be Henry's most beloved wife and her only crime was not giving him a male heir. That's why he wanted her dead and made the whole adultery thing up to discredit her. He even went as far as accusing her own brother of incest and had him beheaded on Tower Hill along with several other innocent men," she recounted. "Of course, there's always the possibility that Henry got wind of the rumor about Anne complaining to her sister-in-law, Lady Rochford, that the king possessed 'neither skill nor virility in the bedroom,' and if the rumors were true and he actually was sexually lame," she teased, "I think he should have been beheaded instead."

Of course, she didn't mean it, but the horrified look on James' face was priceless, and that was exactly the response she was hoping for. If he truly believed that adultery was a crime punishable by death, then she felt the need to counter it with an equally shocking declaration.

James quickly changed the subject by suggesting they go have some lunch before continuing on to the London Eye. "I'm starting to get hungry, and I hear there is a Cornwall Pasty shop in Covent Gardens has delicious Cornish Pasties and blackberry-flavored mead. Doesn't that sound good?" he asked, still visibly miffed by Kerrie's comment.

Kerrie agreed to his suggestion rather than risking another confrontation, but if it were to her, she'd skip both lunch and the London Eye and go straight back to the hotel because the more she was getting to know this man, the less she liked him. There was something not quite right about him, and the sooner their day of sightseeing was over, the better.

James was uncharacteristically silent during the cab ride to Covent Gardens, and Kerrie couldn't have been happier. His silence enabled her to enjoy the sights along the way without having to make small talk.

When the taxi finally dropped them off, Kerrie was surprised to find that Covent Gardens was nothing like she imagined it would be. To begin with, she was under the impression that the area was merely a large outdoor shopping center which housed the Royal Opera House and a few restaurants. Instead, it turned out to be a sprawling city within the city and home to over 6000 residents, more than 1000 restaurants, several hotels, and a myriad of shops, heaters, pubs, and clubs.

The Cornish Pasties were delicious, but the atmosphere at the table was uncomfortable. After lunch, they walked the short distance from the restaurant to The London Eye.

The attraction, which could be clearly seen from many vantage points throughout the city looked like a huge bicycle wheel towering 135 meters over London. Each of the large passenger capsules offered spectacular views 25 miles in each direction. James behaved like any other inquisitive tourist and most of the venom he displayed the night before and his sullen attitude over lunch slowly faded away. By the time they finally arrived back at the hotel, he appeared to be in a good mood once again. He even tried to apologize for his bad behavior, but Kerrie cut him off by telling him all was forgotten. Hoping that she was telling the truth, he asked if they might have dinner together.

"Thanks, but I think I'm going to say have to pass. I'm so full of Cornish Pasties, I won't be hungry till morning. "

James was disappointed by her refusal, but left the invitation open and told her that if she changed her mind to let him know. Then, having a sneaky suspicion that she'd probably try to steal away on her own, James called the front desk and asked the clerk to let him know immediately if Miss Sherman happened to come downstairs at any time, but the call never came because Kerrie spent a peaceful evening all by herself snacking from the honor bar and watching Andy Dickinson movies.

CHAPTER 4

......Much to her amazement, Kerrie's first book signing in the U.K. drew a very large crowd and although she wasn't comfortable being the center of attention, she was thankful it went so well.

......With so many people milling about, Kerrie was pretty much able to ignore James, even though he tried very hard to remind her he was there. Every few minutes, he'd either come up and give her shoulder a reassuring squeeze or bend down and whisper words of encouragement, but because she was busy autographing books, and at the same time keeping a watchful eye on the door just in case Andy Dickinson might be passing by, it was easy to ignore her publicist.

......All the London newspapers knew she was in town and ran stories about Kerrie in every edition. That gave James an excuse to stop by her room with copies of the newest recently clipped articles several times a day. It wasn't that he was becoming a nuisance as much as his presence was all consuming and, to be honest, made her skin crawl.

...... "You don't have to keep running over here every five minutes." she finally told him after his seventh visit of the day. "Why don't you just save them up and give me a whole batch at once?"

...... "Fine!" he shouted, throwing the clippings to the ground. "I'm sorry for being so intrusive, but I'm just doing my job."

......Because she had tried to sound friendly in suggesting he not come by so often, his sudden outburst caught her off guard and when she bent down to pick up the mess, James pushed her away.

"I'm the lowly grunt here, and I'll clean up my own mess," he sneered, gathering the bits of paper together into a pile. Then he shoved them into her hands and stormed back to his room.

......Kerrie had no way of knowing that it wasn't her request for him to limit his visits that had made James so angry. What set him off was hearing Andy Dickinson's voice blaring out of her television set each time she opened the door. In his mind, she'd been holed up in her room watching that prat's movies when she should have been spending her free time with him.

......The media blitz began in earnest early the next morning with a round of interviews and photo sessions and James was constantly at her side. Speculation amongst members of the media was that the two were a hot item no matter how often Kerrie tried to explain that James was 'just her publicist.' Disgusted by all the presumption, she finally took him aside and begged him not to be so clingy in public.

......For the next few days, Kerrie was so busy she didn't really have time to give Andy much thought but was still holding on to the hope that she would somehow have another opportunity to meet up with him one more time before leaving London. She hoped that what Ted had told her about fate and destiny, would shine in her favor.

......Whether Andy believed in destiny or not, Kerrie was very much on his mind. He definitely wanted to see her again and was happy to read her repeated denials about being romantically linked to James, but thought it might be best to wait until she was back in the States and out from under the little bastard's thumb before trying to contact her.

Over the next several nights, Andy's nightmares returned. He kept reliving that fateful morning in October 1862 when he learned that Rachel had been murdered, and woke up every morning with a feeling of great sadness and loss. At first, he didn't make the connection between those horrible visions and Kerrie until the night he dreamt of sitting in his living room mourning over Rachel's photo. Then the realization of what he was looking at jarred the actor awake. He fumbled for the light then reached over to the nightstand and picked up his copy of Kerrie's book. Turning it over to have a look at the author's photo on the back cover, he noticed a slight resemblance between Kerrie and Rachel, especially around the eyes.

The next afternoon Andy was mindlessly flipping through the channels on television when he came across one of those entertainment programs he never watched because he hated slick, gossipy-type shows. He was about to switch it off when he heard the presenter announce that his special guest, Kerrie Sherman, would be coming up after the break.

Andy impatiently clicked the remote to mute so he wouldn't have to listen to a barrage of annoying commercials, then turned up the volume when the show's host came back on and welcomed his first guest. The camera panned over to Kerrie for a quick close up during her introduction then settled back on the host.

"So, Kerrie, welcome to London."

"Thank you, it's a beautiful city and I'm glad to be here." She nervously watched as the host glanced down at his notes and said a silent prayer that the show's researchers didn't dig up anything too personal for him to ask.

"I read in your bio that you have an affinity for Britain because of your distant English roots. Is that a fair statement?"

"Yes, on my father's side, we've actually got the family tree back as far as The War of the Roses so I guess there's a bit of British blood in me somewhere," she joked.

"Well we're happy you've found your way back home after all these years and does that mean your interest in Britain also extends to your interest in British men perhaps?" he asked coyly. "Do you fancy any of our dashing leading men?"

Kerrie wasn't expecting that, but before she could come up with a tactful reply, she heard herself blurting out, "As a matter of fact, I find Andy Dickinson quite fascinating."

James, who had, of course, accompanied Kerrie to the studio was standing just offstage drinking a cup of tea. The moment he heard Kerrie say Andy's name, the teacup and saucer flew out of his hands and shattered on the concrete floor with a loud crash. Both the presenter and Kerrie instinctively turned towards the sound.

Seeing that it was just a minor mishap, the presenter turned back to the camera and said, "Ah, yes. Well as you probably just heard, the mere mention of Dandy Andy Dickinson causes quite a stir." he joked, but Kerrie knew this was no laughing matter because as a couple of production assistants were on their knees gingerly picking up the pieces of broken china and trying to wipe the spill, James was staring at Kerrie with a violent look of rage.

Andy had no knowledge what was happening behind the scenes, and was elated at Kerrie's revelation, even though he hated the presenter's 'Dandy Andy' reference. It was a nickname he picked up early in his career when his onstage portrayal of Casanova was a little too convincing, and the moniker stuck. He hoped this exaggerated depiction was not the reason Kerrie apparently found him so fascinating. Now that he was middle aged and unwilling to hop in and out of bed with every starlet or leading lady who offered him the chance, he preferred to be known for his body of work.

The rest of the interview was uneventful, and as they were winding down, Kerrie mentioned that she was sorry about having to leave the UK the following day, but said she had enjoyed her short stay and promised to come back again soon.

As he clicked off the television, Andy was glad he happened to catch the interview because while he first thought it might be awkward trying to contact Kerrie out of the blue after she arrived home, this new bit of information about her being a fan opened up a world of possibilities. At the very least, now he knew that she would appreciate knowing that he was a fan of hers as well.

Later that night Andy had yet another dream about Rachel, but this one was even more disturbing than any of the others because in it, he actually witnessed the events that led up to her murder.

The movie playing in his head showed Rachel walking along the road on her way to the dressmaker. Suddenly a young man who popped out of the bushes and stood menacingly in front of her.

Rachel seemed more annoyed than frightened as she confronted the intruder. "Martin Smith, get out of my way. I'm late for an appointment."

"I'm sure you are," he sneered, "and we wouldn't want to keep your dear husband-to-be waiting, would we?"

"Not that it's any of your business, but my appointment is with the dressmaker, so if you'll excuse me," she said, trying to push past him.

"Oh, that's right. The big day is almost here, isn't it?" he teased, blocking her way. "You'll have to forgive my lack of enthusiasm, but for some reason I never received an invitation to the wedding. I'm sure it was just an oversight."

"Hardly," she shot back. "Everyone in town knows how much you hate Adam, so there was no reason to invite you."

Martin's face flushed at the mention of Adam's name. "Does everyone in town know that the reason I hate him so much is because he stole you away from me?"

Kerrie was shocked that he honestly believed that. "How can you say he stole me away when I never had any interest in you in the first place?"

"That's only because you never gave me a chance." he countered. "I fell in love with you the day you moved into town. In fact, I was just about to ask you to dance at the church social when Adam pushed me out of the way so that he could get to you first. Just because he is the mayor's son, he thinks he's better than the rest of us."

"He certainly does not!" she argued. "Adam is a kind, compassionate person, and that's why I fell in love with him."

"Oh really?" he asked, reaching out to take her hand. As she tried to pull away, Martin yanked the engagement ring off her finger. "You mean to say that the fact that he's rich enough to buy you this huge diamond didn't have anything to do with it?"

"Give it back, Martin Smith! You're the most hateful person I know," she cried, trying to retrieve her most prized possession, but Martin skillfully kept the ring just out of reach.

"Compared to your saintly Adam, I suppose you think I am hateful, but what you don't understand is that I love you a hundred times more than he ever could, and it sickens me to know that tomorrow night you will be giving yourself to him body and soul."

Embarrassed by Martin's reference her wedding night, Kerrie tried to change the subject by demanding her ring back.

"Give it back to me right now!" she said, once again making a grab for the ring.

"It means a great deal to you, doesn't it?" he asked thoughtfully, rolling the ring between his thumb and forefinger. Then before she could answer, he raised his arm and pitched the ring into the bushes several feet away.

"You stupid man! What have you done?" she screamed, staring helplessly into the thicket.

"Oops. It just slipped out of my fingers." he deadpanned. "Maybe we'd better go look for it." he said, reaching for her arm.

Kerrie tried to pull away, be he was much too strong and was easily able to guide her deeper and deeper into the bushes. When he finally found a suitable spot several hundred yards from the road, he stopped walking but didn't loosen his grip. Instead, he pulled her closer to him.

"Let go of me." she screamed, trying to break free. The determined look on Martin's face that reminded her of a cat stalking a mouse.

"Not until I get what I want," he said, eyeing Rachel up and down. "You want your ring, but I want something as well," he said, reaching down with his free hand to unbutton his trousers. "I'm afraid your dear Adam won't be the first one to have you," he said, forcing her down to the ground then lowering himself on top of her. "In fact, he's never going to have you because I'm going to be the first...and the last."

Andy woke up in a panic to the sound of someone screaming "Nooooo!" and that someone was him. Dream or no dream, it was a terrible thing to witness such a violent act, but even more horrifying by the sudden realization that the victim in his nightmare looked exactly like Kerrie and her cold-blooded killer was the spitting image of her publicist, James.

Andy immediately reached for his phone looked up the number of the only person who could possibly tell him what the dream was all about, Ted Stephens. He hadn't been in touch with the American psychic for a number of years, but dreaming of Rachel's murder jarred some memories of the past life regressions Ted had once performed on him.

"Andy! I wondered when I would be hearing from you." said Ted in a jovial voice. "I saw Kerrie Sherman several months ago and did a past life reading on her." he explained. "I'm sure you understand that I cannot go into any great detail, but I get the impression that she might have something to do with why you're calling?"

"I've got to get in touch with her because I have reason to believe she is in great danger." said Andy, who then recounted his dream to Ted. "Kerrie was once Rachel and I was Adam, wasn't I?" he asked. "That would explain the unpleasant encounter I had with her publicist, James, last week. I have reason to believe that he is the reincarnation of Martin Smith, the man who murdered Rachel."

Ted listened without comment until Andy was through ranting. "Kerrie called me a couple of days ago to tell me that she did indeed meet you, and she also voiced her concerns about her publicist, but I don't think she's made the connection between him and Martin Smith. I think the reliving of her murder was so intense, she's consciously blocked most of it out."

Andy couldn't believe how casual the psychic's tone was, considering that Kerrie was hanging around with the lunatic who once took her life. "Didn't you advise her to break off all ties with the guy as quickly as possible? He's a menace."

"I had no reason to warn her about him, Andy, because this is the first I'm hearing about the connection between her past life murderer and her current publicist, but that being said, only God can change a person's destiny, you know that, and it would be folly to try and interfere."

"Forget about bloody destiny!" yelled the actor. "Kerrie's in danger and she must be warned."

Sensing that Andy was very near the breaking point, Ted tried to calm him down. "We don't know that for sure. Maybe because of your unpleasant encounter with James, you want to believe that he is actually the reincarnation of Martin Smith."

"I know they're one in the same!" shouted Andy, who was now furiously pacing back and forth. "He killed her once because of his hatred for me, and judging by his negative reaction to me when we met, I think he's ready to do it again!"

"If you believe that to be true," said Ted, "then I strongly suggest you stay out of Kerrie's life. Don't give James any reason to harm her and let fate run its course. By doing nothing you might actually save her life."

"She knows I am Adam, doesn't she?" he asked, knowing Ted would probably not confirm his suspicions.

Ted chose his words carefully before answering. "Even if she does, we must assume she hasn't yet figured out James' role in this love triangle of long ago, and if she is meant to find out, that information must be realized on her own."

Andy was getting more and more frustrated. "How can I just sit back and do nothing knowing she is in a perilous situation? Just seeing her the other night brought out feelings in me I never knew I was capable having, and I can't bear the thought of losing her again."

"How can you lose someone you haven't really found?" asked the psychic.

"But that's just it. I have found her, even though it was she who came looking for me." he explained. "We met, we talked, and I was immediately drawn to her, even though I didn't know why until a few moments ago."

"Are you quite sure it wasn't just the possibility of another conquest that drew you to her at the party instead of the attraction being Karmic in nature?" asked Ted. "You've attained quite a reputation as a ladies' man over the past several years, and Kerrie is rather attractive. What is it they call you now? Dandy Andy?"

"Oh, for God's sake, man!" he groaned. "I know the difference between a one-night stand and real feelings for someone, and when I met Kerrie that night, I'll admit I was very attracted to her, but not in the carnal sense. And I certainly had no intention of asking her up to my flat to look at my bloody etchings."

Despite the serious nature of their conversation, Ted couldn't help but laugh at the comment, and then once again warned Andy to stay away from Kerrie.

After the phone call ended, Andy gave a great deal of thought to what Ted had to say. While he agreed somewhat with the psychic's overall assessment that Kerrie might be just fine if he didn't try and get in touch with her, he had a strong suspicion that James would end up harming Kerrie no matter what, because whether it was him or someone else she got involved with, the publicist would not be pleased.

Kerrie was feeling good about her successful book tour, and as she and James boarded the plane for the long ride back home, she was thankful that once they arrived back in the States she would finally be able to get him out of her life once and for all.

He was in a sulky mood when they boarded, so Kerrie thought it would be a good idea to just try and ignore him. Even though she could barely contain her excitement at the thought of never having to see James again once they landed, she knew it would only make matters worse if she appeared too happy.

Several times during the flight he tried to broach the subject of them keeping in touch with comments like, "I'm going to miss you so much," or "Now that the tour is over, I don't know how I'm going to be able to live without you." Kerrie struggled to find a proper response each time, but not being able to come up with a tactful comment that would even come close to expressing the way she really felt, she pretty much ignored him.

To make James' mood even worse, the airline must have decided to prolong their passenger's British experience as long as possible because most of the in-flight movies starred Andy Dickinson. As much as she wanted to watch, she worried that James might flip out at 10,000 feet, so she opted to catnap instead. She had just fallen asleep when he woke her up by yelling, "I don't believe it! Why can't that egotistical bastard just leave us alone?"

At first Kerrie thought he might be complaining about another passenger, but when she shifted around to see who he was talking about, there was James, sitting rigidly in his seat staring straight ahead at the movie screen with an intense look of hatred. Both his hands were balled up so tightly his knuckles were white, and was so consumed in the conversation he was having with himself, he didn't notice her looking at him. But when Kerrie saw Andy's face staring back at her from the monitor, that was all the explanation she needed.

It was bad enough that James had acted badly in front of Andy at the party, but getting worked up about a stupid movie was insane. What made the situation even worse was that while he could have just turned the movie off, James sat there and watched the whole thing, mumbling irritably to himself throughout. By the time the plane landed at LAX, Kerrie was ready to get as far away from her lunatic publicist as possible.

They still had to go through customs, but Kerrie had to take care of something first, so she told James to get in line. She said she had to run to the bathroom really fast and she'd be back in a flash. Then she made a beeline for the nearest ladies' room and even though it was two o'clock in the morning, made a desperate call to Meg.

"Hi, it's me, and our plane just landed, and I need you to come pick me up at the airport right away."

"Kerrie? What time is it?" she asked, still half asleep. "I thought you were going to take a cab home."

"Look, I know this is a big imposition, but it's an emergency and I don't have time to explain. Just get here as soon as you can. I'll meet you out in front of the British Airways terminal and please act like we had this all arranged."

Meg's head was finally starting to clear enough to realize something was wrong. "Are you okay?"

"Yes, I'm fine." said Kerrie, sounding like she was in a big hurry to get off the phone. "Just get over here as soon as you can and I'll explain everything on the way home."

James was holding her place in line, and because she was feeling better about having made the call to Meg, Kerrie walked up next to him and tried to act as though she hadn't just planned her own great escape.

"As soon as we're done here, I'll get us a cab, he said as they edged their way up to the front of the line. "I thought we could share a ride and since you live closest to the airport, I'll drop you off first."

"Oh, thanks, James, but that's not necessary because I already have a ride." she said cheerfully. "My friend Meg should be waiting for me outside as we speak. She said before I left that she'd be happy to pick me up and emailed me this morning to confirm. She doesn't live too far from here and I'm going to spend the night at her place."

As much as he tried to mask his emotions, the disappointment on James' face was quite apparent. "Can't you call her and tell her not to come? I thought we could stop and have an early breakfast on the way home."

"Like I said, I'm sure she's already here." she said, hoping that Meg had been able to drag herself out of bed.

Her prayers were answered when they walked outside the terminal and she saw her slightly disheveled friend leaning up against her car in a nearby loading zone.

"I don't want Meg to get a ticket for loitering, so I'd better get going," she said. Then she reached out to shake his hand. "And I want to thank you for all your help on the tour and wish you good luck in the future."

James looked back at her like she had two heads. *"What is this?"* he thought to himself. *"A curt handshake, an impersonal thank you and a quick dismissal after all I've done for her? She was practically fawning over that prick Andy Dickinson the moment she walked up to him and I'm sure she would have offered more than her hand if he had the chance to ask."*

"James, are you okay? she asked, interrupting his train of thought. He almost looked catatonic.

"I'm fine," he said, regaining his composure. "I'm just a little tired. Must be jet lag or something."

"I'm pretty tired myself," she admitted, thankful that James wasn't going to insist on dragging her off with him. "It's been a long, tiring trip, but thanks again for all you've done."

Before he could reply, Kerrie turned and ran off to join her friend, leaving him standing there very much alone and more than a little perturbed. In fact, he was downright angry. He had hoped to share a cab ride home and tell her that now that the book tour was over he'd like to begin seeing her on a nonprofessional basis. He had no idea she'd already made plans with her friend to pick her up and was insulted that she'd sprung Meg on him at the last moment. Surely, she must know how much he cared for her, and he didn't like the way she handled the situation. But then again, he reasoned, perhaps she didn't understand that their professional relationship was actually over. He would need to remind her again before she did something stupid like trying to get back in touch with Andy Dickinson.

CHAPTER 5

Meg might have been half asleep on the way over to pick Kerrie up, but one look at James and she was wide awake. "Was that your publicist?" she asked, maneuvering the car away from the curb and into the constant flow of airport traffic. "I thought you'd be stuck with some bookish older man, but from what I could see, this one's a lot younger and even though he had his back to me, he looked way better than I expected."

"Believe me, I'd have been better off with the bookish old man." said Kerrie.

The scowl on her friend's face perked Meg right up. "Why? What happened? Please tell me it's something deliciously scandalous because now that Steven and I have gone our separate ways, I need something to cheer me up."

"I wish it was that simple," sighed Kerrie, who then proceeded to tell Meg the details of the trip. By the time she was done with the story, they were sitting in Meg's living room having a nightcap.

"You're making this guy sound like some kind of raving lunatic," said Meg. She was sure her friend was exaggerating.

"He is," Kerrie assured her. "There is something seriously wrong with James, and if you could have seen him at the party with Andy, you'd understand. If this were prehistoric times, he would have hit me over the head with a club and dragged me away by the hair."

Meg still wasn't convinced. "Oh, come on now. Aren't you stretching the truth just a little?" She knew that Kerrie sometimes used her writer's imagination to make things sound more interesting. "He's probably just one of those anal guys who takes their job too seriously. But in any case," she said, getting up from the couch, "it's late, and I'm going to try and get back to sleep, so I'll see you in the morning and we can talk more about it then. Sweet dreams."

Kerrie had too much on her mind to fall asleep right away, but now that she was finally rid of James, she could feel all the tension she'd been living with for the past few days begin to fade. Unfortunately, the same could not be said for Andy Dickinson who, at that moment, was in a meeting with his agent, Kate Milligan. He sat patiently as Kate went over all the urgent business at hand, but she could tell that his mind was elsewhere.

He was, in fact, trying to figure out a way to get a contact number for Kerrie because he was desperately worried about her safety and had to warn her about James despite the caution from Ted to stay out of it. He thought perhaps Kate might have a way of tracking her down, so he casually asked her if she'd ever heard of the author.

"All I know about Kerrie Sherman is that her book is flying off the shelves, and that she's pretty enough to get your attention," she laughed. But later that day, Kate remembered an unsolicited email she received a couple of years ago from an entertainment writer who wanted to do an article on Andy and on a lark, she emailed Kerrie's publishing company and asked them to send her Kerrie's bio to see if she was the same person.

"I think I've solved the mystery," said Kate during a follow up phone call to the star the following day. "I'm just looking over Kerrie Sherman's bio and I think she might have sent me a request...well, several, actually, for an interview with you a while back, which, as always, you declined. But she was so persistent, her name stuck in my mind."

Andy's heart sank at the realization that he might have passed up the opportunity to meet Kerrie before any of this mess with James began. That chance meeting might have changed the course of events in such a way that James might have never been given the opportunity to intrude upon their lives. "Do you still have that email?" he asked.

"Are you kidding? My e-mails are cleared out every two days, and hers would have come in a couple of years ago. But I can see if her publisher will give me any contact information, if that will help."

"No, that's okay, I'll do it myself. Maybe I've got a fan or two working there who would be willing to do me a favor."

The fact that Andy actually refused her assistance really peaked Kate's curiosity. She was used to women chasing after Andy, not the other way around. "If you don't mind me asking, why the sudden interest in Kerrie Sherman?"

"Just call it kismet," he said, offering no further explanation.

As soon as he got off the phone with Kate, Andy put in a call to Kerrie's publisher. He was a bit concerned that if they actually did give him her phone number and he had the opportunity to try and explain his nightmares and warn her about James she'd think he was some kind of a nut, but he hoped mentioning Ted Stephens' name right away would make the situation less awkward.

While it was against company policy to furnish their clients' personal contact information to anyone, including award winning actors, the secretary who answered Andy's call said she'd be happy to take a message. Andy left her his phone number and email address, then asked the secretary to please remind Kerrie that they had met briefly in London and he was quite anxious to speak to her again.

The secretary knew that Kerrie was back in town and would probably be calling in sometime soon. Since she was already late for a lunch date, she hastily clipped the phone message to Kerrie's in-folder then grabbed her purse and hurried out of the office.

She and James passed in the hall and they stopped and chatted briefly about his trip to London. Then she told James that Mr. Walker was expecting him, but was on a long, boring, conference call and suggested James wait in the outer office until he was free.

James was easily bored and with no one to talk to he began nosing around the secretary's desk looking for something to amuse himself. It was then that he saw a bright pink telephone message marked URGENT clipped to the outside cover of a folder with Kerrie's name on it, so of course he had to investigate and see what it was all about.

"I knew it!" he said, after reading the message left by Andy. Then, making sure nobody else was around, James snatched the note off the folder and jammed it into his pocket.

When Meg dropped Kerrie off at her apartment the next morning, there was a huge basket of flowers waiting on the front porch. It was a beautiful arrangement and she carefully maneuvered the bouquet into the house before looking at the card. She knew they were probably from her publisher, as a thank you for a job well done, but she hoped the flowers might be from Andy.

She set the flowers down on the kitchen table, and eagerly plucked out the card. She opened it with great anticipation, only to be disappointed when she read who the bouquet was actually from.

"Beautiful flowers for a beautiful lady." it began. *"Thanks for making my job so easy. I'll call you later. We have lots to talk about. Love, James."*

Suddenly the beautiful flower arrangement wasn't so attractive after all. *'Love, James? What the hell is he thinking?'* she wondered. Her first instinct was to call James and let him know he needn't have bothered wasting his money on flowers because they had nothing more to talk about, but knowing how unstable he could be, she thought it best to wait until he called her, then try to let him down gently.

As anxious as he was to find out what Kerrie thought of the flowers, James needed to calm down first. Not only was he still upset about being dumped at the airport, he couldn't rid himself of that disgusting image of Andy and Kerrie gazing into each other's eyes at the party. They looked like two lost souls who had finally found each other, for God's sake, and just remembering that horrible evening made James so sick to his stomach he had to run off to the bathroom several times during the day to try and purge himself of the ghastly vision.

Throughout the day Kerrie had plenty of time to figure out what she was going to say to James when he called and when his name did finally show up on her Caller ID she was ready for him.

"I hope you had a good night's sleep at your friend's house." he began, sounding like he hoped she hadn't.

"I actually fell asleep right away" she answered, trying to ignore his negative tone. "Oh, and thank you for the flowers. It was a nice surprise, but I wish you hadn't bothered."

James couldn't tell whether or not she was being facetious. "I've done several of those overseas tours and all the other authors

I've worked with were so demanding and disagreeable, it was the least I could do," he explained. "It was such a pleasure working with you, I just wanted to show my appreciation."

"Well, I enjoyed having you there," she lied, "and I'll make sure to give your boss a glowing report next time I speak to him." In reality, she intended her report to be more glowering than glowing.

"There's no need for that," he said, not happy that she was sounding so businesslike, "but you could have dinner with me tonight. I've heard some really good things about the Mucky Duck Pub in Santa Monica. It will almost be like having that pub meal that we didn't get to share while we were in London. Have you ever been there?

The invitation wasn't unexpected but she had hoped to have a little more time to gauge his mood before having to brush him off. "No, I haven't, but unfortunately, I've made other plans for tonight, and besides, we work for the same company and I don't think it's a good idea to mix business with pleasure."

"So, you're saying that if we didn't have a working relationship you would go out with me?" he asked hopefully. "Because if that's the case, there's no problem. Our working relationship is officially over. I was only your publicist for the duration of the London tour.

"It's not that simple, James." she sighed, realizing that it wasn't going to be as easy to break it off with him as she had hoped. "I know the tour is over, but we both still work for the same publishing house and I'm sure they would frown on any fraternizing between the ranks. They've already made me an offer to do a second book and I don't want anything to jeopardize my relationship with them. They've been very good to me."

"So, have I," he snapped, "but you don't seem to mind jeopardizing our relationship, do you?"

That was the very thing Kerrie didn't want to hear and she chose her words carefully before responding.

"Look, James, I'm flattered that you think enough of me to want to stay friends, but I'm going to have to say no. You're a wonderful person, and I'm sure you'll make some lucky girl very happy someday but that someone can't be me. Don't take this the wrong way, but even if we weren't working together, I doubt we could make a go of it. You're just not my type."

Not expecting such a direct brush off, James tried not to display the rage that was quickly building up inside. "May I ask what type of man would suit you better? he asked, trying to sound analytical rather than emotional. "After all, you don't even know me, so how can you make a judgment call like that?"

"I just have to go by the way I feel, and it doesn't feel right between us. So please accept my refusal gracefully, James. I'm not trying to hurt your feelings but I really think honesty is best and I don't want you to be living under any illusions that there could be anything more between us."

"Why don't you give me a chance to prove you wrong?" he argued, "And if we're talking about hurt feelings, how do you think it made me feel when you practically threw yourself at Andy Dickinson, right in front of me?"

Even though she knew it was coming, the accusation about her and Andy made it difficult for Kerrie to stay calm; and once she lost her temper, it was nearly impossible to control the words that came out of her mouth.

"In the first place, I didn't throw myself at anyone. We just shook hands and tried to make small talk. And if you think that my behavior was overly forward, what about your breach of ethics when you put your arm around me like you owned me, then pulled me away from him like a jealous lover? It was humiliating. I can't even begin to imagine what Andy thought about that."

"Why should you care what Andy thought? He doesn't give a damn about you. He just wanted to get in your pants!"

Because their conversation was getting uglier by the moment, Kerrie knew it was time to end it once and for all. After taking a couple of deep breaths to calm down she finally said, "Look, this is getting us nowhere, and I really have to get going. It wasn't my intention to hurt your feelings in any way and I'm sorry if you think I acted inappropriately while we were in London, but we're back home now, and I think it would be best if we went our separate ways."

Before he had the chance to respond, Kerrie hung up.

"How dare she?" he yelled, hurling his cell phone against the wall. 'If she thinks this is over, she's very much mistaken."

Kerrie was equally disturbed because she hated unpleasantness and James had taken it to the extreme. She prayed he would be able to calm down and forget about the whole situation, but was pretty sure it wouldn't be that simple. Then, not wanting to make a liar out of herself about having made plans for the evening, she called Meg and invited her over for dinner and explained her reason for the sudden invitation.

After she was filled in about the phone call, Meg didn't seem to think it was any big deal. "You were right to tell him how you felt," she said, "but it was probably a big blow to his ego and that's why he got so angry."

"It was more than just an angry reaction. He sounded insane," said Kerrie. "He's got a Jack Nicholson in *The Shining* kind of thing going on, and it's really creepy. And then to bring up Andy Dickinson, who is ten thousand miles away and probably hasn't given me a second thought? I swear, Andy and I only said a few sentences back and forth before James came charging in and hauled me away."

"It's not what you said, but the way you were staring at each other that probably set James off. I've seen the look on your face when you watch his movies, and you've got it bad for the guy," she teased. "I'm surprised you didn't jump his bones then and there."

Kerrie had never fully explained her interest in Andy Dickinson to Meg, and hadn't said anything about her visit to Ted Stephens, either. Meg was quite intelligent, but didn't believe in the metaphysical and thought reincarnation only had to do with sacred cows in India, so Kerrie thought it would be easier to let Meg come to her own conclusions about Andy and leave well enough alone for now.

"I probably would have, if I'd had a little more time," she laughed. "Even though I'm not a great fan of the one-night stand, I think I would have made an exception in his case."

CHAPTER 6

James was so furious at Kerrie's refusal to even consider going out with him he thought about calling Andy Dickinson and telling him flat out to leave Kerrie alone. After all, he reasoned, Kerrie's only motive for giving him the brush off was because she was so smitten with the British actor, but after James received a serendipitous phone call from his boss telling him that he was scheduled to accompany another author on an overseas trip, the phone call to Andy was put on hold in favor of an even better opportunity to warn him off once he got back to England.

Andy's fervent quest to locate Kerrie was also sidetracked when he received an offer to star in a pilot for a proposed television series. Because the script had been written by a good friend of his, and was to be directed by a man he highly respected but had never had the opportunity to work with, Andy gladly accepted. While he didn't like the idea of putting his search for Kerrie aside, the shooting schedule for the pilot was very tight. What with learning his lines, wardrobe fittings, photo shoots, rehearsals and endless production meetings, Andy soon found he had little time for anything but work.

One morning a couple of weeks later while he was sitting in the makeup room trying to work out a particularly difficult bit of dialogue, the actor happened to glance over at one of his co-stars who was sitting in an adjacent chair reading the tabloids. There at the bottom of the page facing him was a small photograph of Kerrie.

"May I see that?" he asked, snatching the paper out of his fellow actor's hand before the man had time to respond.

Andy stared at the picture for a very long time before finally reading the accompanying blurb. It just said that Kerrie Sherman had returned to the States after a very successful book tour in the UK and was now planning to start work on a second novel, subject unknown.

In an odd twist of fate, there was also a photo of Andy right alongside Kerrie's and a short note about the pilot he was shooting, so he hastily tore the two articles off the page and stuffed them in his pocket before handing the tattered paper back to his co-star with an apologetic grin.

Unfortunately, Andy wasn't the only one who read those two short articles that morning. Having arrived in England two days earlier, James was having breakfast in his London hotel room, dressed in a utility worker's uniform, when he also came across the side-by-side photos of Kerrie and Andy. Seeing them in such close proximity, even in print, upset him so badly he flew into a rage and ripped the newspaper to shreds. Then after taking a final sip of coffee, James grabbed his jacket and stomped out the door. There was much to do.

The publicist knew where the actor lived because he had surreptitiously followed Andy home after bumping into him in front of the book store during his last visit to London with Kerrie. Now he was anxious to gain entry to the apartment and have a look around because he wanted to make sure that Kerrie and Andy had not been exchanging letters or email. And, if they had been in touch, he wanted to find out exactly what was going on between them.

James knew that Andy was hard at work on the pilot and spent most of his time at the studio, so he hailed a taxi and gave the driver the actor's address. He'd been busy the day before procuring a reasonably convincing fake of a London Energy employee's badge and planned on having the building manager let him in on the guise of checking out a faulty electric meter in Andy's apartment.

After knocking on the manager's door, flashing his phony ID and explaining why he was there, the manager, an overweight, middle-aged man, who wore a grease-stained t-shirt and was holding onto an unusually large sandwich filled with huge hunks of bacon, begrudgingly lead him down the hall to Andy's apartment.

James walked a few paces behind the sandwich man, carefully side-stepping the bits of bacon and grease that were dropping out of the sandwich along the way.

"Just let me know when you're done so I can come back and lock up," he said after unlocking Andy's front door and calling out to announce the unannounced intrusion. Finding the apartment empty, he wasn't the least bit interested in sticking around to supervise the inspection because for one thing, Monty Scott was a very trusting soul, and, at the moment, was much more concerned about the football game on television and finishing his sandwich than a faulty electric meter.

After thanking Mr. Scott for his trouble, James let himself into the actor's tastefully furnished apartment while Monty scurried back to his kitchen, carefully cradling his sandwich in both hands to avoid any further loss.

The first thing James noticed when he walked inside was how meticulous the place was. There were no dishes in the kitchen sink, the bathroom towels looked clean and fluffy, and the contents of the dresser drawers in the bedroom were all neatly folded. James wasn't exactly sure what kind of incriminating evidence he was looking for, but intended to make a thorough search in order to ease his mind that there had been no communication between Andy and Kerrie.

Thinking he might find something scribbled on the note pad that was sitting next to the telephone on the kitchen counter, James was disappointed to find that it had never been used. And the stack of unopened mail sitting on the counter right alongside was made up of the usual assortment of unsolicited ads and a couple of utility bills.

James went back to the bedroom for a further look around and was immediately drawn to the laptop computer on one of the bedside tables. He took the computer over to the bed and sat down and turned it on. There was a saved mail file on the desktop so he clicked on the icon. There was nothing out of the ordinary in the files. Most of the e-mails were from someone named Kate who, judging by the subject titles, must have been Andy's agent or manager. James quickly scrolled down the long list of entries until one in particular caught his eye. The email was from Kate and subject title was 'Kerrie Sherman.' James clicked the file open with shaky hands.

"Hey there," the message began. "I just double checked my files as promised and sorry to say the email address you are looking for is long gone. I've also checked the phone book and the Writer's Guild, but came up empty. I think your only option is to contact her publisher, if you haven't already done so. I'm sure they'd be happy to pass on your message. By the way, you never did say why you've taken such a keen interest in Kerrie. Could it have anything to do with that gorgeous photograph of her on the back of her book? Inquiring minds want to know. LOL."

James immediately clicked on the sent mail icon for Andy's reply.

"Re: Kerrie Sherman"

As much as it pains me to withhold any juicy bits of information regarding my personal life from you, and I dare say you know far too much already, I'm afraid I'll have to keep this little tidbit to myself. I owe you one. XOX."

James slammed the laptop shut. Now had all the proof he needed to confirm his suspicion that Andy's interest in Kerrie was more than just professional courtesy. He then tore through the closet and even checked under the bed for anything else he might find regarding Kerrie, but aside from a copy of her book laying prominently on one of the night stands, he found nothing else.

James was so wrapped up in searching for clues, he'd lost all track of time and now suddenly realized he'd better leave before the manager, who was surely done with his lunch by now, came back and found him rummaging around.

He was just walking out of the bedroom when James thought he heard voices outside in the hallway followed by the sound of a key in the door. Because James was not sure if the actor would recognize him from the party in spite of the disguise, James dove into the hall closet and silently prayed that Andy hadn't returned for a jacket.

"I'll just be a moment," he heard the actor say to an unidentified companion. "The computer is in the bedroom."

James held his breath when Andy walked past the closet door. A moment later, he walked back into the living room. The men were talking so softly that James couldn't make out what they were saying but a few moments later, both men laughed, followed by the sound of the front door opening and closing, and then all was silent. Peering out of the closet to make sure they'd gone, James then ran into the kitchen, out the back door and down the stairs.

James was afraid he might run into Andy as he exited the alley, so he crouched under the stairwell and waited impatiently for the actor to leave the building. It took quite a bit longer than he had anticipated because on his way out, Andy and his friend ran into Monty Scott in the hallway. "Ah, Mr. Dickinson, I was just on me way to your apartment to check on the man from the electric company," he explained. "I hope he didn't startle you."

Andy gave Monty one of those unyielding stares that he was so famous for. "There was nobody in my apartment, Mr. Scott."

"Well of course there was," he said impatiently. "I let the bloke in about an hour ago. He said something about checking a faulty meter in your apartment and I told him to come get me when he was done so I could lock up. But if you say no one was there, I reckon it must have slipped his mind."

"Well, there's no harm done, I suppose," said Andy, "but from now on, I'd appreciate it if you'd call me and let me know about such things. I don't like the idea of strangers in my house when I'm not there. Faulty meter or not, they should have scheduled an appointment."

Not giving the manager a chance to respond, Andy and his friend turned and walked away.

James watched from the alley as the two men finally left the building, climbed into a car parked out in front and drove off. He was thankful he hadn't been caught because he wouldn't be able to proceed with his plans if he'd been arrested for trespassing and stuck in a London jail with nobody to bail him out.

Ted Stephens had only spoken to briefly Kerrie since she got back from the UK and she sounded just fine then, but after the disturbing phone call from Andy, the psychic was in the midst of a moral dilemma. On the one hand, he wanted to let her know that he'd been in touch with Andy and share the actor's distressing information, but at the same time he knew he should take his own advice and stay out of it. Ordinarily that would not have been a problem, but Ted had a bad feeling about James because people carried specific traits, both good and bad, from one lifetime to another. What a person does in one life experience influences how they behave in the next. A murderer's soul, for example, could easily continue to murder in subsequent incarnations if he chose not to repent. And because we usually surround ourselves with the people we were with in previous lives, patterns often repeat themselves. James was already proving this by his jealous and controlling behavior towards Kerrie, and Ted felt certain it would only get worse.

After meditating on the subject for several nights, Ted came to the reluctant conclusion that he would not interfere, but that didn't keep him from calling Kerrie the next day to see how she was.

"I'm fine thanks, and am anxious to get started on the new book, but I'm still disappointed that I couldn't spend a little more time with Andy Dickinson while I was in London," she sighed. "The more I think about it, our brief meeting probably didn't do anything to jolt his memory about me, and I'm quite sure that witnessing my ugly row with James probably did more harm than good as far as making him want to get to know me any better."

"I wouldn't be so sure," said Ted. "Andy Dickinson is intelligent and very intuitive. I'm quite sure he has no ill feelings about it. After all, from the way you described the scene to me, it was James who made an ass of himself, not you."

"I know, but that was a once in a lifetime chance to connect with Andy and James made a big mess out of it. Who knows if I'll ever see him again?"

"What have I always told you? Any negativity you put out there will come back to you tenfold," he reminded her, "so rather than dwelling on that unfortunate incident, make up your mind that you will see Andy again. And pray that when it happens, your publicist won't be around to muck things up."

"I'm not worried about that because I'm done with James. He called me the day after we got back and suggested we have dinner together, and I pretty much told him to bug off for good."

"Good." said Ted, happy to hear that Kerrie had done something to get James out of her life. "It's been a long time

72

coming, but you're now a successful author and you don't need any negative energy around you to hamper all the good that you've been working so hard to achieve."

"I agree with you, Ted, but I just can't shake the feeling that I haven't seen last of James Goldman."

Ted knew Kerrie was right, but didn't want to say so. He knew in his heart that James probably wasn't going to leave her alone and there was no stopping him.

After he left Andy's apartment, James went back to his hotel room to figure out what he was going to do next. Now that he knew for sure that Andy was trying to locate Kerrie, he had to be stopped. Maybe arranging some sort of "accident" to maim or incapacitate Andy would be the best way to go, but violence could be so unpredictable. What if Andy actually died? It wasn't that James had any qualms about taking the actor's life because Andy's demise would be a blessing, but how could he be one hundred percent sure he wouldn't get caught? After all, no matter how carefully laid out his plans might be, the odds would still be against him. He blamed Kerrie for his current dilemma because if she had just accepted his invitation to go out for dinner the day they got back, he could have made her forget all about the British heartthrob and none of this unpleasantness would have been necessary.

Over the next couple of days James thought carefully about several different ways to get Andy Dickinson out of the way and although his final plans were put on hold when the author he was hired to look after arrived in England, James had a pretty good idea of what needed to be done.

After returning to the States the following week, James began putting his plan into action. His first task was to find out what Kerrie was up to, and the best way to do that was by asking her best friend, Meg. Kerrie had talked about her during their trip abroad so he knew Meg's last name and that she was a yoga instructor. Now all he had to do was hire a private investigator to track her down.

It didn't take long to find out that Meg was working at an upscale yoga center near the beach and the following day, James went down there and signed up for a trial membership. By four o'clock that afternoon, he was properly outfitted and standing

73

outside the door of Meg's beginner's class with the rest of the students waiting for the teacher to arrive.

Because he was the only man in the class, several of the women found excuses to walk up and say hello but rather than feeling flattered, all the attention made him feel like a piece of prime meat hanging in a butcher shop window.

He spent a few uncomfortable moments making small talk with the fawning females, and James was thrilled when Meg opened up the door to let them all in.

"Welcome to Basic Yoga. For those of you who are new to the class," she said, looking directly at the good-looking man smiling back at her from the front row, "just try and keep up, and you'll soon get the hang of it. As for the rest of you, please try hard to make me look good in front of the newcomers," she said with a wink. "Okay, places everyone."

James worked out every morning on a home gym, but he wasn't used to placing his body in the unusual positions that Yoga required, so he struggled at first. Meg walked over and helped him out several times during the hour-long class and because there seemed to be a lot of innocent flirting going on between the two, she began to wonder if this man was purposely messing up just to get her attention. She really didn't care. It had been quite a while since anyone had flirted with her so openly and she was enjoying it.

After the session ended, Meg spent a few minutes tidying up the room in preparation for her next class, then walked across the street to the neighborhood juice bar for a pick-me-up. She saw that there was an empty table out front as she was getting her order and she walked over, sat down, set her glass down on the table in front of her and was reaching into her purse for her cell phone to make a quick call to Kerrie when someone whispered in her ear. "Would you consider me a suck up if I offered to buy the teacher a muffin to go along with that drink?"

Meg was startled and spun around quickly in her chair. In doing so, her knee hit the underside of the table, knocking over her smoothie. The sticky goo began to ooze towards her and she jumped out of her chair a split second before the spill landed on her.

"Oh that's just, great!" she fumed, fumbling for a napkin to stop the flow. Then, remembering the reason she was startled in the first place, Meg looked up accusingly to see who was responsible for the mess.

"I'm sorry," he said with a sheepish grin. She immediately recognized him as the good-looking guy in her class. "I didn't mean to frighten you, and now it looks like I owe you more than just a muffin. Let me get you another drink."

"No, that's okay," she snapped, tossing her smoothie-soaked napkin on the table in defeat. "It really wasn't very good and I was just about to leave anyway. I've got to get ready for my next class."

"I really think I need to make it up to you," he insisted. "Could I buy you a cup of coffee later or would that be breaching the teacher-student ethic?"

Even though she was still annoyed that he snuck up on her like that, there was something about this guy that Meg found irresistible to ignore and wanted the chance to find out why. "I won't get fired for fraternizing, if that's what you mean."

"Great." he said, thankful he hadn't scared her off. "I'll pick you up at nine, if that's okay."

"Okay. That'll give me enough time to take a quick shower and get changed after my last class, so I'll see you then," she said, feeling like a teenager who was about to go out on a first date.

The thought of going out for coffee with this guy was a little unnerving because she hadn't socialized much lately and because her long-term relationship with Steve ended so badly, Meg had sworn off men for the time being. But, she reasoned, a harmless cup of coffee certainly wasn't a lifelong commitment and it'd be good practice for when she was ready to start dating again.

CHAPTER 7

James was waiting for Meg in the lobby of the Yoga Center and greeted her with an endearing smile. "I'm not too familiar with the neighborhood," he explained. "Is there someplace nearby that makes a wicked caramel latte?"

She didn't feel comfortable about getting into a total stranger's car anyway, so Meg suggested a neighborhood coffee house a couple of blocks away. She'd been there once or twice before and really like it. "The Coffee Klatch is within walking distance, and everything they make is wonderful."

"Off we go then," he said, gallantly extending his arm. Meg couldn't remember the last time anyone had made this kind of polite gesture and thought to herself that perhaps chivalry wasn't dead after all.

After they got their order, they found a small vacant table. James pulled out Meg's chair for her, set her drink and a plate of biscotti in front of her, then sat down across from her. He didn't say anything at first, and just stared at her hands. After a moment, apparently content at what he saw, he broke into a wide grin.

"What was that all about?" she asked, looking down to make sure she wasn't walking around with a big blob of ink or something on her fingers.

"I was just looking for symbols of attachment," he explained. "You know, wedding rings, engagement rings, things like that. I know we're just having an innocent cup of coffee, but I don't want to worry about a jealous husband bursting in on us and punching my lights out." he joked.

Meg didn't think it was funny because his comment raised suspicions. Maybe this guy made a habit of picking up married women. "You make it sound as though it's happened to you before.

"Just once." he said, staring at his coffee cup with a scowl. "It was a first date, and we were sitting in a restaurant waiting for our order when this huge guy walks in, sees me sitting with his wife and went into a rage. Fortunately, he was in such a foul mood he didn't take careful aim when he took a swing at me and missed. I had just enough time to get the hell out of there before he had the chance to try again."

"Didn't you know the woman was married?" she asked, worried that maybe she should have gotten to know him better before accepting his invitation for coffee.

"I knew she and her husband were recently separated, but she told me that her ex had lived out of state. She had no idea he was stalking her until he showed up at the restaurant"

"Did you see her again after that?"

"Well, she called several times to apologize, and hinted that she'd like to go out with me again, but, no. I don't need that kind of stress in my life, so please tell me your past isn't going to come back to haunt me because I'm not fond of physical violence, and I'm very attracted to you," he said, reaching out across the table to take her hand. "In fact, I'm so attracted to you, I don't think I'd be able to run away and leave you to face the consequences of a jealous lover all by yourself. Instead, I'd be forced to defend your honor and would probably end up in the emergency room with multiple injuries because I'm a lover, not a fighter."

She thought he was laying it on a bit thick, but James was charmingly irresistible so it was easy enough to forgive his sappy approach.

"I don't think you have anything to worry about. My last relationship ended a couple of months ago. We were together for two years and he's now married to the woman he was cheating on me with. Nice, huh? And from what I understand, they're living happily ever somewhere on the East Coast, so I'm sure he won't be interrupting our coffee date."

"Coffee date?" he asked in a comically shocked tone. "That's all I am to you? A pitiful coffee date?"

"Well I hardly know you well enough to think of this as anything else," she laughed.

"I'm wounded to my very soul," he said with dramatic flair, "but you do make a rather good point. We are practically strangers and the only way to remedy this awkward situation is to ask you out again. Tomorrow perhaps? For dinner? Please don't say no. A rejection would render me hopelessly despondent, and I can't afford years of psychotherapy to put me right again, so what do you say?" he asked, getting off the chair and down on one knee. "Please?"

One of the things Meg couldn't resist in a man was a sense of humor, so she happily agreed to another date.

"Well, thank God for that." he said, getting up off the floor and brushing off his trousers. "I'm a great beggar, but not so adept at groveling. Thanks for saving me the embarrassment."

"Anytime," said Meg, taking the last bite of her biscotti. She was feeling really good about this guy and was glad he wanted to see her again, but for some reason, she didn't remember him ever telling her his name. "So now that I've agreed to another date, it might help if I knew what to call you."

Because he was usually a stickler for details, James was horrified to realize that coming up with an alias was the one element in his scheme to win Meg over that he had somehow overlooked. He had to think fast.

"Am I that forgettable?" he asked, cleverly shifting the blame to her. "I distinctly remember introducing myself to you in class the first time you came over to help me with the Down Dog position. Maybe you didn't hear me because you were distracted by my tail wagging," he laughed.

Meg decided he probably did tell her his name and feeling guilty for not having paid attention to him during class, she apologized for the oversight.

James was pleased with himself and decided to play the game a bit longer. "Well, since I'm not one to hold a grudge I do accept your apology, but at the same time, I shouldn't be letting you off so easy," he teased. "Maybe I should try the Rumplestiltskin approach and give you three days to figure out my name."

"And if I don't get it by then?" she asked. "Don't make the stakes too high, because it's not like I'm asking you to spin thread into gold, you know."

James was glad to see that Meg was going along with his little ploy because it bought him some time to reinvent himself. "Don't worry, I'm not interested in your firstborn child," he said, referring to the price the young fairy tale queen would have to pay Rumplestiltskin if she didn't guess his name, "but I think spending the weekend with me at a cozy little lodge up in the mountains would be a fair penalty, don't you agree?"

It was too soon to commit herself to an overnight date with a total stranger, so Meg just smiled and said a silent prayer that sometime within the next three days she'd get lucky and remember this guy's name.

They exchanged phone numbers before they left the coffee shop, and James walked her back to the Yoga Center where they said their goodnights.

As soon as Meg got home, she called Kerrie to tell her all about it. Kerrie was thrilled to hear that Meg had finally decided to come out from under her rock. She was worried that the pain of her breakup with Steven would have kept her out of circulation for a very long time.

"I'm really happy for you, and he sounds terrific," said Kerrie. It's about time you got out of the house and had a little fun."

"I could say the same about you," said Meg. "Ever since you've been back from England, you've been cooped up in your apartment, and I'm pretty sure you're having another Andy Dickinson movie marathon as well.

"I'm also working on my book," Kerrie said defensively, "but don't worry. If Prince Charming happens to knock on my door, I won't turn him away."

"Maybe I should see if my new friend has a single best friend."

"And maybe you should at least find out your friend's name and get to know him a little better before dragging me into it," laughed Kerrie. I thought James was a nice guy at first, too, and look what happened."

"This guy is nothing like James." Meg protested. "He's actually quite charming, not overbearing, and has a great sense of humor. And speaking of your psychotic publicist, have you heard anything more from him?"

"No, but like I told Ted the other day, I have a strange feeling he's not done with me yet and I'm getting kind of paranoid about it. Every time I leave the apartment, I feel like he's lurking about. It's kind of unsettling."

"Don't let your imagination run wild. James has probably set his sights on a new victim by now," said Meg, in an attempt to be reassuring.

"I hope you're right," sighed Kerrie, "but I feel sorry for whoever she might be because nobody deserves to get involved with Psycho Jim."

By their third date, Meg still hadn't correctly guessed her new friend's name, but they'd been out together every night since they met and she felt comfortable being with him. She was also looking forward to a weekend in the mountains.

James picked her up at the Yoga Center after her last class on Friday night, and after a little coaxing by Meg on their long drive up to the mountains, he finally revealed his newly made up identity to her. He said his name was Curt Bachman, that he'd only recently moved down to L.A. from the San Francisco Bay area, and he ran his own business, a computer services company which was similar to the Geek Squad. He went on to that since the business was still relatively new, he was the only geek and that kept him quite busy.

As far as Meg was concerned, he was far from being an unattractive, socially awkward man, except when it came to being romantic. Not once during the entire weekend at the lodge did he try and make a move on her. At first, she was hurt, thinking that he wasn't attracted to her after all, but when he explained that he wanted to take things slow and get to know her better before taking the relationship to the next level, she was impressed that he was such a gentleman. And by the time he dropped her off at her apartment on Sunday night, Meg knew she was falling in love.

Meg was still worried that Kerrie was home brooding over Andy Dickinson way too much, so she called Curt the next day and asked if he could possibly fix her friend up with any of his friends. He apologized and said that all his buddies were living up in San

Francisco but if any of them came down to visit, he'd see what he could do.

She thought it was kind of odd that he hadn't made any new acquaintances since moving to Los Angeles, but he explained that he was a bit of a loner, and since he since had her in his life, he wasn't the least bit interested in making any other new friends.

Now that they were officially a couple, Meg wanted to introduce Curt to Kerrie and some of her other friends, but each time she set up a date for everyone to get together, he always canceled at the last minute, sighting commitments at work. Although he had warned her that he was on call 24/7 for emergency response, she didn't like the fact that his work schedule was miserably unpredictable and also thought it was strange that he never seemed to get called away when they were alone together.

"It's just the luck of the draw, I guess." he explained after she brought up the subject one night at dinner. That was a red flag for him and he made a quick mental note to cancel a date or two in the future to make his excuse seem more plausible.

"Sounds more like Murphy's Law to me. Whatever can go wrong, will go wrong when making plans for all of us to get together," she shrugged. "And my friends are beginning to either wonder if you really exist at all, or maybe I'm trying to hide you from them because there's something terribly wrong with you."

Actually, the only one who questioned Curt's invisible man status was Kerrie. She had invited Meg and Curt over for dinner two weekends in a row, but both evenings Meg arrived alone with a bottle of wine and the usual apologies.

Kerrie was concerned that something was wrong with the whole situation, but didn't want to voice her opinion quite yet. "So, do you think I'm ever going to meet this Prince Charming of yours?"

"Of course, you are," said Meg. "I'm sure once his business is more stable and he can hire a few other technicians to go out on calls, you'll be seeing a lot of him. These things just take time."

"If I didn't know you better, I'd swear you made this guy up."

"Think what you like, but I'm not making him up, and there's nothing wrong with him either. In fact," she said, extending her arm and showing off a very expensive diamond bracelet, "look what he gave me this morning."

Kerrie knew that there was no way Meg could afford such a costly piece of jewelry on her meager salary, so she had to admit that it must have been a gift from the elusive Curt. "It's beautiful," she said, admiring the bauble, "but if his business is just getting started and he can't even afford employees, how can he manage to come up with enough money to buy that? It must have cost a fortune."

"I'm sure it did, but when I tried to tell him it was way too expensive for me to accept, he told me that nothing was too good for me, then mumbled something about paying it off on time. He looked so hurt, I was sorry I'd brought it up."

"I hope he can make the payments, or the repo man will be pounding on your door," laughed Kerrie.

"Let's hope not," said Meg, shuddering at the thought of a big, burly, cigar-smoking guy with no neck snatching the bracelet off her wrist. "But I don't think that's going to happen. Curt told me this morning he's going to Europe at the end of the month to attend some kind of international computer conference in Paris and said he'd come back with some innovative ways to improve his company and make lots of money. I think he said he's going to be gone for three weeks and I'm really going to miss him." she sighed. "We haven't gone without seeing each other for more than a day since we started dating."

"How can he afford a trip to Europe?" Kerrie wondered, thinking it was really odd that he could manage paying for both a trip overseas and the bracelet.

"He said he couldn't afford not to," said Meg. She was clearly annoyed by Kerrie's comment. "And why are you giving me the third degree? It really sounds like you don't trust him."

"How can I not trust someone I don't even know?" said Kerrie, trying to hide her suspicions about Meg's new boyfriend. "And anyway, Curt's finances are none of my business, so as long as you're happy with him, I trust your judgment and wish you all the best."

Later that evening as she was getting ready for bed, Kerrie couldn't seem to get the mysterious Curt out of her mind. He sounded too good to be true, and that worried her. The last thing she wanted was to see was Meg getting hurt by a con artist, but what could Curt possibly want from Meg, anyway? It wasn't like she was a heiress or something.

The following evening when Curt came to pick up Meg for their date, she brought up the details of her conversation with Kerrie the night before in the hopes he'd explain more about what was going on in his life. Up until this point, he'd actually said very little.

"She was asking all these questions about why you were never around to meet my friends, and wondered how you could afford this beautiful bracelet and a three-week trip to Europe when your business is just getting off the ground."

"Doesn't she have anything better to do than question my financial stability?" he asked, a little too harshly.

She was startled by his sudden change of mood, so Meg chose her words carefully before answering.

"Of course, she does. Kerrie keeps herself very busy. I think I told you that she's an author, and her first novel landed on the New York Times best seller list. She was in Europe a couple of months ago promoting the book and has started work on the sequel. I guess she's just a little leery of men right now because she had an awful episode with the creepy publicist who went along with her on the book tour. She said he was controlling to the point of obsession and even went so far as to ruin a meeting she had with her favorite actor, Andy Dickinson."

Curt shifted slightly in his chair at the mention of the actor's name.

"She was so upset by his behavior, she called me in the middle of the night from the airport begging me to pick her up. She said she wanted to get away from him as quickly as possible, and even though she ditched him, the guy had the nerve to call and ask her out on a date the next day. What a loser."

After hearing that Kerrie had lied to him about her arrangement with Meg to pick her up at the airport, it was all he could do to keep his rage under control. If she lied about a little thing like that, what else had she been untruthful about? Maybe she hadn't gone to Liverpool after all and had spent the day with Andy Dickinson instead, and then at the after party was only pretending not to know him.

In James' twisted mind it was all becoming painfully clear. Kerrie had given him the brush off so that she could devote all her attention to Andy Dickinson.

He was so deep in thought, he didn't realize that Meg was still talking.

"...and I don't blame her," she continued. "So, what do you think about a guy like that?"

Ignoring her question, he immediately asked one of his own. "Did she say anything about ditching her publicist to spend any time with that actor while she was in England? You know, the one you said she's so interested in?"

"Oh, no, nothing like that," said Meg, wondering about Curt's sudden interest in Kerrie. "All she told me was that James, that's his name, ruined her whole trip, and I for one think she'hs well rid of him."

Even though James didn't like what he was hearing, he was glad to finally have an excuse to pump Meg for information about Kerrie. "Has she been in contact with the guy since she came back? I mean, it's only logical that if she was so attracted to him, she'd try to keep in touch."

"I think she's hoping that he'll find her," she explained, "but she's kind of embarrassed about the ugly scene James caused at that party and is worried that he ruined her chances of getting to know Andy. I think she wants to call him and apologize, but doesn't have enough nerve."

Finding out that Kerrie hadn't been trying to track Andy down was the first bit of good news he'd had all night. "I'm sure he would have called by now if he was interested, but that's a long shot, isn't it?" he asked cheerfully. "I mean, he must have thousands of women dying to go out with him, so why would he be interested in an American author he'd only met for five minutes?"

"I was thinking the same thing," she admitted, "but Kerrie said there was some kind of instant chemistry between them that went far beyond casual flirting, and she's almost certain he'll try and find her. Kerrie is very interested in the metaphysical world, so maybe she thinks they once knew each other from a past life or something," she joked.

"I hope you don't believe in all that nonsense," he said with a sneer. "It's a lot of rubbish, if you ask me. People who believe in reincarnation, karma, ghosts or the bogey man should have their heads examined."

CHAPTER 8

Even though James and Meg had planned to go out to eat and then catch a movie that night, he cut their date short and, citing a headache, took her home right after dinner. Meg's revelation that Kerrie had lied to him put James in the foulest of moods and he needed some alone time to sort it all out.

In his paranoid way of thinking, James was now certain that Kerrie and Andy were somehow plotting against him. Of course, he didn't totally blame Kerrie. She had no doubt been brainwashed by the actor, and James knew it would be easy enough to set her straight when the time came. Meanwhile, he needed to figure out a way to discredit Andy in her eyes so she'd realize what kind of conniving, devious devil the man really was.

His first thought was to contact the tabloids, both in the U.S. and in the U.K. and plant a salacious story. Surely that email he came across on Andy's computer regarding the juicy tidbits of his personal life would be a good place to start. While it was true that Andy's reputation as a ladies' man was legendary, what about all the speculation that it wasn't just the ladies that Dandy Andy fancied?

Since he was going to be back in England the following week, he'd be able to check into Andy's personal life more thoroughly. Perhaps there was a spurned male lover out there somewhere who'd be willing to come forward with some scandalous information. And if that didn't work out, it would certainly be easy enough to hire an out of work actor to portray Andy's jilted boy toy. Meanwhile, he needed to confront Kerrie about her lies and was on the phone to her first thing the next morning.

Kerrie was in the middle of reediting a particularly challenging paragraph of her new book when the phone broke her train of thought. Her normal routine would have been to check the caller ID before answering, but because she was expecting a call from the cable company to confirm an appointment later in the day, she distractedly reached over and picked up the phone without checking to see who it was.

"How's my favorite author?" he asked, trying to sound as friendly as possible. "Hard at work on your new book?"

Kerrie didn't recognize his voice at first, because she was still focused on her laptop. "Who is this?"

James was certain that she was trying to provoke him by pretending not to know who he was, but managed a composed response nonetheless. "After all we've been through, my *friend*, was it really that easy to erase me from your memory?"

It took a moment to clear her head, but that accusing tone was instantly recognizable and Kerrie was tempted to hang up on him, but rather than risk making him angry again she knew it would be better to see what he wanted, and that she'd have to be careful how she responded.

"No, of course not, James," she said, trying not to sound as flustered as she truly was." I'm sorry. I guess my mind was somewhere else."

He tried to be gracious because he didn't want to let her know how truly angry he was.

"No apology necessary," he said, gritting his teeth, "but since you've now hurt my feelings, the least you could do is join me for dinner tonight to make up for it. How's eight o'clock?"

"That's impossible, James," she said, hoping he wouldn't belabor the invitation, " I'm busy tonight."

"I won't take no for an answer so cancel your plans and I'll pick you up at eight." And before she could argue the point any further, he hung up.

Kerrie couldn't believe that James was too much of a coward to remain on the line and graciously accept her refusal, so she hit redial to call him right back because there was no way she was going to allow him to force his way back into her life. She was pretty sure he wouldn't bother to answer her return call and she was right. When his voicemail finally did pick up, Kerrie left a message.

"James, please don't play games. I said I was busy and can't have dinner with you tonight, so don't bother coming by." Then, thinking she should probably end the call on a more upbeat note, she added, "Perhaps another time."

Kerrie left James three more messages throughout the day to make sure he understood that she was not going to be coerced into having dinner with him, but when her doorbell rang at seven forty-five, she knew her efforts had been completely wasted and begrudgingly answered the door.

"I know I'm a wee bit early," he said, pushing his way past her and into the living room before she had the chance to turn him away, "but I just wanted to make sure I caught you before your *other plans* showed up."

Of course, there were no other plans, so Kerrie had to think fast and make up some sort of excuse to get rid of him.

"I was supposed to be going out with my friend Meg, but she just called a little while ago to cancel. I know I must have mentioned that she taught yoga, but anyway," she stuttered, "one of the other instructors called in sick at the last minute so they asked Meg to take over her eight o'clock class."

"Oh, that's too bad." he said, trying to sound sympathetic even though he knew she was lying. He had just spoken to Meg on his way over to Kerrie's and knew she didn't have to go to work. "Well, your friend's loss is my gain because now you're free to have dinner with me. I've made reservations at this great place in Malibu that overlooks the ocean and they have..."

"I don't think so, James," she interrupted, hoping to stop him before he got too carried away. "Since Meg can't make it, I think I'm just going to stay in and watch a movie."

Seeing a stack of DVDs on the coffee table, James walked over and began looking through them, then immediately pulled his hands away in disgust, looking as though he had just grabbed hold of a pile of steaming poop. "I see that you still haven't had your fill of Andy Dickinson, have you?"

Kerrie bristled at the tone in which James said his name, and even more upset that he decided to show up uninvited and force his way in, she forgot all about trying to keep him calm. "What I watch is my business, and who I choose to spend my time with should be my decision as well and tonight I want to be alone."

James listened to what she had to say, but rather than taking a hint and walking out the door, he strolled over to the couch and sat down instead.

"Don't you get it, James?" she said, throwing her hands up in exasperation. "I don't want to go out with you tonight or any other night because all we had was a brief working relationship and now that it's over, we're done. You and I have nothing in common, and I've got all the friends and dinner dates I can handle right now, so let's just leave it at that, okay?"

"I know for a fact that you've found a way to handle another new friend," he said, reaching for one of the DVDs off the coffee table then waving it accusingly in the air. "How is it that you've managed to find room enough in your cluttered life for him but can't seem to find any time for me?"

"What the hell are you talking about?" she said, grabbing the DVD out of his hand. "You were with me when I met Andy for the first and only time, and thanks to your meddling, that meeting ended on a rather sour note."

James immediately jumped up off the couch and got so close to Kerrie that they were practically nose to nose. "Quit lying!" he said, "I know you've been in touch with him since then and you were probably seeing him behind my back the whole time we were in London, weren't you?"

"It's really none of your business, but just so you know," she shouted after taking a couple of steps back, "I haven't been in touch with Andy since that horrible night in London, thanks to you."

"Temper, temper," he cooed. "Why are you getting yourself so worked up? Is it because you're still mad at me for ruining your little flirtation, or are you worried that I'll find out that you've been lying to me all along about your relationship with Andy Dickinson?"

"I'm getting worked up because once again you're sticking your nose where it doesn't belong," she said, staring him down. "My personal life is none of your business, I don't owe you any explanations and, to be honest, you don't mean enough to me to waste my time trying to think up lies."

"Oh really?" he said, toning his voice down so that he sounded like a wise old owl. "Then why did you lie to me about having previously arranged for your friend Meg to pick you up at the airport? I know you called her from the ladies' room to come and pick you up."

Kerrie was stunned. How could he possibly know that? But rather than trying to deny it, she tried to change the subject by once again asking James to leave.

Unfortunately, James refused to be dismissed and kept right on talking. "...and if you lied to me about a small thing like that," he continued, pacing back and forth across the living room like Sherlock Holmes pondering a clue, "I'm quite certain there's a great deal more to this Andy Dickinson thing than you're willing to admit."

Finally, at her breaking point, Kerrie decided that maybe if she made him angry enough, he'd leave. "Well maybe there is something going on," she lied, "but that's between Andy and I, so why don't you just shut up, get over it and get the hell out of my house?"

James stood up in a rage and ran towards Kerrie. He grabbed her by the shoulders then, pinning her arms to her sides, he shoved her up against the wall. Kerrie struggled to break free, but James was much too strong.

"Andy doesn't deserve you!" he yelled. "He couldn't possibly love you as much as I do, and there's no way I will ever allow him to come between us, do you understand?"

If Kerrie had been frightened before, she was now, terrified because she knew she was staring into the eyes of a madman.

Before she could respond, James pressed his body up against hers and began grabbing at her blouse. Kerrie started to panic but knew she had to do something to stop him.

Because his upper body was pressed tightly against hers it was impossible to squirm away but her legs were unimpaired so with all the strength she could manage, Kerrie thrust her left knee hard up into James' crotch.

The force of the well-aimed blow was so intense, he let out a horrible scream, then immediately doubled over in pain.

She wanted to make sure he was completely incapacitated, so Kerrie then swung hard at his head hoping to knock him out long enough for her to call the police. As soon as her hand connected with his head, he fell to the floor in a fetal position with four deep scratch marks on the side of his face.

Kerrie immediately raced over to the coffee table and grabbed her cell phone, but before she had the chance to dial 911, James sprung up, snatched the phone out of her hand and threw it across the room where it smashed to bits against the brick fireplace.

"There's no need to get the police involved," he said calmly, although she could tell that he was still in a lot of pain. "And now that you know where we stand, I'll leave you be to give it some thought."

James couldn't straighten up all the way, so he slowly hobbled across the room to the front door, took hold of the doorknob to steady himself before turning around and said, "Remember what I said. Andy Dickinson will never come between us. I'll see to that." Then, he reached into his pocket and pulled out a money clip and carelessly tossed it onto the side table next to the door. "This should be enough to pay for a new phone and then some. Get yourself an upgrade. That piece of crap you were using was bound to fall apart sooner or later anyway." And with that, he let himself out.

Kerrie immediately dead-bolted the door behind him then ran to the phone next to the sofa and called the police. She was put on hold for a very long time, but when the desk sergeant finally answered, he sounded less than sympathetic after Kerrie told him what has just happened with James.

"Since you're not hurt, you weren't raped and he paid for the broken phone, there's not a whole lot we can do," the officer told her. He'd had many calls like this one in the past and experience told him it was just a lover's spat.

"But he assaulted me," she argued, "and he threatened an acquaintance of mine, Andy Dickinson, the actor."

"Look, lady," said the officer, sounding less cordial after hearing the actor's name because his horrible ex-wife had been a big fan. "From what I read in the papers, old Dandy Andy is nothing but trouble and I imagine he's in hot water with dozens of angry husbands and boyfriends on both continents so I wouldn't worry too much about him. As for you, all I can suggest is that if you insist on pursuing the matter, the best thing to do is serve your boyfriend with a restraining order."

"He's not my boyfriend." she said loudly, trying to get her point across. "He's my ex-publicist, and he's crazy."

"Crazy in love, is what it sounds like," the officer chuckled, "and I'm sure he'll call you first thing tomorrow morning to apologize."

Kerrie was frustrated that the officer just didn't get it. "I don't want him to call," she explained. "I want him arrested for assault."

All of the precinct phone lines were now ringing and the desk sergeant was anxious to end the call. "Like I said before, unless you're injured in any way, there's nothing we can do. If you don't want him to call, change your phone number, and if you don't want to see him, get the restraining order. You can come down to the station tomorrow morning and whoever is working the desk will give you all the necessary paperwork. In the meantime, lock your door and have a safe night."

The policeman's cavalier attitude was uncalled for, but Kerrie intended to take his advice about the restraining order, Kerrie cleaned up the cell phone debris then called Meg to tell her what happened.

"Oh my God, are you okay? Do you want me to come over?"

"No, I don't think he'll be back tonight, and I'm not hurt, but I would like you come to the police station with me in the morning, if that's okay. That officer who I spoke to really made me angry."

"Of course, I'll go," said Meg. "I'd hate to have to bail you out of jail for assaulting an officer," she laughed, "I'll come by and pick you up around nine, but in the meantime, make sure your door is locked, and if anything comes up between now and then, call me, okay? I'll keep the phone next to me all night."

Meg was worried about Kerrie and wished there was something she could do, but her concern was sidetracked when the doorbell rang around midnight and she found Curt standing on the stoop patiently waiting to be let in.

"I know it's late, but I was in the neighborhood," he laughed, giving her a kiss on the cheek as he walked into the living room. "You're not busy, are you?"

"No, but I'm really glad you're here because I just got off the phone with Kerrie a little while ago and I'm kind of upset."

Meg then recounted their phone conversation and Curt hung on her every word.

"My God, that's awful!" he said, trying to look as sympathetic as possible. "Is there anything I can do?"

It was then that Meg noticed the scratches on his face and momentarily forgot all about Kerrie. "What happened to you? Are you okay?"

"Oh, you mean these?" he asked, dismissing the angry scratch marks as though they were nothing more than a smudge of dirt. "Don't worry. It's nothing. I just had a run in with the neighbor's cat," he explained. "The darned thing got stranded up a tree, and the old lady who owned him begged me to get him down, but if you ask me, that cat was quite content up there because he put up quite a struggle when I tried to rescue him, as you can see." he shrugged, pointing to his cheek. "Now, back to more important things. How's Kerrie doing?"

"She says she's physically fine, but I could tell by her voice that she's really scared. I know she'll feel better once she files a restraining order on James tomorrow morning."

James was silently glad for the advance warning, but was angry that Kerrie called the police despite his warning not to. He got up from the couch and began to pace back and forth. "Those things are worthless," he declared, hoping to convince Meg to change Kerrie's mind. "I've never heard of a piece of paper stopping someone who is intent on harming someone else. It's a waste of time."

"Maybe so," she sighed, "but if it makes her feel better, why not do it? The only problem I have with restraining orders is that I've heard they aren't any good unless they are personally served on the person you're trying to keep away, and that can be difficult sometimes, especially if the offender thinks that they're coming after him and decides to go into hiding."

"Yeah, I've heard the same thing," he said, wondering if Kerrie had somehow been able to get access to his address. "Does Kerrie know where this jerk lives?"

"I don't think so, but she has his cell phone number, so maybe they can trace the address from that."

"Could be," he said distractedly, thinking about what time his plane was leaving in the morning and glad he'd be far away until

93

all this blew over, and after hearing about the restraining order, thought it would be a better idea to extend his stay overseas indefinitely, so he quickly made up a good viable excuse.

"Oh, by the way, one of the reasons I stopped by was to let you know that I'm going to be away on my trip a little longer than I first thought." he told her. "I got a call this afternoon from a friend of mine who is also going to the seminar in Paris, and he wondered if I would be available to accompany him to Italy after it's over. The guy's an old friend and was very instrumental in helping me get my company started, and I just couldn't say no," he said, looking convincingly sad. "I hope you understand."

The disappointment on Meg's face was obvious, but she tried to put on a brave front.

"I'm really sorry, but it can't be helped," said Curt, pulling her close. "I promise we can Skype or Facetime every day."

"I know it's not your fault," she said, putting her arms around his waist, "and I want your business to do well, but I'm really going to miss you."

Curt pulled her even closer. "I like hearing that, and I think I have just figured out a way to make you miss me even more," he said, with a knowing smile.

"Oh yeah? How?"

"Follow me." he said, taking her hand and pulling her towards the bedroom.

CHAPTER 9

Andy couldn't shake the feeling that something was terribly wrong, but couldn't figure what it was. All he knew was that he woke up in a terrible mood and had spent the rest of the day preparing for the worst.

Logically, he knew the feeling was probably his imagination because things couldn't have been going better. His biggest worry, the filming of his tv pilot, had wrapped the day before and the network was very pleased with the outcome. The show was almost guaranteed a spot in the new season line up and that alone should have bolstered the actor's spirits. So why all the doom and gloom?

By mid-afternoon, Andy decided that his dark mood could be a combination of the damp and dreary London weather and exhaustion, so he and decided to treat himself to a short vacation and booked a room at his favorite hotel on the Isle of Sark, one of his secret getaway spots. The tiny island, only three miles long and a mile and a half wide, was the perfect place to unwind. Just 80 miles off the south coast of England, visitors to the enchanted isle were taking a step back in time. No cars were allowed to pollute the 40 pristine miles of picturesque coastline, and visitors felt they were miles away from the hustle and bustle of everyday life. He immediately called the airlines and booked the next flight out.

Arriving late the next afternoon, Andy thought it was a good omen that he'd come to the island on this particular day because May 10 was Liberation Day on Sark, the anniversary of the island's liberation from occupation by the Germans at the end of World War II. The Channel Islands had been the only part of the British Isles which were captured, and each year residents came together to remember and celebrate their freedom. Andy was also celebrating a freedom of sorts. A loner by nature, he didn't get the chance to get away all by himself often enough, and after running himself ragged the past couple of months with the responsibilities of shooting the pilot, he was glad for the opportunity to finally spend some much-needed time alone.

After checking into the hotel, he took a leisurely stroll down to the Maison Pommier Restaurant and had a delicious dinner. He was perfectly content to dine alone and watch the rest of the world go by, and was finally able to shake off some of the previous day's doom and gloom but the ominous feeling of doom wasn't completely gone.

Because of his Bedouin lifestyle of traveling all over the world from one movie location to another, Andy didn't usually have trouble falling asleep in a strange bed, but after returning to his room after dinner, the actor discovered that this night was to be the exception. Every time he managed to doze off, a series of nightmares about Rachel's disappearance kept waking him up in a panic and it was the last dream of the night that ultimately caused the most anguish. It started out with Andy once again witnessing the final confrontation between Martin and Rachel but then it suddenly morphed into something else. In this updated version, the year was not 1862 and the participants were not Rachel and Martin, but Kerrie and James.

He watched in horror as James threw Kerrie up against the wall and tried to force himself on her. Andy instinctively knew that if Kerrie tried to fight him off she might end up dead. "He killed you once before and he'll do it again," he screamed. "I can't bear the thought of losing you another time!"

He never did find out whether Kerrie heard him or not because Andy was yelling so loudly, the couple in the next room called the front desk fearing that a terrible crime was being committed in the actor's room. The assistant manager rushed to Andy's door and hearing all the commotion, used his master key to let himself in.

"Are you all right, Mr. Dickinson?" he asked, after finding Andy all alone and thrashing about in his bed with a look of sheer terror. He realized that the actor was having some kind of nightmare, he tried to wake him up by calling his name, but when that didn't work he reached over and gave Andy's shoulder a hard shake.

Andy immediately sat up in bed and shoved the hapless manager away, taking a swing at him in the process. Luckily, the manager saw it coming and was able to dive out of the way just in time, but the force of the intended blow caused Andy to lose his balance and fall out of bed. The shock of hitting the floor was what finally woke him up.

By now, several other hotel guests who had been awakened by the ruckus had gathered outside the actor's door and were looking in with expressions ranging from worried curiosity to great amusement. Andy hated to be the center of attention when not on screen and quickly stood up and hastily walked over to the door and shut it in the faces on his uninvited audience without further explanation.

"You gave us quite a fright, Mr. Dickinson," said the manager, picking himself up off the floor. "Are you all right?"

"My ego is a little bruised, but otherwise, I'm fine," he said, looking slightly embarrassed. "I'm very sorry for all the trouble my little nightmare might have caused."

"No trouble, sir. It happens to the best of us, but I dare say that was more than just a little nightmare. It looked like you was trying to stop a murder or something," he joked.

Not wanting to go into details, Andy just sighed and shook his head sadly. "I hope to God I did."

Kerrie hadn't been sleeping well the past couple of days either. She was sorry she hadn't insisted that Meg go with her to the police station right after James left, and when she tried to call her friend back to tell her she had changed her mind and didn't want to wait till morning to file the report, there was no answer.

By the time Meg showed up at nine the next morning, Kerrie was already on her third cup of coffee, still was still peeved that Meg didn't answer the phone the night before. That animosity had to be put on hold though, because Right now she was anxious to get going.

On the way to the police station, Kerrie noticed that her friend seemed to be in a fairly decent mood but was quieter than usual. Finally, she broke the silence.

"Curt left for Europe this morning, and said he would probably be away longer than he first expected." she explained, neglecting to mention that they had also spent the night together.

"Business is business, I guess." shrugged Kerrie who at that moment didn't give a damn about Curt. "Is it really going to bother you that much? I mean, you've only known the guy for a few weeks.

Meg began to fiddle with her key ring to avoid eye contact. "I know, but I think I'm falling in love with him.

That unexpected revelation caught Kerrie off guard and she snatched the keys from Meg's hand to get her undivided attention. "I think it's way too soon for that," she said, sounding every bit as exasperated as she felt. "You guys are still pretty much strangers. All of your bad habits and irritating quirks are still in hiding. You can't fall in love with someone until you get to see who they really are, warts and all."

"I can't help the way I feel, and so far, I haven't been able to find anything wrong with him at all. In fact, he's practically perfect," she boasted. "For example, when he stopped by late last night, he looked a little beat up and I was worried that he might have gotten into a fight or something, but guess what happened?" she asked, sounding like a school girl playing twenty questions.

"I have no idea, but I can't believe you actually look pleased that he came over with battle scars," said Kerrie

"I'm pleased because he was wounded doing a good deed," she said, trying to convince Kerrie how noble Curt was. "He's so kindhearted, he climbed up a tree to rescue a neighbor's cat. Isn't that wonderful?"

"Wonderful isn't exactly the word I'd use to describe it, but I'm glad you think so," said Kerrie, not sounding the least bit impressed. Then she noticed the look of disappointment on Meg's face and she quickly apologized.

"Look, I'm sorry for being so cynical but I'm still a little edgy about what happened last night with James," she explained. "Of course, it was a noble deed, and I'm glad you found such a thoughtful and caring person to share your life with."

Meg gave Kerrie a hug. "I know you didn't mean it and I'm sorry to be rambling on about Curt all the time, but he makes me so happy, I can't help it. But enough about that. Let's go get that restraining order, and then I'll take you out for breakfast to make up for it, okay?"

Once they got to the police station, filing the restraining order was no problem, but it was only a temporary injunction. Kerrie was told that she would have to appear at a hearing and convince the judge there was just cause to make it permanent. The court docket was so full that the hearing was set for July 6, which was almost two months away, but knowing that once the temporary order was served, James could do jail time if it was violated made her feel better.

"I hope they're going to let me know that he was successfully served.," said Kerrie, nervously stirring her coffee as the friends waited for their breakfast order to arrive.

"I'm sure they will," said Meg, who then reached across the table and gently took the spoon out of Kerrie's hand because the constant clink of metal on glass was very annoying.

"But in the meantime," said Kerrie, who immediately switched to drumming her fingers, "they better hope he doesn't try and bother me again, because if he does, I'll be the one committing the violent act. If he comes anywhere near me, I swear I'll kill him."

Andy was so disturbed by the horrible dream that he couldn't get back to sleep and spent most of the next day trying to figure out its significance. Was it just a nightmare, or could something that actually happened between Kerrie and James? In order to ease his mind, he called Ted Stephens the next morning to ask if the psychic knew whether or not Kerrie was okay and told him about the dream.

"I think she's perfectly safe. I'm getting the impression that James isn't anywhere around."

"Well that's good to know," said the actor. The relief in his voice was quite palpable. "It's just that the dream was so real, I thought it might be precognitive. You know, some sort of warning."

"While we both know that James is certainly a menace and could potentially cause problems for Kerrie, I think this time it was your subconscious digging up your worst fears. Of course, if these dreams continue, then there may be a reason to worry, but as it stands, I'm not the least bit concerned. According to Kerrie the last time we spoke, James is long gone and as you know, spirits never lie, so just enjoy the rest of your vacation, and don't hesitate to give me a call back if you have any other concerns."

Andy trusted Ted the psychic implicitly and tried to put the whole incident out of his mind and did manage to enjoy the rest of his week on Sark. He slept soundly, ate heartily, exercised moderately and even found time to finally read Kerrie's novel, which he thoroughly enjoyed.

It had been a long, boring flight back to London and James spent a great deal of the time recounting the events in Kerrie's apartment the night before. He hadn't wanted any sort of unpleasantness between them, but when she out and out lied about her relationship with Andy Dickinson, he couldn't control his temper. And then, when Meg mentioned that Kerrie was planning to take out a restraining order, he nearly lost his mind altogether. He'd done nothing but try and express his devotion to Kerrie, and even if he had come on a little too strong, was that any reason for her to knee him in the groin, scratch his face and then call the police?

James checked into a hotel not far from where Andy lived, then spent the next couple of days lurking around the apartment building hoping to catch the actor coming or going because they needed to talk. He thought of himself as a reasonable man, and was hoping that a stern, verbal warning would be enough to convince Andy to stay away from Kerrie, but after three days with no sign of the actor, James was getting nervous. Where in the hell was he?

In order to find out, James pretended to be a casting agent and called Andy's manager to find out if the actor might be available for a bogus audition later that afternoon. Kate was obviously insulted that this guy expected anyone as famous as Andy to actually show up for a casting call, and curtly declined on behalf of her client. Then she went on to pointedly explain that even if Mr. Dickinson was not out of town on vacation, he was too big a name to subject himself to the indignity of a lowly cattle call.

That's when James really started to panic. It would certainly be a cruel twist of fate if Andy taken a vacation to the States at the same time he had come back to the UK and now he had to make sure that wasn't the case. The thought of Andy and Kerrie even being on the same continent together was infuriating so posing as a producer of a new reality series, James called Andy's manager in the United States on the guise of inquiring whether Andy would be interested in hosting the show. He was relieved to find out that the actor was vacationing somewhere in the British Isles and was asked to leave his name and address so they could get back to him upon his return to London.

After giving the manager's secretary a fictitious production company name and telephone number, James went out and had a celebratory dinner. He couldn't have been happier knowing that Andy and Kerrie were still thousands of miles apart but now he was more determined than ever to keep it that way, even if it meant going to great lengths to do so.

His original idea of trying to discredit Andy was a good place to start, so James combed through back issues of all the London tabloids for bits of unflattering information on the actor, but could not dig up anything bad enough to merit Kerrie's complete disapproval. Then he searched the public records for weddings, birth announcements and criminal records, but found that Andy had never been legally married, never fathered any children of record and had had not spent even one night in jail. James then turned to the gay community and spent many evenings in gay bars looking for information that would suggest Andy was at the very least bisexual, but all he got for his trouble was the unwanted attention of several lovesick men and a very costly bar bill.

James knew that he could easily make up a story and sell it to the American tabloids, and he gave the idea some thought, but all his ideas fell short in the end because he didn't really think Kerrie would believe anything bad about the actor, no matter how credibly it was presented.

A few nights later, while James was absentmindedly flipping through the channels looking for something to watch, he happened across a rerun of a recent interview with Andy on a local news program. The actor was discussing his new pilot, then mentioned that he was planning to go away for a few days and relax. While he declined to say where he was going, he did say he loved to curl up with a good book and was planning to spend several contented hours reading Kerrie Sherman's new novel which, he understood, was quite good.

"You're probably the only one in all of England who hasn't read it yet." chided the presenter. "Did you at least get the chance to meet the author while she was here on tour?"

"Only briefly," said Andy, without further comment. Being reminded of the unfortunate incident at the after party still made him uncomfortable.

"Maybe after you finish reading her novel, you could arrange another meeting to, er, discuss her work." he suggested. From the twinkle in his eye, James could see that the man was egging the actor on. "She's quite a looker, that one. And talented, too. Surely you must have gotten her phone number because I can't believe the amorous Dandy Andy would let someone like that get away."

That was a very discourteous line of questioning and Andy was about to respond in the same manner, but before he had the chance, the presenter realized that he might have gone a wee bit too far with his little joke, quickly cut to a commercial.

James wished he'd been fly on the wall to hear what had happened during the break, but it was fairly clear when the presenter finally came back on screen looking slightly unnerved and with an empty chair next to him. He made some feeble excuse about Andy having been called away, then showed a clip of the new pilot and wished Andy well before introducing his next guest, an anger management specialist.

James was feeling pretty angry himself because he hated that they were talking about Kerrie in such a frivolous manner. While a normal person would have taken Andy's nonverbal reaction to the presenter's prying as a way of standing up for her and protecting her honor, in James' twisted mind, the actor's silence was an affirmation that there really was something going on between them and that he was trying to cover it up.

CHAPTER 10

James had been skulking around Andy Dickinson's apartment building for the better part of a week while waiting for the actor to make an appearance, and had way too much time on his hands which resulted in him having *crazy thoughts,* as his mother used to call them.

By definition, crazy thoughts are akin to having one's imagination run wild and create scenarios that either don't or couldn't possibly exist.

"I've never known a person to have as many crazy thoughts as you do," his mother used to say. "If you put as much effort into your homework as you do thinking about nonsense, you'd be a straight A student."

In truth, James did very well at school, but his mother's expectations were impossibly high and there was no pleasing Rose Goldman. She was a self-centered, bossy hypochondriac who complained about everything. Maybe that's why James' father ran off soon after his son was born, leaving Rose to raise their baby alone.

Having been dumped by the only man she ever loved fine-tuned Rose's peculiarities, resulting in an overprotective mother whose exaggerated fears for her son's safety caused the boy to grow into a neurotic, fearful, and overly dependent child.

James had no friends to pal around with because Rose refused to let him participate in normal childhood activities. He wasn't allowed to ride the school bus with the rest of his classmates because she was certain the bus driver was "a crazed lunatic who drove like a speed demon." When the other kids went off to camp each summer, James stayed home because Rose was worried that if he were allowed to go he'd either get bitten by a black widow spider and die, or get lost in the wilderness and be eaten by hungry wolves. He was forbidden to go to the Saturday matinee for fear a child molester would be lurking in the darkened theater, and even the neighborhood playground was off limits because Rose felt that the swings and slides were unsafe and the sandbox was toxic.

In short, James' childhood was devoid of any of the necessary social interactions that would have allowed him to develop into a healthy, normal child. Instead, he spent all his time at home reading the books his mother bought him (library books were off limits because she felt they were unsanitary), watching television (but only those programs she deemed acceptable) and worrying about his mother's "failing" health because each and every day she complained of feeling unwell and offered up a laundry list of symptoms that were always exaggerated into potentially fatal diseases. If Rose had a mild headache, she knew it must be a brain tumor. A simple cough was self-diagnosed as tuberculosis, and if a scratch or scrape didn't heal quickly enough or happened to get infected, she was sure that flesh eating bacteria was the culprit.

Rose also overreacted when it came to her son's health. Every sneeze, cough or sniffle resulted in a trip to the pediatrician who eventually gave up trying to convince Rose that James was perfectly healthy and all he needed was a daily dose of fresh air and exercise.

"I will not have my son exposed to those horrible ultraviolet rays and die of skin cancer before he's 20," she huffed before storming out of the office during one of her many visits.

While James agreed with the doctor and knew there was really nothing wrong with him, Rose had done such a good job of playing the invalid that James was convinced that his mother was forever at death's door despite the fact that she had the capacity to attack her daily chores with such vigor, it was a wonder she wasn't bedridden from the exertion of it all. The woman was filled with so much nervous energy, she couldn't sit still.

To say that James' lived through an unfortunate childhood would be an understatement, but as he got older, life got no better because puberty and the realization that his mother was far from perfect arrived at about the same time. As his body began to change, so did his opinion of Rose. It had been a long time coming, but James eventually found his voice and began to rebel.

One evening shortly after this 12th birthday, James told his mother that he was going out alone, after dark, to the Circle K market up at the corner because he wanted a root beer. He wasn't sure how she was going to react to the news, but hadn't expected her to throw herself up against the front door to block his way. "I won't allow it! It's much too late for you to go out by yourself!" she screamed, hanging onto the door jambs for dear life. "There are degenerates and drug dealers out there. You could be killed."

"It's not late, Mother," he argued. "It's only six thirty and the park across the street is full of kids much younger than I am. Apparently, their parents aren't worried about degenerates and drug dealers."

"Their parents don't love them as much as I love you," she cried. This was a phrase Rose commonly employed whenever she couldn't think of a better excuse and James was sick of hearing it.

"Sometimes I think you love me too much." he mumbled, before angrily stomping back to his room.

While Rose may have won that first battle, she didn't win the war because with every passing day, James became more independent, less eager to please, and was finally able to see that his mother was not an invalid who needed constant attention, but merely an emotional malingerer.

By the time James started high school, he felt that he had finally become his own man. That's not to say he totally disregarded his mother's opinion or ignored her completely. All those years of brainwashing were deeply ingrained, so he still tried to be a good son, but at the same time, made many attempts to exercise his newfound freedom.

Rose tried her best to adapt and loosen those apron strings just a bit when she realized that her hold on James was loosening, and all went fairly well until the night that James announced over dinner that he met a new girl at school and thought he was falling in love.

"That's impossible," said Rose, dismissing what he had to say with an impatient wave of her hand. "You're much too young to even know what love is, much less fall in love with the first tramp who smiles at you."

Infuriated by Rose's reaction, James threw down his fork and pushed away from the table. "Mindy is not a tramp!" he shouted. "And in case you hadn't noticed, I'm not a child anymore. I'm nearly seventeen years old and I know my own feelings."

Her son's sudden outburst didn't upset Rose in the least. "What you are feeling is raging hormones," she said, "and it's no wonder. The way the young girls dress these days is shameful. They're all a bunch of self-centered heathens, if you ask me."

James knew better than to argue with Rose's convoluted logic. "I'm not asking for your opinion, Mother. I'm just telling you how I feel and whether you like it or not, Mindy and I are officially a couple."

Rose's composure quickly turned to anger. "Well, I don't like it," she declared, "and I forbid you to have anything more to do with that little whore. It'll only lead to heartbreak."

"I'll take my chances," he sneered, "and from now on you're not going to tell me who I can or cannot see. I'm not five years old anymore, and I've had enough of your smothering ways. I'm going to live my life the way I want, without asking your permission."

Rose didn't want to lose the upper hand and decided to make use of her best defense, laying on the guilt. "How dare you raise your voice to me like that? Don't you realize that I gave up my life for you, and never asked anything in return? And then as soon as some little bitch comes around and pays attention to you, you're ready to choose her over me."

James was at the boiling point and not able to control his temper. He ran over to where his mother was sitting, grabbed Rose by the shoulders and began shaking her violently. "So that's what this is all about! You're afraid I'm going to run out on you like my father did," he yelled. "Well in case you haven't noticed, I'm not your husband, I'm your son, and that gives me every right to run away whenever I want to."

Then, suddenly realizing that he might be hurting her, James forced himself to let go and take a step back before continuing his tirade. "I used to wonder how dad could just walk out of our lives with no regrets, but I'm starting to think that you drove him out. I bet he couldn't even go to the bathroom without your permission, could he?" he said, happy to see the horrified look on his mother's face. "You're an impossible woman to live with, and if you're not careful, history will soon repeat itself and I'll be gone, too." That said, James stormed out of the room and Rose was so unsettled by his outburst that she immediately took to her bed.

For the next few weeks, she wouldn't even look at, much less talk to James, and despite his attempts to ignore the guilt trip she was trying to lay on him, James was deeply affected by her actions. It was as though a black cloud hung over the Goldman house and followed James everywhere he went. He was helpless to make peace with Rose no matter how hard he tried because she was a stubborn, vindictive woman who wanted to see her son suffer for treating her so badly. And as if things weren't bad enough at home, his relationship with Mindy was also in serious trouble.

James was, after all, his mother's son, and his smothering ways were driving a wedge between the young couple. Because he was afraid to let her out of his sight, James walked Mindy to school, walked her home, made sure he was with her between classes and during breaks, then called her several times an evening when they weren't together to make sure she was at home. If Mindy so much as looked at another guy, James flew into a jealous rage. Eventually, she couldn't take it anymore and decided to end their relationship.

They were standing out in front of her house after school one day when she finally got the courage to break it off.

"I'm sorry, James, but as much as you can't live without me, I can't be with you." she blurted out, knowing he wasn't going to handle the news too well. "At first, I was flattered by all the attention, but you don't give me any room to breathe. You act like you own me, and I can't deal with it anymore, so I think it's best if we break it off and just be friends."

James was in shock because he hadn't seen it coming, and her words were so painful, he hardly knew what to say. It was as though Mindy had reached into his chest and ripped his heart out with her bare hands.

"I can't just be friends with the woman I love," he cried. "I'd rather die than see you with another man."

His tears didn't phase Mindy at all. In fact, she was rather annoyed at his childish behavior. "Oh, quit being so dramatic, James. I'm not breaking up with you because there's anyone else.

Didn't you hear what I just said? I just can't be with someone who thinks they own me. It's as simple as that."

Just then, a car drove by and honked to get their attention. "Hey, Mindy!" yelled the passenger, who James immediately recognized as Bob Ross, the hunky and handsome star quarterback on the school's football team. "I need to talk to you about those biology notes you loaned me yesterday. I'll call you later, okay?"

Mindy was horrified at the look on James face as the car sped by. He had turned bright red, was clenching his teeth and his fists, and a big fat vein on his forehead looked as though it was going to rupture.

As soon as the car was a safe distance away, James grabbed Mindy by the arm and spun her around. "So, it's not another guy, is it? Well what was that all about?"

"Oh, for God's sake, James, Bob is in my biology class and was out sick for a couple of days, so I let him borrow my notes. What's the big deal?"

"I saw the way you looked at him, and I'm sure there's more going on than a little note lending, isn't there? And it's a good thing he's not in your health class or you'd be offering to personally tutor him in human anatomy!"

"You see?" she fired back, flailing her arms in frustration. "That's exactly why we can't see each other anymore. It's all those crazy thoughts in your head."

He was stunned by her comment, because he hadn't heard those two words put together in a sentence since he was a child.

"What do you mean by 'crazy thoughts?' Have you been talking to my mother?"

"You know perfectly well I've never even met your mother. What does she have to do with anything?"

"Nothing." he muttered. "It's just something she used to say."

"Your mother accused you of having crazy thoughts?" she asked, wondering if his mother said it jokingly or if she really meant it.

"Forget it. It's nothing," he said, trying to pretend the whole thing was unimportant.

Mindy always hated the way James tried to change the subject if the topic was the least bit uncomfortable, and she didn't usually kick up a fuss, but since they were breaking up anyway, she didn't think there was anything to lose if she spoke her mind. "You know, James, if my mother said I was crazy, I wouldn't think it was nothing."

He couldn't believe she was taunting him like this and flew into a rage. "I said drop it, will you?" he screamed, looking as though he was about to explode.

She had never seen him so angry. "Okay, fine! Have it your way and I hope you enjoy it because this is the last time I'm ever going to speak to you. And if you really want to know the truth," she said, staring him down, "I agree with your mother. I do think you're crazy, so leave me the hell alone!"

James never even considered the possibility that Mindy might be right. He was too intelligent to be crazy, he reasoned, forgetting about that fine line between genius and madness, which he apparently did cross that afternoon.

Avoiding Mindy for the rest of the semester wasn't a problem, but he was keenly aware of the odd stares and whispering going on behind his back from her large group of friends. By the time graduation rolled around, James had to get away from it all and after scoring high on his SAT exams, he applied to, and was accepted by a college very few of his classmates would even consider because it was so far from home. So far, in fact, he needed a passport to get there.

James enrolled in The American University in London, England, and his first two years there were idyllic. Being a continent away from his neurotic mother, who was so distraught over his leaving she threatened to kill herself, was like being reborn. He knew that Rose loved herself entirely too much to carry out her suicide threat, so he walked out the door with a clear conscience.

He was able to secure a rare single room, and even though he much preferred his own company, he made a few acquaintances in case he ever felt like socializing. And seeing no reason to venture back to the States, even for holidays, he spent his leisure time taking in the sights of London or nipping down to the local pub for a pint.

While his long-term goals were to remain in England and pursue a career in Media Communications after graduation, fate stepped in and cut his studies short when, at the beginning of his third year, Rose fell seriously ill and James had no choice but to return home at once.

He was full of resentment for being pulled back into the life he thought he had left behind and James was certain that his mother was perfectly well and that she was once again feigning illness to make him feel guilty. She had been miserable living on her own, and called him incessantly, begging for his return.

When he arrived home after the long flight, James was greeted at the door by a hospice nurse who sadly explained that Rose's condition was terminal. "You should go upstairs and make your peace with your mother while you still can," she urged. "She doesn't have much time left."

He was still thinking this was one of Rose's ploys as he slowly walked up the stairs and was totally shocked to find his mother lying in bed looking as though she really was at death's door. Rose had lost a great deal of weight, looked very pale and had dark circles under her eyes. It was as though she had aged 100 years overnight.

When she heard her son walk into the room, Rose opened her eyes to greet him but was much too frail to sit up. "Come sit beside me," she whispered, looking as though the slight effort of moving her lips was too much to bear.

Reluctantly, James pulled a chair over to the bedside and sat down. He knew it would have been a nice gesture to take his mother's hand and offer her comfort, but he just couldn't. He blamed Rose for getting sick on purpose in order to have him back home.

"There you go having those crazy thoughts again," she said, as though reading his mind. "I can assure you that it was not my choice to leave this world quite so soon."

Rose could have been reciting the Gettysburg Address for all he knew, because he didn't hear anything after she said those two disgusting words.

"I am not having crazy thoughts!" he yelled, jumping up from the chair and bending close to his mother's ear, he started in on a tirade. "You're the crazy one in the family and you know it," he began. "That's what drove my father away and after he was gone, you tried to control me like you wanted to control him but all you succeeded in doing was to rob me of my soul.

"Don't you understand that all these crazy thoughts you accuse me of having are nothing more than a difference of opinion?" he continued. "Just because I don't always agree with you doesn't make me crazy, and I've had enough! But if you think I'm crazy, old woman, you can rest in peace knowing that you drove me to it!"

Having said that, James stormed out of the room without a second glance, went downstairs, grabbed his suitcase, went out the front door and headed back to the airport.

When James left the house that day, he never looked back. He arranged for an estate attorney to handle the details of his mother's funeral, settle the rest of her affairs, and open a trust account for him from the proceeds of her somewhat sizable estate. If he was careful, there would be enough money for him to live on for the rest of his life even if he never found work.

The final two years of college flew by and after graduation, James changed his mind about remaining in England and returned home. Now that his mother was long dead, there was no reason to stay away.

He interviewed with a wide variety of jobs, he accepted an offer from a prestigious publishing house as their junior publicist. It was a terrific entry level position and he was up for the challenge. He hoped that in a few years down the line his employer would recognize his extraordinary capabilities and make him a full partner. In the meantime, his main priority was to be recognized for his good work.

Because James had attended college in London and knew the city well, his new employer began using James to accompany a few of the company's lesser-known authors on their book tours to the UK. It was on his third overseas trip that he was assigned to Kerrie.

James was elated at the prospect. He studied her bio then read the book in preparation for their trip, but it was her publicity photos that clinched the deal. He was instantly smitten with the author and hoped this would be a match made in heaven. Little did he know it truly was heavenly forces that brought them together.

CHAPTER 11

Kerrie felt certain that James was still lurking around somewhere nearby and whenever she called the police department to find out if the restraining order had been served, all they would admit to was that they were working on it and would contact her when they had any news.

She was continually on edge and tried to keep busy during the day by spending long hours at the computer working on her novel, and spent her evenings in front of the television watching movies. Before going to bed she always double checked the doors and windows then diligently punched in the security code to her newly acquired alarm system.

As much as she loved the solitude of her apartment, all the extra precautions made her feel as though she was under house arrest, and she looked forward to the opportunity of getting out of the house. Thankfully, Meg's new boyfriend was still away on business, so the two friends went out to dinner at least two or three times a week. The thought that James might be stalking her was always on Kerrie's mind, but being out in public in a crowded restaurant seemed to ease the tension.

The downside to being out with so much Meg was her friend's constant references to Curt. "I can't believe how much I miss him," she would sigh, and while Kerrie did feel sorry for her lonesome friend, she also wished that Meg would change the subject once in a while.

Once, when she politely joked that the whole world didn't revolve around Curt and suggested they try and talk about something else, Meg had a quick comeback. "You mean like the center of your universe, Andy Dickinson?"

"My whole world does not revolve around Andy Dickinson," Kerrie argued.

"You could have fooled me," said Meg. "At least Curt and I have been able to spend time together and have gotten to *know each other.* In your case, you've only met Andy once and you hardly had the chance to say hello before that nut case dragged you away. Face it, Kerrie, you're obsessed with a total stranger."

She was just about to defend herself when Meg's sly revelation finally registered in her mind. "What exactly do you mean when you said you've gotten to *know* Curt a lot better?"

"Well, I meant to tell you about it sooner," she giggled, "but I wasn't sure how you'd take it because it happened the night you had the problem with James, and I didn't want you to think that I was off having a good time while you were sitting there worried about being killed in your sleep."

"But that's exactly what you did, wasn't it?"

Meg was starting to feel guilty. "Oh, come on, Kerrie. You know it's not like that. And don't forget, I asked you if you wanted me to come over, and you said no. Then Curt showed up unexpectedly and, well, things just sort of happened."

"No wonder you didn't bother to pick up the phone when I tried to call you back. You were too *busy.*"

"I would have called you back if you had bothered to leave a message," said Meg, "but you didn't, so it must not have been very important, was it? "

"No, I guess nothing is as important as Curt these days," she snipped. "Even when he's not around, that's all you talk about and just so you know, nobody is as perfect as you believe him to be. You make him sound like Mother Teresa."

"I never said he was a saint and I'm sure he's got a skeleton or two in his closet. I just haven't found it yet, but if it'll make you happy, I'll be sure that you're the first to know when I do."

As much as Kerrie wanted to continue lashing out about Curt, she knew she was being unfair and decided to put an end to the disagreement. "You'd better hope a skeleton or two is all you find in his closet," she joked, "and as soon as Curt gets back from his trip, we should all have dinner together. And no more excuses about him having to work, okay? I really do want to meet him."

"I want you to meet him, too, and someday, I hope to meet Andy as well. Have you heard anything from him?"

"No, not yet." she admitted. "I guess there's really no reason for us to be in touch, but it's really frustrating because when we shook hands, I could feel something between us, like the feeling you get when you hug a long-lost friend, and I know he felt it, too. But if that's the case, why hasn't he tried to contact me?"

"Well, James was acting like you were his private property so maybe Andy is being gallant and doesn't want to interfere. For all he knows, the two of you could be married."

Kerrie thought Meg was probably right and knew she'd have to find a way to let him know otherwise."

While the girls were busy talking about Andy, the actor was preparing to check out of his hotel room on the Isle of Sark. It was the kind of place most people visited to get away from city life and never wanted to leave once they had settled in, but for Andy, he could never stay away from the hustle and bustle of London for very long. Even though he was solitary by nature, he liked being able to exit his cocoon and blend in with the lively masses at will and was looking forward to getting back home.

Except for the unfortunate nightmare incident, his short vacation had been pleasant and productive. He had brought along a script that Kate wanted him to read because she thought the starring role was perfect for him. It wasn't the type of character he would normally be interested in playing, but the storyline was compelling, the characters were well written and he had a feeling that the movie would do well at the box office, so he decided to accept the part. Because the movie was already in preproduction, he had to let her know if he was interested as soon as possible and that's another reason he was anxious to get back to London.

A Bad Case of the Collywobbles was a fantasy film set in contemporary times. It was the story of a young American woman, Shelly Gordon, a freelance writer who finds out she is no mere mortal, but actually a witch. She also learns that she must fulfill a legacy left to her by her great grandmother Sophie, an elite sorceress. The legacy requires her to seek out and destroy a very powerful amulet, before the evil Witches of Rue can steal it away.

In order to do so, Shelly must first learn "the craft," then successfully complete a series of tasks assigned by the guardian of the Seal, but while possessing supernatural powers is one thing—knowing what to do with them is quite another. Shelly is sent a tutor, Thomas Wakefield, headmaster of Wakefield Academy, a prestigious wizarding school located just outside of London. It was the wonderfully complex role of Thomas Wakefield that Andy would be playing and the actor loved a good challenge.

While Andy was on his way back to London, James was busy making a few plans of his own. His ultimate goal was to make sure Andy would never contact Kerrie again, but how?

He thought of himself as a reasonable man, so his first option was to contact the actor directly and warn him to stay away. He hoped a man to man talk would be enough to convince Andy to leave Kerrie alone, but he was also mindful that he might eventually have to resort to more drastic measures, so a contingency plan needed to be put into place as well.

For the first few days after Andy's return to London, James staked out the actor's apartment and followed him around as he went about his daily routine. Lurking just out of sight, James accompanied Andy to his manager's office, to the film's production office, the dry cleaners, the Chinese take-out down the street, a poetry reading on the West End and an outdoor charity concert where the actor made an impassioned plea to the concertgoers to do whatever they could to help in the fight against poverty.

While the activities of his busy lifestyle varied greatly from day to day, Andy never failed to stop at a small neighborhood cafe every morning to read the newspaper and have a cup of coffee. James thought this would be a good place to confront him and was waiting for him the following morning.

James was seating a few tables away from Andy's usual table, and hidden behind a potted plant. He watched as the waitress brought Andy his order and waited until she left before walking over to him.

The actor had his head buried in the entertainment section of the daily news and was so engrossed with what he was reading, he didn't see James approach. After a moment or two of impatient waiting, James finally spoke up. "Excuse me, Mr. Dickinson, if I might have a word?"

Andy peered over the top of the paper and obviously bothered by the intrusion, politely tried to shoo James away. "I'm sorry, but I never sign autographs on personal time."

Ignoring the brush off, James pulled out the chair opposite Andy and sat down. "Please don't confuse me with any of your adoring fans,' he said in a quiet tone. "It's not an autograph I'm interested in. It's quite a bit more important than that."

Andy lowered the paper and although he was quite irritated by this man's gall, he managed not to show it.

"If you'd like me to read a script you've written, it must be submitted to my agent by your agent. If you'd like me to make a donation to a noble cause, I'm already doing a great deal of work for a few select charities that I consider to be worthy. And if you'd like me to ring your wife and wish her a happy birthday because she considers herself to be my biggest fan I'll have to respectfully decline."

That being said, Andy once again picked up his newspaper and hoped the intruder would just go away, but James was not to be dismissed so easily. He reached over the table, tore the paper out of the actor's hands and tossed it aside. "Get over yourself, Andy. This has nothing to do with your money, your popularity or your illustrious career."

"Then I don't think we have anything further to discuss," said Andy, turning towards the counter to try and get the waitresses' attention. He wanted this lunatic gone.

"Before you call anyone over to throw me out," James warned, "I think you should know that I'm here on behalf of Kerrie Sherman."

Just hearing Kerrie's name was enough to get Andy's undivided attention, and he quickly turned back to James. "Kerrie? What about her?" he asked indifferently, masking the worry that something might actually be wrong with Kerrie. "And who, may I ask, are you?"

Before his table mate had the chance to answer, Andy suddenly realized he was sitting across the table from the very man he had been worried about all along. Then, thinking it would be best not to let on that he recognized James, he waited for the publicist's response.

"I didn't think you'd remember me," said James in a sullen tone, "but the name Kerrie Sherman sure got your attention, didn't it? Well let me reintroduce myself to you. I'm James Goldman, Kerrie's publicist."

"Ah yes, Mr. Goldman, I believe we met briefly at the party after my play a few weeks ago, did we not?"

"That's right."

"Well, it's very nice seeing you again," said Andy, reaching out to shake James hand. When James did not return the gesture, the actor quickly pulled his hand back and continued the conversation as if that awkward moment hadn't happened. "Is Kerrie back in London, perhaps? I've been meaning to get in touch with her to let her know how much I enjoyed her book."

James bristled, but managed to keep his anger in check.

"Actually, no, she's not here. I'm in London on other business." he explained.

"Then you've been heaven sent, because I haven't had the time to track down her contact information myself," lied Andy, fumbling around in his pockets for a scrap of paper and a pen. "Could I trouble you for her phone number or email address?"

"You won't be needing those." said James, watching Andy produce the writing implements.

"Surely you don't expect me to memorize the information." said Andy, putting the pen and paper on the table.

"What I expect you to do, is leave Kerrie alone," warned James. "Don't think for a minute that I don't know what's on your mind. I saw the way you looked at her that night at the party, and I won't allow you to come between us. Do you understand?"

The look on James' face was frightening. This was no jealous lover, but someone who was completely unstable.

"It seems you're living under some kind of misconception, James, because I have no romantic interest in Kerrie whatsoever," said Andy, trying to calm the situation. "I'm just an appreciative fan who wants to offer her my congratulations on a job well done."

"Liar!" shouted James, banging his fists on the small table, knocking over Andy's cup of tea and causing everyone in the cafe

117

to turn and see what all the commotion was about. "Your interest in Kerrie is far from literary. You want to get into her pants!"

Andy looked around the room silently hoping that there were no tabloid reporters lurking about to witness the heated exchange. "I can assure you my interest in Kerrie is completely professional, and if you'd rather not give me her phone number, then please just pass on my congratulations. It is not my intention to cause any sort of unpleasantness between you. Now if you'll excuse me," he continued, quickly pushing back from the table and standing up, "I have a pressing engagement."

"I'm warning you, Dickinson," James shouted as Andy hurriedly exited the cafe. "Stay away from Kerrie!"

Instead of going to the studio as originally planned, Andy made a hasty retreat to his apartment. He was happy to find out that Kerrie and James were thousands of miles apart and that she was safe, at least for the time being, but after seeing how crazed James really was, he was even more worried about Kerrie than he had been before, and called Ted Stephens to voice his concerns.

Ted was alarmed to hear about Andy's encounter with James, but assured the actor that Kerrie was just fine. "She's had to take out a restraining order on James, but now that you tell me he's in England, that explains why the police have been having difficulty serving him with the papers.

"Why does she need a restraining order?" he demanded. "What happened?"

Ted could hear the panic in Andy's voice. "I don't think there's anything to worry about. From what I understand, James showed up at Kerrie's apartment trying to sweet talk her into going out with him, and when she refused, he flipped out and tried to force himself on her. She managed to fight him off with a good swift kick to the groin, then called the police and filed for a restraining order the next day."

"What do you mean it's nothing to worry about?" yelled Andy. "You just said that James tried to force himself on her, and that's the same thing that happened to Rachel in my dream. The only difference is, this time Kerrie managed to escape." Then after taking a couple of deep breaths to calm down, he added, "She shouldn't be living alone. Isn't there anyone she can stay with until something can be done about James?"

"We talked about it, but the only one she would even consider moving in with would be her best friend, Meg, but Meg's got a new boyfriend, and Kerrie thinks she'd be in the way. She doesn't want to interfere in a budding relationship."

"That's insane!"

"No, that's Kerrie." Ted chuckled. "Always more concerned about everyone else than she is for herself. But really, Andy, as soon as James returns home, they'll find him and serve the papers, and hopefully that will be the end of it. Meanwhile, you need to stay out of it because as long as you're not a threat to James, Kerrie will be okay."

"I don't agree." said Andy. "If I weren't already a threat, he wouldn't have bothered to confront me in the coffee shop and try to warn me off. Do you honestly think he's going to give up now? He's intent on breaking up a love triangle that doesn't exist. And how in bloody hell did he get the impression that I've been trying to get in touch with Kerrie?"

Ted was silent for a moment before answering and even though Andy had meant the question to be rhetorical, he was happy to know that Ted was trying to come up with an answer.

"I get the feeling it has something to do with your computer. Has anybody had access to it lately?"

"No, of course not. I was out of town for a few days, but I left strict instructions with the building manager not to let anyone in my apartment." he explained. "The prat allowed a man from the electric company in without my permission a few days before I went on holiday, but they are bonded, aren't they?"

"I'd get that man's description from your manager, if I were you, and see if there is any resemblance to James," said Ted.

Andy was appalled to think that James might have been rummaging through his apartment, and with barely a proper goodbye, he hung up the phone and went straight to the manager's office. Unfortunately, it was just as Ted had suggested. The description the manager gave of the electric company employee matched James perfectly.

He didn't remember exactly what correspondence he'd left undeleted in his email's inbox, so Andy rushed back to his apartment and started going through his old mail. It didn't take long for him to come across the flirty correspondence to and from

119

his manager about Kerrie. Even though the messages were written innocently enough, Andy could see how James could have misinterpreted their content.

The whole scenario worried him greatly because if James was capable of breaking and entering, reading his email, and then forcing himself on Kerrie in her apartment, Andy was sure the man was capable of much worse.

CHAPTER 12

The only downside to keeping James' promise to Meg about video conferencing was that he had to make sure that Kerrie wasn't around when he and Meg would be chatting so he suggested they rendezvous in the wee hours of the morning, her time, just to make sure she'd be alone.

Meg always made an effort to be in good spirits during their nightly conversations, but after three long weeks, her cheerful façade began to crack until she finally broke down and cried because she missed him so much.

"I really hate being away from you, too," he cooed, trying to look convincingly regretful, "but it just can't be helped. These conferences seem to go on forever, but if I want my business to succeed, I need to be here for as long as it takes."

"All alone in Paris, the city of romance," she pouted. "I am so jealous."

"Don't be," he laughed. "I've been so busy, I haven't even had the chance to take in any of the sights. I can see the Eiffel Tower from my hotel room, but that's about it."

It would have been nothing short of a miracle if James could actually see the Eiffel Tower from his hotel room, because he was talking to Meg from London.

"Maybe I should book a flight and come visit for a few days." she suggested. "I've never been to Paris, and I'm sure I could find plenty to do all day while you are in your meetings. Then we could stroll down the banks of the Seine at night and take in the sights."

Her proposal set James into a panic. "That's not a good idea," he shot back. They hadn't known each other long enough for him to be sure whether or not she was kidding. "I mean, as much as I'd love to have you here, this isn't the right time for us to explore Paris together," he explained, "but how about coming here on our honeymoon?"

Meg was speechless and needed a moment to think of a tactful way to make sure she hadn't misunderstood what he just said, so she accidently on purpose hung up the phone.

They had been disconnected several times before so James just thought it was just another glitch and immediately called her back.

"Wow," she said, looking rather flustered, "those gremlins are really garbling things up tonight because right before we got disconnected, it sounded like you said something about a honeymoon."

"No, you heard me right." he assured her. "I said we would be honeymooning in Paris and I don't want to spoil that special moment of walking the city together until we are husband and wife."

"I don't know what to say," she stammered, hoping this wasn't a dream.

"Just say you love me as much as I love you, and know that I'll be home before you know it."

"I do love you, Curt, and can't wait to see you, but I'm about to burst and I've got to call Kerrie and tell her the good news, so I'll talk to you later, okay?"

"Give her my regards," he said, laughing to himself as he closed the chat window. He was glad to see that Meg was so gullible because without a doubt, there would be a great deal more deception to come.

Kerrie had turned the ringer off her phone the night before because she was afraid that James might try to call, then left to do errands early the next morning without checking her voice mail so she wasn't surprised to find half a dozen messages waiting for her when she got home, but she didn't expect them all to be from Meg.

The messages were urgent, but cryptic. They ranged from, "Hi, it's me. Call me back as soon as you can." to "Kerrie, it's Meg. Pick up the phone!" and finally, "Where the Hell are you? We need to talk!"

Thinking that something was terribly wrong, Kerrie called her friend right back and Meg answered on the first ring.

"Hi, are you okay?" asked Kerrie, steeling herself for bad news.

"I'm better than okay," gushed Meg. "I'm getting married!"

It took a moment for the news to sink in and before Kerrie could think of anything to say, Meg offered a bit more information. "Curt and I are getting married, and we're going to Paris for our honeymoon. Isn't that exciting?"

Although this wasn't the sort of bad news she was expecting, Kerrie didn't like what she heard nonetheless and blurted out the first thing that came to mind. "Don't you think it's a little too soon to be planning a wedding? You hardly know each other."

"Since when does true love follow a timetable?" asked Meg rather defensively. She was hurt that Kerrie wasn't as excited as she had hoped. "It's not like we just met yesterday."

"Close enough," sighed Kerrie. "Two months is hardly enough time to really get to know a person, and you haven't even introduced him to any of your friends. I, for one, would at least like to get a look at this guy before you ask me to be your maid of honor."

"Then why don't you come with me to the airport when I pick him up? We could surprise him."

"When is he getting back?" she asked, not entirely sure whether or not that was a good idea.

"Well, I'm not sure, but I hope it's soon, so please say you'll come with me. I know you're going to love him as much as I do."

"Let's hope so," mumbled Kerrie. There was something not right about this whole relationship, but she still couldn't figure out what.

In the days that followed his encounter with James at the cafe, Andy couldn't shake the uncomfortable feeling that he was being followed. While he suspected that James might still be in London, he hoped the publicist wouldn't be stupid enough to make a further nuisance of himself.

James was, of course, trailing the actor, but had no intention of doing anything stupid. He had already warned Andy to keep away from Kerrie, and now it was just a matter of reminding the actor, in a not so subtle way, that he meant it.

Day after day, he continued his diligent pursuit, always keeping a safe distance in case Andy decided to do something foolish, like call the police and report him as a stalker. At the same time, James was so brazen about the whole situation, he even called Meg several times during his stakeouts, chatting away about the sights and sounds of Paris and professing his undying love.

By the fourth day, James was getting tired of the cat and mouse game because in reality, it was serving no purpose. While he was sure that Andy wasn't leaving the country for a rendezvous with Kerrie, he had no idea of what the actor was doing behind closed doors. It got to the point where the mere sight of Andy was making James physically ill with worry, and he began to think his world would be a better place if the actor weren't in it.

James' previous aggressive acts against his mother, Mindy, and Kerrie notwithstanding, he never actually thought of himself as a violent person. Sure, he admitted to having a bad temper at times, but it had never gotten to the point of thinking about doing any real harm to anyone, until today.

Several murderous plots came to mind, but James wasn't sure how he could pull off a crime of such magnitude without getting caught until he picked up a copy of the Los Angeles Times at the international news stand near his hotel and came across an article on the recent surge of freeway shootings in the L.A. area. Snipers were targeting innocent people at random and the police were at a loss to stop the crime spree because they had no motive, witnesses or suspects.

This, thought James, was the perfect crime and later that afternoon he went shopping for a gun.

Procuring a lethal weapon wasn't quite as easy as he might have hoped due to England's strict gun control laws, the toughest firearm restrictions of any democracy. Unfortunately, England's firearms restrictions seemed to have had little impact on the illicit underworld and James knew that a weapon could always be found through means open to any criminally minded individual. For him, it was simply a matter of calling up a few of his old college chums and asking around. Once properly armed, all that was left to do was carry out his plan.

Andy took the motorway to the studio every morning and left quite early when there wasn't much traffic to contend with. In fact, it was such an easy drive, the actor had gotten into the habit of reading his lines into a digital voice recorder the night before and then playing it on his way to work. Andy's mind was shut off from the rest of the world when he listened to the playback and nothing could break his train of thought.

He and the car were both seemingly on autopilot when he maneuvered the vehicle into the fast lane at half past five the following morning.

The scene he was preparing for this morning's shoot was particularly long and tedious. His character, Thomas Wakefield, was lecturing his new charge about the history of witchcraft.

"The belief in witches dates back to antiquity," he heard himself say. *"According to the early Christian church, witches never existed. But by the Fifteenth century, the church had modified its opinion. Even though they had finally acknowledged our existence, they mistakenly believed that in order to obtain our powers, we sold our souls to Satan. This fictional belief was used as justification for the church's subsequent burning at the stake of hundreds of thousands of religious heretics of all types."*

Because he had a photographic memory, Andy was able to memorize the scenes as he read them into the recorder, and used the tapes to improve his inflections and timing.

"True witches do not acquire their powers from Satan or anyone else," he continued, repeating his lines out loud along with the recording. *"We are neither man nor demon made. Our powers are passed down through bloodlines, from one generation to the next. We can choose to either embrace those powers or ignore them. It's a personal choice. But whether we choose to utilize these gifts or not, we can never disclaim them, because that is who we are."*

Andy wasn't quite sure he sounded enough like the strict taskmaster the character called for him to be, and wanted to make certain he carried the proper authoritarian tone throughout. This intense concentration was the reason he didn't notice James's car following him onto the highway's onramp.

James was feeling quite serene as he cruised along a few car lengths behind the actor. As predicted, traffic was light, and the one or two cars that were also on the road took advantage of the open lanes and sped by with blatant disregard of the posted speed limit.

"Even though most modern-day mortals think of themselves as literate in the ways of the world, their image of witches is still very archaic," droned the recording. *"They think our sole purpose is to fly through the air on broomsticks at Halloween, shift our shapes to resemble animals, or to dedicate our lives to harming and killing our victims,"* he repeated with a disdainful sniff. *"While it's true that some of our kind still choose to use brooms as a mode of transportation, its more for the fun of it than out of necessity. And while shape shifting, is, of course, possible, all that nonsense about us harming and killing victims is pure tripe! Magick is neither black nor white, good nor evil. It just is."*

When James looked into his rearview mirror to check for oncoming traffic, he was pleased to see that there were no other cars in sight so he reached into the glove compartment and pulled out the gun. He then made a quick lane change so that he was driving right next to Andy's car, quickly rolled down the driver's side window, took careful aim and pulled the trigger.

The sound of shattering glass as the bullets penetrated the passenger side window of Andy's car broke the actor's concentration, but before he could figure out what was happening, it felt as though he'd been punched hard in his right shoulder and then once again on the left side of his neck. It all happened so fast he had no idea he'd been shot but when Andy looked up and saw his windshield was spattered with blood, he knew something was very wrong.

James watched with glee as the actor's car swerved out of control across the empty lanes of the highway. It was all he could do to keep from slowing down and watch the horror unfold, but knowing that it was prudent to get away from the scene as quickly as possible, he floored the accelerator and drove off, satisfied that he'd hit his mark.

Andy's car continued to veer out of control. The actor was struggling to rationalize what had just happened, not to lose consciousness, nor lose control of the vehicle, but he was bleeding badly. The car ran completely off the road and right before he passed out, Andy saw that he was speeding towards a big rig truck that was parked at a rest stop about a quarter of a mile up the road. Unfortunately, he was not coherent enough to put on the brakes to avoid the imminent collision.

The owner of the rig, a middle-aged man named Derek McGee, had pulled off the highway for a quick nap just a few hours before, and it was fortunate that Andy's car ran into the back of his truck and not closer to the cab where Derek had been sound asleep just seconds before impact. The force of the crash was so powerful it threatened to turn the rig over on its side. Thinking it was an earthquake, the bleary-eyed Mr. McGee jumped out of his sleeping compartment wearing not much more than a horrified expression on his face and got himself out of the teetering truck and a safe distance away before stopping to see what had actually happened.

Horrified to see Andy's mangled car wedged tightly underneath the truck's rear axel, Derek immediately ran back to the rig, climbed into the still-teetering cab, grabbed his phone off the passenger seat and called for help then grabbed his trousers before running to the back of his trailer to try and assess the damage to both his truck and the car that ran into him.

The front end of Andy's car was so crumpled, Derek very much doubted that the poor man laying across the front seat could still be alive. The steering wheel was lodged tightly against his chest and there was blood everywhere. Fearing the car would burst into flames and incinerate the unfortunate man before the body could be identified, Derek made a valiant effort to pry the driver's side door open so that he could try and pull the man out of the wreckage, but what was left of the door wouldn't budge.

"Oi, mister, can you hear me?" he yelled, hoping the accident victim would respond in some way.

He wasn't sure whether it was just his imagination, but Derek thought he heard the man moan.

"Help is on the way, so try and hang on," he pleaded, not knowing what else to do put pray.

By the time the paramedics arrived, Andy was still drifting in and out of consciousness, and had no idea what happened. The last thing he remembered before waking up in the hospital two days later was hearing one of his rescuers say, "Blimey! That poor bloke looks just like Andy Dickinson."

After they freed Andy from the wreckage, the paramedics did a quick examination and found the bullet wounds right away. The highway was immediately shut down as a crime scene and the critically injured actor was rushed to a nearby hospital where he spent the next several hours on the operating table.

While the surgeons managed to remove the bullets and repair the extensive damage they caused, Andy's condition was touch and go. His vital signs were unstable and due to his weakened condition and severe blood loss, the consensus was that the actor might not survive.

Round the clock nurses hovered over him in the intensive care unit, and a priest was called to perform the last rites, but miraculously, Andy somehow managed to make it through the night.

By nine the next morning, he was still barely clinging to life while a press conference was being held in the hospital parking lot in response to the large number of grieving fans and members of the media who had come find out whatever they could about Andy's condition. They had been alerted to the tragedy by a hospital orderly who made an anonymous call to a local newspaper, and bad news did indeed travel fast.

"Ladies and gentlemen, my name is Clive Storey, and I am the chief of surgery at this facility. As I am sure you're aware, Andy Dickinson was brought here early yesterday morning as the result of a traffic accident. He arrived in grave condition, and was admitted with multiple injuries including internal bleeding due to a ruptured spleen, a collapsed lung several broken ribs, and two gunshot wounds, one to the left shoulder, which traveled to his lung, and another to the left side of his neck which nicked his carotid artery.

Everyone was listening quietly until Dr. Storey mentioned the bullet wounds, and then sounds of anger and disbelief rumbled through the crowd.

"Please settle down, everyone and let me finish," said the doctor, trying to get on with the briefing.

"There was a great deal of blood loss and Mr. Dickinson was immediately taken to surgery. During the course of the seven-hour operation, we excised his spleen, removed the bullets, he received a blood transfusion and patched him up as best we could."

"Is he gonna make it?" interrupted a reporter who was standing right beside the podium.

"While Mr. Dickinson's condition has improved slightly overnight, we still can't be sure. His injuries are severe and the next 24 hours will be critical, but we are doing everything we possibly can, and it is our hope that he will continue to improve."

"If Andy was shot, what are the authorities doing to find out who did it and why?" yelled another reporter.

"Be assured that they are conducting a full investigation," said Dr. Storey. "They have recovered the bullets and are doing ballistic testing on them as we speak, but at the present time, they are still unsure why this horrible tragedy occurred."

Immediately following the shooting, James spent the better part of the day driving around the countryside listening to the car radio for news of Andy's demise, but none was forthcoming. He stopped only long enough to get rid of the gun in an abandoned barn a hundred or so miles out of town and then went straight back to the hotel where he booked a flight out of London for the following morning.

The disturbing news that Andy had somehow managed to survive the attack came on the radio while James was in a cab on his way to the airport, and he was furious. More than anything, he was mad at himself for having botched the job because if he had been more aware of his surroundings and not so quick to pull the trigger, he might have noticed the big rig truck by the side of the road. If he'd only waited a few minutes longer and chose a better location, Andy would have bled to death before anyone had the chance to come to his rescue.

Now all he could do was get out of the country while he was still a free man and pray that Andy's condition would take a turn for the worse.

CHAPTER 13

The following afternoon, Kerrie was just getting ready to walk out the door for a quick run to the post office when the phone rang. Ordinarily she would have just ignored the call and checked her voicemail when she got back, but for some reason, she felt compelled to answer it.

"Turn on channel 7, quick!" yelled Meg, without even bothering to say hello.

The last time Meg called and demanded she drop everything and turn on the television, it ended up to be some human interest story about an old organ grinder's monkey who bore an unmistakable resemblance to Groucho Marx. She was thinking this call was of a similar nature, so Kerrie explained she didn't have time.

"I'm out of stamps and want to get to the post office before it closes. So unless the world is coming to an end, it can wait until I get back."

"No, it can't wait!" Meg shouted. "It's about Andy!"

By Meg's tone of voice, Kerrie could tell something was wrong, so she grabbed the remote and turned the set on. Andy's picture was up on the screen and the newscaster looked grim.

"...and we have it on good authority that the British actor is near death in a London hospital today following a freeway shooting incident early yesterday morning. There were no witnesses to the senseless crime and police have no suspects in custody. Mr. Dickinson had just completed a starring role in a television pilot for the BBC and had recently begun shooting a new movie, *A Bad Case of the Collywobbles*, which was supposed to be released in April of next year. Studio executives declined comment on either the actor's condition or the status of the movie. In other news..."

Although Kerrie didn't hear the whole story, she'd heard enough to make her blood run cold. Andy had been shot and even if the police didn't have any suspects, she had a terrible feeling about who the shooter might have been.

"Kerrie? Hey! I'm still here!" shouted Meg, trying to get her friend's attention.

She stood there staring blankly at the television screen and it took Kerrie a moment to remember that Meg was still on the phone but when she finally responded, she blurted out the only thing that was on her mind. "James shot Andy and we've got to tell someone."

"You don't know that for sure," said Meg, hoping that Kerrie was wrong. "Look at all the freeway shootings we've had around here. Maybe some nut in the UK read about it and went on a copycat spree. It happens all the time."

"No, it was James," said Kerrie, completely convinced that he was capable of such a terrible crime.

"Look, before you go accusing anyone of murder, you'd better get a few more details." said Meg, trying to be the voice of reason. "Last you heard, James was in town, right? So why don't you call your publisher and find out if they sent him away on another European book tour?"

"Okay, hang on. Let me call them."

After a couple of minutes, Kerrie had her answer. "They said James has been away and came back just last night. "

"Really?" said Meg. "What a coincidence. Curt came home last night, too."

Kerrie was annoyed that Meg still managed to inject Curt's name into every conversation they had, and couldn't help but come back with a sarcastic reply. "I'm really glad to hear that *your* boyfriend came back safe and sound."

"Well of course I am," snapped Meg. "but he's not just my boyfriend anymore, remember? He's my fiancé. And what was that snide remark about '*my* boyfriend?' she wondered aloud. You make it sound like Andy Dickinson is yours, and I don't think a brief five-minute meeting meets the criteria for any sort of meaningful relationship, you know."

She hadn't meant to sound so mean spirited and was immediately sorry for the dig. "Look, I'm sorry to hear about Andy and I really do hope he survives, but I still don't understand your obsession with the guy and I hate to see you so upset over this."

As much as she wanted to tell Meg about her connection to Andy, she didn't think this was the right time. "Maybe someday I'll fill you in, but right now I've got to call Ted, so I'll talk to you later."

Flipping channels to an all-news station so she'd be sure to hear any updates on Andy's condition, Kerrie then called the psychic. Before he even had the chance to say hello, she blurted out the news that Andy had been shot and said she knew it was James who tried to kill Andy. Then she pleaded with Ted to call Scotland Yard and tell them to have him arrested.

"In the first place," Ted began, "you need to calm down. And secondly, I can't make that call. You know very well that a client has to contact to me, not the other way around. If Scotland Yard needs my help in solving the case, they will have to call me and it's common knowledge that the Yard does not endorse psychics in any way. They never approach psychics for information, there are no official police psychics in England, and according to them, there is no recorded instance in England of any psychic solving a criminal case or providing evidence or information that led directly to its solution, so I doubt that I'll be hearing from them."

"But you know it was James who did this to Andy. Don't tell me you don't," she argued. "And if you won't do anything about it, I will."

"Look, Kerrie, I agree that James had a hand in this, but we have no solid proof. If you called Scotland Yard, you'd have to explain why you think James did it, and if you try and explain to an inspector that you and Andy are soul mates and James murdered you in a past incarnation, they won't think you are the least bit credible. It's ridiculous to even try."

"So, you're suggesting I sit back and do nothing?"

"I'm afraid there's nothing we can do for the time being," he sighed, "except pray that Andy has a speedy recovery, which I'm fairly certain he will."

"How can you be so sure?" she asked, already knowing what Ted's answer would be.

"Hey, I'm psychic, remember?" he laughed. "And besides, Andy has a whole legion of his fans who are praying for him, and the power of prayer is a wonderous healing device. You know that."

Kerrie was bolstered by Ted's positive attitude. "I know you're right, but I can't stand the thought of James getting away with this."

"He won't." the psychic assured her. "Just be patient, and have faith that everything will work out the way it's supposed to."

Shortly after she spoke to Kerrie, Meg got a call from Curt inviting her to his house for dinner.

"I'd like to take you out to celebrate my homecoming, but I'm dead tired after that long flight back from Paris," he said, sounding convincingly exhausted, "I thought we might order in, if that's okay."

"I don't care where we meet or what we eat, as long as I get to see you."

"Great. I live over by the Marina, so I'm not too far away. The address is 752 Captain's Way, unit 167. I'll see you around seven."

Meg was so excited to see Curt that she left an hour early just in case traffic was bad but as it turned out, it only took her fifteen minutes to make the drive to the Marina. Instead of going straight to Curt's, she did a little bit of window shopping, wandering through a nearby mall. She was pleased to see that Kerrie's books were still prominently displayed in the window of the local Barnes and Noble and made a mental note to let Kerrie know. Then she popped into a gourmet shop and picked up a bottle of her favorite wine, a wedge of brie and a package of crackers before walking the short distance to Curt's condo. She was still a bit early, but just couldn't wait any longer.

There was a little nervous flutter in her chest as she walked into the lobby of apartment building. She had never had such strong feelings about anyone before, and she quickly checked herself out in the mirrored wall next to the elevator to making sure she looked as good as she hoped she did.

She fidgeted all the way up to the third floor and was glad to see by the numbers on the information plaque on the wall that Curt's condo was only a couple of doors down from where she stepped out, because suddenly her legs felt like jelly, and when she went to ring the doorbell, her hand was a bit shaky as well, but all that nervous tension immediately dissipated the moment he opened the door and swept her up in his arms.

As he spun her around in a big hug, she had a quick glance around and was pleased to find that Curt's condo was much nicer than she expected and after he gave her the grand tour, she was even more impressed. The third-floor unit had a terrific view of the Marina, and rather than being decorated in "frat boy chic" as she expected, the rooms were so tastefully furnished, her own apartment seemed dingy by comparison.

"This is really nice," she commented once they were both back in the living room and settled down on the sofa. "Did you hire an interior designer to put it all together?"

"Nope. It's all my doing, for better or for worse," he boasted.

"I'm impressed." she admitted, then jokingly asked "So now that you've revealed a completely new side to your personality, are there any other deep, dark secrets that you're keeping for me?"

Rather than being flattered by the compliment, Curt turned this innocent bit of teasing into an accusation. "Why would you ask me something like that?" he snapped.

Seeing the quick change in both his expression and demeanor, Meg felt horrible about inadvertently hurting his feelings. "I wasn't accusing you of anything," she explained, "It was just a feeble attempt at humor. Sorry"

James knew he'd overreacted, and in an attempt to diffuse the situation, he apologized, explaining it was the jet lag talking and then he quickly changed the subject.

"So, what shall we have for dinner? Thai, Mexican, Italian, Chinese, Ethiopian?" he asked, and without waiting for an answer, he got up from the couch and walked over to the kitchen counter, opened a drawer that contained several well-worn take out menus, and waved them in the air.

"You choose," she said, trying to be accommodating. "As long you didn't acquire a taste for frog legs and escargot while you were in Paris, anything is fine."

"Actually, I spent a great deal of time at the neighborhood McDonalds," he admitted. "I'm not a picky eater, but snails, amphibious creatures and rich sauces don't set to well with me, so how about Thai food tonight. Does chicken larb, beef satay and some Mee Krob sound good?"

"That sounds great, but can you also add a Thai iced tea for me please? And I hope they hurry, because I'm really hungry."

"Yeah, so am I," he said, patting his stomach. "I was so excited about seeing you tonight, I forgot all about having lunch."

After Curt called in the order, he made his way back to the sofa and hunkered down close to Meg.

While they waited for dinner to arrive, Meg asked Curt about his trip, then, noticing the big screen smart tv on the living room wall, she asked if it would be okay to turn on the news.

Meg rarely watched television, but she told him she was thinking about getting a similar tv herself and wanted to see if they were really as spectacular as she had heard. Her real motive, though, was to hear an update about Andy's condition.

James was happy to oblige. He flipped thru the channels and was kind of glad she asked, because he didn't feel like struggling to make small talk quite yet. He was waiting till after dinner for them to have a little pillow talk so he could get an update on Kerrie.

Meg was so enthralled with the television, she didn't hear the doorbell ring.

"That was fast," he said handing her the remote and giving her a kiss on the cheek. "I'll be right back with our feast."

Meg surfed through the channels until something on the screen caught her eye. It was the scene of a horrific traffic accident with a small, mangled car wedged tightly underneath the back of a very large truck. A visibly upset reporter was standing alongside the wreckage and Meg turned up the volume so that she could hear what he was saying.

"...and as you can see, it was a very close call for our Mr. Dickinson. It's hard to believe anyone could survive such a terrible crash but a hospital spokesman says he is resting comfortably. While not out of danger yet, Andy's doctors have high hopes that he will make a full recovery. This is Edward Grant in London reporting for the BBC."

"Kerrie will be glad to hear that," said Meg when Curt came walking back into the room with an armful of food.

"Huh? Sorry. I wasn't paying attention," he said, setting the take out down on the coffee table.

"It was a news report on Andy Dickinson's condition," she explained. "He's that British actor Kerrie is so crazy about and someone tried to kill him on the freeway yesterday morning as he was driving to work."

Trying to look as disinterested as possible, Curt began taking the food out of the bags. "Really?" he said, as he handed her a pair of chopsticks. "Is he dead?"

She was startled by the blunt question, but recounted what the reporter had just said. "It was touch and go for a while, but he seems to be doing better and they are hoping he continues to improve. Poor Kerrie really flipped out when she heard about it."

"Why? You said she was crazy about him but they don't actually know each other, so what's the big deal?" he asked, carefully avoiding her eyes.

"Well," she began, not remembering how much she had told him about Kerrie and Andy, "I mean, she met Andy while she was in London for the book tour, but only for a minute because that idiot publicist of hers got jealous and dragged her away. She was livid and so embarrassed. But aside from that one brief meeting, she doesn't know him from Adam and that's why I can't figure out why she's so obsessed with the guy. She's seen all his movies dozens of times, and reads everything about him she can get her hands on. I've heard of people having crushes on movie stars before, but this is no simple infatuation. She's determined to hook up with Andy no matter what, and knowing how determined Kerrie can be, I'm pretty sure she'll be able to figure out a way."

Curt was seething. Kerrie had always defended her interest in the actor to him by saying that while she really enjoyed his work, she wasn't the least bit interested in him as a person, but now, hearing from Meg that Kerrie was practically in love with Andy was almost too much to take.

"The whole thing sounds rather unhealthy to me," he said, trying to make it sound as though this was just a casual conversation.

Even though Meg agreed, she didn't want Curt to think that her best friend was a love struck lunatic. "I'm not sure I'd call her interest in him unhealthy, but I agree that she's gone a little overboard about him. In fact," she said, opening up one of the food containers and helping herself to the chicken larb, "I was sure she was going to tell me that she was catching the next plane to England to be by his bedside, and I'm pretty sure the only reason she didn't actually go is that she knew she'd never get within a hundred yards of the hospital. There are a million fans outside holding prayer vigils for the guy."

Even though that he had hooked up with Meg for the express purpose of extracting information about Kerrie, hearing all this was torture for James but had to find out more. "Well, from what you said, it appears that Dickinson is going to pull through, so that should make her feel a little better. Did she happen to say anything about going to London to try and see him if he manages to make it out of the hospital?"

"No, but she's pretty sure she knows who tried to kill him."

Curt, who was in the process of spooning white rice onto his plate, nearly dumped the whole container into his lap. "How could she possibly know that?" he asked, trying to appear less rattled than he actually felt.

"Well, remember what I've told you about her publicist, James?" she asked, taking the rice container out of his hands and scooping up the mess.

"Yeah, you said he not only spoiled their rendezvous in London, but came to her apartment after they got back and tried to force himself on her or something so she was going to get a restraining order on him, but I don't see what this James fellow has to do with Andy Dickinson getting shot. I mean, does she think James flew to London just to seek his revenge on a two bit actor? That's absurd."

"Well, it does sound a little far-fetched," she admitted, "but from what I've heard about James, I wouldn't put it past him. He's more obsessed with Kerrie than she is with Andy, and that's saying a lot."

"I'm sure James meant her no harm," he said, reaching for a skewer of sate. "She was probably just upset that he came on to her and she blew the whole incident way out of proportion."

"I don't think so," she said, pouring liberal amounts of peanut sauce over her rice. "Kerrie had to display good cause before the judge would issue a permanent restraining order, and after hearing what she had to say, he apparently felt that Kerrie really was in danger because he signed the papers with no problem."

James suddenly lost his appetite. "Our whole legal system is in such disarray, that judge probably signed the damn thing just to get her out of there," he said, pushing away from the table. "No doubt she was at the head of a long line of similarly misguided people who think it's okay to clog up the court system with a bunch of nonsense."

"I think she's right about James, and he should be locked up," she said in defense of her friend. "Nobody has the right to force themselves on anyone, and that's what he did from day one, but I'd rather not get into a lengthy debate about Kerrie, James or our legal system right now," she added, seeing how angry he was getting, "so can we please talk about something else?"

There was so much more he wanted to ask, but while he knew it would be best to drop the subject for now, he couldn't resist one more question. "Kerrie's not dating anyone right now, is she?

Hoping this would put an end to the Kerrie-Andy saga for the evening, Meg told Curt that Kerrie hadn't had a boyfriend in a long time.

James was relieved to hear that Andy was the only one he had to get out of the way to get to Kerrie. "Well that's the problem, isn't it?" he chuckled. "She hasn't got anyone in her life, so all she can do is fantasize about getting together with some movie star who has probably forgotten all about her by now."

"All I know is that Kerrie won't be satisfied until she manages to see him again and her obsession with him does worry me because I've tried to fix her up on blind dates several times, but she flat out refuses. It's like, if she can't have Andy, she'd rather not have anyone and she's missing out on a lot of great men."

"I know," said Curt, reaching out and pulling Meg closer to him. "You've got one of those great men right here, and I'm sure you wouldn't trade me in for all the Andy Dickinsons on Earth, would you?"

"No, not for all the Andy Dickinsons," she said, snuggling closer, "and especially not for all those horrible James Goldmans either. I feel sorry for anyone who gets involved with someone as dangerous as he is," she said with a shiver.

CHAPTER 14

Kerrie had been trying to call Meg all night and when her friend didn't answer the phone after several failed attempts, she began to worry. She stopped calling around midnight and left a message warning Meg that if she didn't hear back from her by nine the next morning, she was going to come over and break down her door.

When Meg picked up her messages at eight fifty-nine, Curt was in the shower, so she had a moment to call Kerrie back to explain her mysterious absence. "I'm at Curt's house. He invited me over for dinner and I ended up staying for breakfast," she chirped. "We had so much to catch up on."

"Yeah, I bet you did," mumbled Kerrie, who then continued her questioning in a livelier tone. "So, have you set the date yet or were you too busy making up for lost time?"

"Actually, we were too busy rehearsing the honeymoon to talk about the wedding," she giggled, "but when we did talk, it was mostly about you."

"Me? How did I manage to qualify as a topic of conversation?"

"When I first got here, they were doing a news report on Andy Dickinson on television, so naturally your name came up," she explained. "Oh, and by the way, you did hear he was doing much better, right?"

"Yeah, I did." she said, sounding almost cheerful. "The reports this morning said he was off life support and starting to come around."

"Well, anyway, we were watching the news about Andy, and I mentioned to Curt that you were a big fan and were really upset about the shooting."

Kerrie knew there was more to it than that. "What else did you tell him?"

"Only that you were madly in love with Andy in a deranged sort of way and would do anything to have him in your life," she teased.

"You did not!"

"No, of course I didn't. Do you think I want my future husband to think my best friend is an obsessed neurotic?"

"Is that what you think?" asked Kerrie after the magnitude of what Meg just said sunk in.

"Obsessed yes, neurotic no," said Meg, not realizing how strongly her little joke affected Kerrie. "But you've got to admit you've gone a little overboard about this guy."

She knew it must have seemed that way to Meg, but this was not the right time to explain, all Kerrie could say was, "I have my reasons.

Andy was only vaguely aware of his surroundings because he was so heavily sedated. It wasn't until the third morning after the accident that he was able to clear away the cobwebs long enough to understand that something was terribly wrong. If the uncomfortable breathing tube stuck down his throat wasn't enough of a clue, the tubes and wires attaching him to several ominous-looking machines were a dead giveaway.

There was a privacy curtain drawn around his bed and at first Andy thought he was alone, but then he heard two people talking nearby and strained to hear what they were saying.

"He's doing much better today, doctor," said the woman. "His vital signs are stabilizing and he seems to be trying harder to wake up."

"I'm glad to finally hear some good news after all he's been through," said the man. "What a terrible thing to have happened. All those broken bones, shot twice, horrible car crash. It's a miracle he's made it this far," he sighed. "If his vital signs continue to remain stable and he fully regains consciousness, we can remove the breathing tube and make him more comfortable."

"Such a pity to have our Andy end up like this, a target for murder," sighed the nurse. "The police haven't come up with any new leads, have they?"

The doctor shook his head. "None, I'm afraid, but given Dandy Andy's reputation, half the men in the UK could be suspect," he chuckled.

Horrified by what he'd just heard, Andy tried to think back to the circumstances leading up to him being in the hospital but the only thing he could remember was getting into his car and driving to the studio. He was so unnerved to learn that someone had actually tried to kill him that he closed his eyes and prayed for sleep so he wouldn't have to think any more about it.

It was well into the night before Andy woke up again. The room was dark and silent except for the beeping of a nearby monitor and the sound of the artificial respiration machine. His eyes quickly adjusted to the darkened room and he saw that a nurse was busily scribbling something on a chart that was attached to the foot of his bed. He needed to get her attention and managed to muster up enough strength to wiggle his foot slightly, but she was so engrossed in what she was doing, she didn't notice.

He watched in frustration as she finished her charting then looked at her watch and turned to walk away. Desperate to make himself be known, he tried calling out to her, but the breathing apparatus made it impossible to be heard, and tears of frustration welled up in his eyes. Andy had no idea what time it was, but he was determined to remain awake until somebody came in and realized he was back among the living.

After what seemed like an eternity of struggling to stay awake and trying to remember anything at all about the events that led up to him being in the hospital, the sun finally came up and Andy was grateful to hear the sounds of a brand-new day. People were chatting quietly in the background, traffic droned in the distance, and he could smell the faint aroma of freshly brewed coffee. How he wished he were sitting in his neighborhood cafe reading the morning paper.

His thoughts were interrupted by the sound of heavy footsteps walking towards the bed and recognized the doctor's voice as he stopped and spoke to the nurse. "Good morning, Miss Webster. How's our patient doing this morning?"

142

"Oh, good morning," she chirped. "I was just about to go check on him, but the night nurse said all his vitals were stable and that he was resting comfortably."

"Well, let's have a look then," he said, pulling back the curtain surrounding Andy's bed.

"Ah, Mr. Dickinson," said the doctor, pleasantly surprised to see that Andy seemed to be waking up. "You're quite a bit more alert than you were yesterday. How are you feeling this morning?"

Given the fact that he could hardly move, had tubes running out of him from every appendage, and was hooked up to a breathing machine so that he couldn't reply even if he wanted to, Andy thought the answer was rather obvious.

The doctor went around to the foot of the bed to check the medical record, then came back and leaned down so that he and Andy were practically nose to nose. He then reached into his pocket and pulled out a pen light to check Andy's pupils. Apparently happy with his findings, the doctor put the light back into his pocket and finally introduced himself. "I'm Dr. Winston, and I've been taking care of you the past few days," he explained, in a voice that he might have used when talking to a two-year old. "Do you understand?"

The doctor's solicitous tone made it sound as though he thought his patient was brain dead, and because Andy resented the implication, he scowled and blinked his eyes furiously to assure the man that he not only understood, but that his brain was in fine working order.

Completely ignoring Andy's attempt at an angry gesture, the doctor stood up, added a few notes of his own to Andy's chart, then turned back to his patient. "I'm glad to see that you've made some progress," he said in an annoyingly cheerful tone. "According to what the night nurse wrote, you've been trying to breathe on your own and since your latest chest x-ray shows that your collapsed lung has now re-inflated, I think we can take the breathing tube out and see if you can get by without it." Then, taking a glove off a tray next to the bed and putting it on, the doctor then took off the tape that held the device in place, grabbed hold of the tube and said, "Take a deep breath, then try to cough."

The tube felt twenty feet long as it uncomfortably snaked its way out of Andy's throat, and once his airway was finally free of the annoying apparatus Andy gagged a couple of times then went into a coughing jag.

The doctor stood back and watched his patient desperately trying to catch his breath, but didn't seem to be the least bit bothered. "Coughing is a good sign, Mr. Dickinson. It means you're lungs are in good working order."

Andy tried to answer back, but his throat was very sore and the best he could manage was a guttural croak.

"Oh, no. Don't try to talk just yet," he instructed. "Just take a couple of deep breaths and try to relax."

Ignoring the doctor's suggestion that he remain silent, Andy once again tried to make himself heard. "What exactly happened and what is my prognosis?" he whispered.

"Well, to begin with, I'd say you are doing remarkably well, considering what you've been through," the doctor began. "You were shot twice while driving on the freeway and then your car ran off the road and crashed into a large lorry off the side of the road. You suffered multiple injuries in addition to the gunshot wounds, arrived at the hospital in extremely critical condition, underwent seven hours of surgery to correct the damage, and it was touch and go for a while, lad, but thankfully, you're still here."

"Do they know who did it? Or why?"" he whispered.

"Not a clue, I'm afraid. There was very little traffic that early in the morning, so I'm afraid there weren't any witnesses, but I'm sure Inspector Stratton will go into further detail when he comes by to see you this afternoon. That is, if he can manage to get through the huge crowd of adoring fans that have taken up residence in our parking lot." he chuckled. "I dare say you've got quite a loyal following, Mr. Dickinson. They've been out there holding a candlelight vigil since the day you were admitted and now that you're back among the living, I think they'd appreciate a word or two from you. Is there anything you'd like me to tell them?"

"Just thank them for their concern." he whispered, too overcome with emotion to say any more.

Over the next couple of weeks, Andy's condition improved so rapidly, it was decided he could be discharged from the hospital earlier than expected. The newspaper headlines championed his speedy recovery with headlines reading "Dandy Andy Back From

The Dead, " "It's A Miracle, But He Made It!" and "Andy Won't Let the Collywobbles Get Him Down." The last headline referring, of course, to the movie he was supposed to begin working on prior to the accident.

"Pack your bags, Mr. Dickinson, you're going home," said Dr. Winston. "I've arranged for you to have a private nurse on duty 24 hours a day, and you'll be coming back here three times a week for therapy, but there's certainly no reason to keep you as an inpatient."

Although still very weak and having difficulty moving about, Andy was thrilled to know that he would finally be able to sleep in his own bed. With the nurse's assistance, he put on his robe and slippers and maneuvered himself into a waiting wheelchair.

He wasn't prepared for the cheers and applause from the sea of fans who were waiting outside the hospital, all eager to catch a brief glimpse of the actor as he was wheeled into the ambulance. He smiled, then slowly raised his arm and waved at the crowd as best he could. By the time he arrived at his apartment and was helped into bed, Andy felt like the luckiest man on Earth.

Not everyone was elated by Andy's miraculous recovery. The moment he heard that the actor had been released from the hospital with an excellent prognosis, James was so angry he couldn't see straight. He prayed night and day that Andy's condition would take a sudden turn for the worse during his recuperation to no avail. Why was this bastard so lucky when millions of others developed raging infections, deadly blood clots or other complications after surgery? He was tempted to fly back to London and pull the plug on the actor himself during those first critical days, but was smart enough to realize that he had to stay as far away from the crime scene as possible and spent hours on end berating himself and trying to figure out where he went wrong.

Because he was spending a great deal of time with Meg, James knew that Kerrie was elated about Andy's recovery and had even sent the actor a huge Get Well bouquet of flowers with a sweet little note. He'd have sent flowers, too, if they could have been in the form of a funeral wreath.

James knew that there was no way he could return to London, so now faced the task of trying to devise another way to get Andy out of Kerrie's life once and for all. He had a few random ideas of how to go about it, but this time had to make certain he could successfully pull it off. Rather than rushing into another poorly constructed plan, James decided to take his time and make sure he wouldn't fail again. After all, Andy would be recuperating for quite a while, so time was definitely on his side. The main thing he needed to do at the moment was to keep tabs on Kerrie and make sure she didn't do anything stupid, like fly to London and try and nurse Andy back to health.

CHAPTER 15

Andy's Get Well bouquet from Kerrie arrived slightly wilted due to a mix-up with the actor's address, but he found the accompanying note much more meaningful than the arrangement itself.

It read, *"Dear Andy, I'm so happy to hear that you're on the mend and wish you the speediest of recoveries. Even though we only met briefly during my London book tour, I'd really like to see you again. I know that your movie has been put on hold indefinitely, but I read that you will be here in Los Angeles sometime during the shoot, so please get in touch with me when you arrive and, perhaps, we can meet for dinner. Call my publisher and let them know where you'll be staying. I look forward to hearing from you. All my best, Kerrie Sherman."*

While he was disappointed that Kerrie didn't enclose *her* phone number with the flowers so he could get in touch directly, the thought of getting together with her again was all the medicine he needed to get him through the long and painful days of physical therapy.

Eight weeks and many grueling therapy sessions later, the actor received a call from the Collywobbles production office telling him the doctor had cleared his return to work and shooting was to begin in ten days' time. Because the movie was to be shot in both London and America, it was decided that they would do the London shoot first and then travel to Los Angeles for the final scenes. This redesigned schedule would allow Andy to continue to regain his strength and endurance throughout.

Since the police still had no suspects in the case, the film's new shooting schedule and its locations would not be publicized. Everyone working on the movie was asked to sign a confidentiality agreement, the studio was under tight security and additional security personnel were hired to make sure Andy was protected at all times, both on the set and at home. While Andy hated the thought of being under constant surveillance, he knew it had to be.

Even though some people said that since there had been no witnesses or probable motive, the incident had possibly been a random shooting, but Andy disagreed. He read everything he could find about the numerous freeway sniper attacks in Los Angeles, and the attack on him didn't seem to follow the same pattern. In L.A., the majority of victims were shot during rush hour when the freeways were crowded, not in the wee hours of the morning when few cars were on the road. And there was usually more than just one victim. No other assaults had been reported in London, which lead him to believe that his was not a random act of violence or copycat crime. He had been the intended victim, and all fingers pointed to James.

Now that he was back in Los Angeles, James saw to it that he and Meg were inseparable. They were together every day and went back and forth between his place and hers each night. Meg loved having him around. They got along well, and she could see no reason for them to be living apart. When she finally broached the subject of moving in together, he was all for it, but instead of inviting her to move to the Marina with him, like she had hoped, James said that he wanted to move in to her apartment instead.

His main reason for wanting to give up his spacious condo for Meg's tiny apartment was because he just didn't feel safe anymore, even though the condo was leased under his pseudonym. Too many people knew where he lived and he didn't want anyone to be able to track him down. He knew the police were still attempting to find him in regards to the restraining order, and he also worried that the FBI might come knocking on his door if Scotland Yard somehow happened to link him to their investigation. He'd have a better chance of remaining untraceable if he were hiding out at Meg's.

That settled, he had two more obstacles to overcome: running into Kerrie because he was going to be living with her best friend, and being sent back to London on business.

To ensure that he wouldn't be sent back to the UK, James cashed in on all the vacation time he'd accumulated at work over the past several years and told his boss that he was going to take a couple of months off. As for Kerrie, he decided to keep Meg so busy with him she wouldn't have any time for her best friend, except over the phone.

The night before the move, James packed up all his personal belongings and piled them into his car then hired a moving company to take his furniture to a nearby storage facility. Meg's tiny apartment was already overcrowded, and just finding enough drawer and closet space was going to be enough of a challenge.

Early the next morning, he arrived at his new home with a car full of stuff and a big bouquet of flowers for Meg.

In all the excitement, Meg had forgotten all about letting Kerrie know that Curt was moving in, so while he was unloading the car, Meg called her friend to tell her the good news.

"Don't you think it's a bit premature?" was Kerrie's immediate response. She was trying to choose her words carefully so that she wouldn't sound so negative about what she considered to be a huge mistake.

"Quit worrying, will you? We love each other, we're good together, and I was hoping you'd be happy for me," said Meg, feeling slightly put out at Kerrie's implied negativity. "And if you're worried about him interfering with our friendship, rest assured. There's plenty of me to go around."

"It's not us I'm worried about, but I guess time will tell," mumbled Kerrie. She knew from past experience that once Meg got involved with a guy, everyone else in her world was put up on the shelf, but not wanting to end the call on a negative note, she wished her friend all the best and said she hoped to hear from her soon.

Meg wasn't happy about the way their conversation ended, but knew that in time, Kerrie would learn to love Curt as much as she did. Then, seeing the beautiful flowers lying on the kitchen counter, she got a vase down from one of the cabinets and put them in water. When Curt came upstairs with another load of clothes a few minutes later, she was walking around the apartment, vase in hand, trying to figure out where to display them."

"Now that I've brought all my stuff up, I don't know if there's going to be any room for those," he joked, "but you'd better find the perfect spot because the florist has a standing order to deliver a similar bouquet twice a week."

'*I can get used to this.*' she thought, still dazzled by the enormous bouquet. "I'll find room if I have to wear them on my head," she laughed. "Oh, and by the way, I've made room in the hall closet and also cleared out a few dresser drawers, so why don't you finish bringing your stuff in and I'll make us some breakfast "Sounds great." he said, giving her a quick peck on the cheek.

How do you like your eggs?"

"Over easy, just like I like my women," he teased, but judging by Meg's stern glare, she didn't think it was funny.

"I was just kidding," he said, looking properly remorseful. 'Oh, and just so you know, "I prefer my eggs runny because I like to cover them with a ton of catsup and mush them together with the hash browns."

"As disgusting as that sounds," said Meg, forgetting all about his tacky comment, "you'll probably have the same reaction when you see me eat a liverwurst sandwich on dill rye bread with mayonnaise, sweet pickle relish and onion."

"Oh my God, that's truly offensive," he said in mock horror. "Don't tell me I'm going to be living with someone who's eating habits are even more nauseating than mine."

"I'm sure we'll manage to get through it. I can think of a lot worse things than a vile-sounding liverwurst sandwich or runny egg and potato hash," she laughed. "I suppose it's kind of late to ask, but you're not a terrorist, bank robber or serial killer, are you?"

He was a bit startled at first by the question, but quickly assured her he was not guilty of any of those crimes and was secretly glad she didn't include *sniper* to the list. "Hey, you're looking at a man who rescues kittens out of trees for little old ladies so don't think for a minute I could possibly think of harming anyone. It's just not in my nature," he explained, hoping that a bolt of lightning wasn't going to shoot down from the ceiling and strike him dead. "So, I think I'll just calmly sit here and watch you make breakfast, if that's okay. I can unpack and get settled while you're at work. It'll give me something to do other than miss you terribly."

Meg's classes began at three o'clock that afternoon and she wasn't done until eight, so James thought it would be a nice gesture to have a romantic dinner waiting for her when she got home. He knew he had to do everything he possibly could to keep her happy because a happy girlfriend was a chatty girlfriend, and he had to keep tabs on Kerrie.

Unlike a lot of men, James enjoyed grocery shopping and was very adept in the kitchen. A creative cook who didn't need to follow a recipe to come up with some wonderfully delicious meals, he hoped to impress Meg with one of his specialties, a spinach and mushroom lasagna with rustic garlic bread, a tossed green salad and some fresh fruit for dessert.

By six thirty, dinner was in the oven, he'd cleaned up the kitchen, set the table and was just about to step into the shower when the phone rang. There was no reason to answer it because none of his acquaintances knew where he was living, but curious to see who was calling, James walked back into the living room to see if whoever it was would leave a message. After three rings, the voice mail picked up and he immediately recognized the caller's voice.

" Hiya. I'm just calling to see how you two lovebirds are doing, but I guess you're too busy to pick up. Whenever you finally manage to pull yourself out of bed," Kerrie teased, "give me a call. I've got some great news about me and Andy Dickinson. It looks like we'll be getting together soon. Hopefully the next time you try to call me, *I'll* be too busy to pick up the phone, too. Talk to you later!"

James rewound the message and played it again. He hoped he'd misinterpreted Kerrie's message, but that wasn't the case. She had finally made contact with Andy and was planning a little get together. The only thing he didn't know was when and where, but that would be easy enough to find out.

By the time Meg got back from work, he was in a truly foul mood. He wasn't going to admit that he'd listened to her voicemail, but over dinner, but she could see that something was really bothering him.

"Are you feeling okay?" she finally asked as they were having dessert. "You're awfully quiet."

"Just tired, I guess," he explained, trying to muster a smile. "It's been a long couple of days and all the excitement must have finally caught up with me. So, if you don't mind, I think I'm just going to go lay down for a while."

"Of course, I don't mind. Go take a nap and I'll put the leftovers away and do the dishes. If there's anything you need, let me know."

He wasn't the least bit tired but James climbed into bed and listened to Meg putter around the kitchen. All through dinner, he kept hearing Kerrie's voice over and over happily repeating Andy Dickinson's name and wondered what sort of arrangements had been made between them. The news reports said that Andy was on the mend, but surely, he wasn't well enough to make a trip to the States. And why would he be coming here anyway? Last he heard, the new movie had been shelved indefinitely.

After a few minutes of pondering, he just had to know more. "Meg? Did you check your phone messages?" he shouted from the bedroom. "I think someone called while you were out. I heard the phone ring while I was in the shower."

"It must've been Kerrie and I've already talked to her. She called me at work because she had some exciting news that couldn't wait," she answered, walking into the bedroom so she didn't have to yell back. "But thanks for letting me know."

Seeing her standing in the doorway, James scooted over to make room for her on the bed. "Why don't you lie down right here and tell me all about it?" he said, patting the bed suggestively.

"If I'm going to come in and lie down next to you, it won't be to talk about Kerrie," she teased.

James threw back the covers and invited her to join him. Romance was the last thing on his mind, but rather than passing up an opportunity for some pillow talk, he didn't think it would hurt to go through the motions.

So many questions were running though his head, but Meg had fallen asleep in his arms before he had the chance to get any answers. He laid awake staring at the ceiling going through all the possible scenarios. Did Kerrie manage to get in touch with Andy and invite him to visit? Did he somehow manage to get her phone number? Was he coming here on business, or was she traveling to London? Had this meeting been somehow prearranged before the actor's *unfortunate accident*? He waited until they were having breakfast the next morning before asking Meg more about it.

"I didn't really have a chance to talk to her in detail," she said, pouring liberal amounts of blackberry syrup over her pancakes, "but she said that Andy was going to be in Los Angeles in a few weeks and she invited him out for dinner when he's here."

"Well that's what she's always wanted, isn't it? Some alone time with Andy? She must be thrilled, "he said, pushing back from the table because once again he'd completely lost his appetite. "Is he going to be staying in L.A. for a while or is he making a special trip to share a meal with an adoring fan?"

"She didn't say, but I have a feeling that if Kerrie has her way, there will be more to it than a dinner date." she laughed.

A chill ran up James' spine at the very thought. "I still don't understand her fascination with that man," he said, getting up from the table to get another cup of coffee. "He's old enough to be her father, for God's sake. "

"All I know is that she's got it bad for him, and so what if he's a little bit older? Age shouldn't get in the way if people are in love."

"Don't be ridiculous," he said, sounding very judgmental. "How can she possibly be in love with someone she hardly knows?"

"Love, lust, I don't know, but he must be interested in her, too, or he wouldn't have accepted the invitation."

James began to pace, trying hard to keep his anger in check. "Well of course he's interested. He's a man, isn't he? I just hope she's not too disappointed when he slinks away in the middle of the night and she never hears from him again."

"I don't think that's going to happen," said Meg, reaching out to stop him from pacing. She could tell something was still bothering James but wasn't sure what it was. "I can't explain why, but I really do think there is some sort of a connection between them. Even though they met just the one time, I get the feeling that this upcoming meeting is going to lead to something more. It may sound silly, but I think it's fate bringing them together, and so does Kerrie. She told me the other day that thinks the reason he wasn't

153

killed in that assassination attempt as she calls it, is because they were destined to be together, and I'm starting to believe that myself. I mean, the man was mortally wounded, yet managed to pull through, and the fact that she's been so obsessed with him for the past year or so, when it's not her nature to be that way about anyone, kind of clinches it in my mind."

"Andy didn't die because he got lucky, that's all," he shot back, pulling away from her. "The guy who tried to kill him just didn't take careful enough aim."

Meg couldn't believe he said that. "You sound like you're defending the shooter."

It did sound like he was sorry that Andy wasn't dead, so he tried to cover up. "Do you think I'm the sort of person who would condone such violence?" he asked, with a wounded expression. "On the contrary, I think if they ever find the guy who did it, he should face the death penalty! "he said with mock conviction. "All I meant to say was that I don't think fate or destiny had any part in Andy Dickinson's survival."

"Don't ever let Kerrie hear you say that," she warned. "I want you to make a good first impression on my best friend, and Andy bashing isn't the way to do it. She's a big part of my life and we're going to be spending lots of time with her, so don't start off on the wrong foot."

"I hope you're not planning any of those cozy, little get togethers anytime soon," he said, reaching out to Meg and pulling her over to him. "I know this may sound selfish, but I want you all to myself for now."

She playfully pulled away from him and said, "You can have me all to yourself for the rest of the day, but I've already invited Kerrie for dinner tonight. She's been dying to meet you, and since you've taken some time off from work, I thought this would be a great opportunity. I hope you don't mind."

His mind was racing. He couldn't possibly have dinner with Kerrie, but what could he do to get out of it?

"No, of course I don't mind." he said, figuring he had the whole rest of the day to dig up some excuse for not being able to attend. "I'm looking forward to meeting your pitifully love-struck friend."

CHAPTER 16

Meg was busy in the kitchen all afternoon preparing a special dinner for Kerrie's visit, and Curt was definitely in her way. It wasn't that his constant presence made her feel claustrophobic, exactly, but she wasn't comfortable with him watching her every move, making suggestions on how to improve on her recipes or having to sidestep him whenever she had to get from one side of the room to another, so she decided to send him on an errand.

"Honey?" she asked, after having been bumped into one time too many, "Could you please do me a favor and run to the store for a bottle of wine?"

The reason he'd been dogging her all day was because he wanted to be in on the conversation in case Kerrie called again to gush about her upcoming visit with Andy. He was also still trying to come up with an excuse not to be there for dinner, and she'd just given him the out he needed.

"I thought we already had some," he said, trying not to sound too eager about getting away from the house.

"All we have is Chardonnay, and I'm in the mood for Shiraz." she explained. "You don't really mind, do you?"

"No, I guess not. Any particular label?"

Meg didn't care if he came home with the cheapest wine there was as long as he left her in peace for a while. "Whatever looks good to you will be fine, but don't get sidetracked because Kerrie will be here in an hour."

"I'll be back in a flash." he lied, giving her a quick kiss on his way out.

He had no intention of going to the store and headed to his favorite sports bar at the Marina instead. After ordering a beer, he found himself a vacant table and sat down to watch the baseball game that was being shown on several of the bar's big screens. At the same time, he ironed out the details of his plan to stay away from Kerrie that evening.

Five minutes before Kerrie was due to arrive, he called Meg and told her that he wouldn't be making it home for dinner.

"You're not going to believe it, but I ran into my old college roommate, Edward Morris, from England, on my way out of the store and he asked me back to his hotel for a drink. He's been in town for a week and has been trying to get in touch with me, but lost my number." he explained. "He's leaving first thing tomorrow morning so I know you won't mind if I skip dinner tonight. This is my one and only chance to spend any time with an old friend."

Meg didn't answer right away, but from the tone of her voice, he could tell she was upset even though she tried to mask her feelings. "Kerrie's going to be very disappointed because she was really looking forward to finally meeting you, but I'm sure she'll understand."

"If she's as sweet and understanding as you are, I know she will," he cooed, slathering it on just a bit too thick. "I'll call you back in a couple of hours to let you know what time I'll be home. Right now we're going to go grab some dinner and then maybe hit that pub over on Montana for a pint or two. I'll try not to be too late and tell Kerrie I'm very sorry."

Meg was just about to hang up when she suddenly had a brainstorm. "Hey, I have an idea. Maybe we could hook up with you guys at the pub after dinner. That way, you and Kerrie will finally be able to meet, and maybe she and your friend would hit it off. Is he single?"

Quick-thinking Curt was at no loss for words. "I don't think that would be a good idea, Babe. Edward is single, but I'm sure Kerrie wouldn't be interested in him, nor he in her because he's not exactly a lady's man, if you know what I mean."

It took her a minute to figure out the message Curt was politely trying to convey. "Oh! So, what you're saying is that *you're* more his type?" she teased. "Well, don't go switching sides on me halfway through dinner, okay? "

"In case you haven't noticed," he said, trying to keep her on the defensive, "I only have eyes for you."

"It's not your eyes I'm concerned about, but after last night," she said, alluding to their very romantic evening, "I'm not the least bit worried, so have a good time and I'll see you later."

James was elated that he was able to come up with such a plausible excuse, and proceeded to ordered dinner, another beer, and settled back to watch the rest of the game.

Meg was just getting out of the shower when the doorbell rang. It was seven o'clock and Kerrie was right on time.

"Come in, it's open." she yelled. "Pour yourself a glass of wine and I'll be right out."

"Hey, you two, is that any way to greet a guest?" she hollered back. "Has opening the door and inviting your guest inside become a lost art?" Then, noticing an unopened bottle of Chardonnay standing next to two wine glasses on the kitchen counter, she glanced over at the dining room table, and saw that there were only two place settings.

"I know I'm horrible at math, but isn't there supposed to be three for dinner?" she called out.

"No need to shout," said Meg, who was now standing in the doorway to the living room. "Curt sends his apologies. I sent him out to get a bottle of wine and he ran into an old college friend at the store. He said the guy is leaving to go back home to London first thing in the morning, and they wanted to spend a couple of hours together to catch up on old times."

"He ran into a classmate from England at the local grocery store?" asked Kerrie, who didn't try and mask her suspicions that her friend was covering up for Curt once again. "How convenient."

Meg didn't like Kerrie's accusing tone. "What are you suggesting?"

Kerrie poured them both a glass of wine before answering.

"Don't you find it odd that every time we all plan to get together, Curt always has some excuse not to join in? What's the matter with this guy, anyway? Is there something you're not telling me?"

Of course not," said Meg, looking rather defensive. "He has nothing to hide and his excuses have always been valid. It's not easy getting a new business off the ground, you know. He puts in a lot of hours and can't help being on call night and day. And running into Edward today was just a coincidence."

"Maybe so," she shrugged, "but something just doesn't seem right. "

"The only thing that's not right is that we're standing her quibbling over nothing while a delicious dinner is in the oven, so put your suspicions aside, sit down and let's eat. I'm dying to hear all about your plans with Andy, and you'd better not leave out a single detail."

By the time they'd finished eating, Meg was totally filled in on the events that led up to Kerrie's date with the actor.

"So, when do you think you'll be hearing from him?"

"Oh, did I forget to mention that I already have?" she said coyly. "He called me this afternoon and we had a nice chat."

Meg was genuinely surprised. "I have to admit, I thought maybe he was just being polite when he responded to your invitation. I never thought he'd actually follow through."

"He said he'd be in town next week," said Kerrie, completely ignoring Meg's apparent amazement, "but he made me promise not to tell anyone because the studio doesn't want the media to find out that they're ready to begin filming. It's all very hush hush since there's that nut case on the loose who still may be gunning for Andy."

"You know you can trust me. I won't tell anyone."

"Not even Curt, okay?"

"Not even Curt," he promised, wishing Kerrie hadn't said that because she was dying to tell him all about it. "So what else did he say? Were you nervous? If someone I liked that much called me out of the blue, I'm not sure I'd be able to carry on an intelligent conversation."

"We only talked long enough for him to say he was looking forward to meeting me again, and that he'd call me as soon as he got into town."

Meg was still in awe. "I can't believe you actually managed to land a date with Andy Dickinson, but it's like I told Curt the other day, when you set your mind to something, you usually figure out a way to make it happen, so I shouldn't be too surprised."

For some reason, Kerrie was a little uncomfortable hearing that Meg said anything about it to her new boyfriend. "You told Curt about me and Andy? He must think I'm some sort of lovestruck idiot."

"Well, he didn't use those exact words, but he seemed concerned that you were chasing after an impossible dream and was worried you might get hurt."

"Why is he concerned about me getting hurt? I don't even know the guy," she said, thinking it odd that a total stranger gave a damn about her feelings.

"He's a very caring person, you know."

"I'll have to take your word for it," said Kerrie, still convinced that something about Curt just didn't seem right.

"Trust me. Curt is a wonderful man, and I know you're going to love him as much as I do. Now, how about some dessert?"

Meg was sound asleep by the time Curt arrived home from his night out with his imaginary friend. He had stayed out especially late because when he called home around ten, Kerrie was still there and he didn't want to take the chance of running into her if he came back too soon, so he explained that he and Edward were having a great time and told Meg not to wait up.

Over breakfast the next morning, he tried to find out what Kerrie had to say about her upcoming meeting with Andy, but Meg lied and said that their plans were still up in the air. He knew there must have been more to the conversation than that and was annoyed that Meg wouldn't say any more, but if he couldn't get any information from her, he'd have to do a little checking around on his own.

For the next few days, he combed the Hollywood trade papers for news about *A Bad Case of the Collywobbles*, called a few media contacts he knew and even emailed the film's production office in England to see whether or not they had resumed production. There was nothing in the papers, his friends hadn't heard anything, and the production office said they couldn't give out any information at this time.

In addition to finding out about the movie, he also visited the Scotland Yard and BBC News websites every day for updates on the Andy Dickinson case, and was glad to learn that although the investigation was ongoing, the authorities were still clueless about the shooter or his motives.

Every couple of days he asked Meg if she'd spoken to Kerrie but always got the same response. "Not really. She's been working hard on her new book so it's always just a quick hello."

"I can't believe she hasn't said any more about getting together with Andy. The anticipation must be driving her wild."

As much as she hated lying to Curt, she had made Kerrie a promise and intended to keep it. In truth, she had spoken to Kerrie earlier in the day and found out that the dinner with Andy was going to take place that evening.

"Call me the first thing tomorrow and let me know how it went. I've got to hear all about it," Meg insisted.

"I'll be on the phone to you first thing in the morning," said Kerrie with a giggle. "We're meeting for dinner at his hotel, and he said something about calling room service, so I guess he's trying to stay out of the public eye as much as possible."

"I would, too, if there was a killer after me," said Meg. "And since I don't hear you complaining about having to suffer through a very private dinner in his suite, I'm assuming the arrangements are to your liking?"

"Are you kidding? How could they not be?" she asked. "Andy Dickinson has millions of lovesick fans who'd give their right arms to be able to share a not so private meal with him at Burger King, and I get to have him all to myself in his hotel room. Could it get any better than that?"

"Only if he doesn't kick you out after desert." she teased.

Kerrie liked the idea that her meeting with Andy sounded romantic, but had no preconceived notions of how things were really going to turn out. She was in a quandary about whether or not to broach the subject of past lives because she needed to find out if he believed in such things, but didn't want to risk it on their first meeting. Hopefully he'd like her well enough to invite her out again, and maybe once they got to know each other better, she'd feel more comfortable about bringing it up.

Andy Dickinson was a happy man when his plane touched down at LAX that afternoon. Although he still wasn't feeling completely well and it had been a long flight, he was glad to be out and about after his painfully long convalescence. The movie was coming along quite well, and he was looking forward to his visit with Kerrie. The only thing that was still bothering him was trying to figure out the best way to warn her about James without having her think he was some kind of lunatic.

During a phone call to Ted just before leaving London, the psychic didn't hide his frustration and dismay when he found out that Andy and Kerrie had been in touch. "You must let fate run its course, Andy," he warned. "Remember, even though Kerrie knows who you were in 1862, she doesn't know that you do. Moreover, she hasn't yet recognized James for who he really is and you can't be the one to tell her."

"Well, she invited me to dinner when I was in L.A. and it would be rude to refuse such a heartfelt invitation."

Given the circumstances, Ted was stunned that Andy would even consider another meeting with Kerrie, but knew there was nothing more he could do than voice his opinion against it.

"Are you worried that she or I would mention our past?" he wondered, thinking that Ted was being an alarmist about the whole thing. "I have no doubt that was the reason she contacted me in the first place."

Ted didn't totally agree. "Don't be so sure. She has no idea whether or not you even believe in such things, and I think she would be cautious about mentioning it for fear you'd think her a bit odd. My advice is that you do not meet up with her, but if you do, say nothing, even if she finds a way to tell you what she knows. Play dumb, and for God's sake do not let on that you and I have been talking. There could be dire consequences if you tamper with fate, and I, for one, don't want to see history repeat itself."

How am I supposed to look Kerrie straight in the eye and not say anything? Andy wondered as he gathered his bag from the overhead luggage compartment. *What are we supposed to talk about? The weather?* But recalling Ted's warning that history could repeat itself, he vowed to follow the psychic's advice and not bring up the past—but that didn't mean he couldn't still warn her about James in the present.

It had been a long time since Kerrie felt butterflies in her stomach, but when she drove into the valet parking area of the historic Hotel Roosevelt on Hollywood Boulevard, she had a fairly severe case of the jitters. Andy had given her the pseudonym he was registered under, and when she told the desk clerk she was there to see Thomas Wakefield, he called upstairs immediately to announce her arrival. Then turning to Kerrie, he said, "If you'll just wait one moment, the bellman will escort you to the private elevator. Mr. Wakefield is staying in one of our penthouse suites."

"I didn't know the hotel even had a penthouse," she said, trying to make chit chat while waiting for the bellman to arrive. "I'll bet there is a lovely view of the city lights from way up there."

"I'm sure you'll be quite pleased with both the room and all its amenities," he said with a knowing wink. Before she had time to respond, the bellman walked up and politely asked Kerrie to follow him.

They walked across the lobby and past the elevator banks until they came to a nondescript doorway leading into a small, wood paneled cubicle. Thinking the bellman must have taken a wrong turn because there was no elevator in sight, Kerrie was about to turn around and walk out until she saw the man flip a switch on the wall. Suddenly, two of the large wood panels slid apart to reveal a small elevator car. "We jokingly refer to it as Lover's Lift, since most people who stay in the penthouse check in by themselves but never stay lonely for long, if you know what I mean," he explained in a tone suggesting that her reason for the visit was more than innocent.

That was two accusations in less than five minutes, and Kerrie didn't like being thought of as some cheap, one-night stand. "Then maybe I should be taking the stairs, because I'm Mr. Wakefield's daughter," she answered back, trying her best to look righteously indignant. Her quick thinking worked perfectly because the bellman's demeanor immediately changed.

"Oh, I'm so sorry. Miss Wakefield. I didn't mean to infer that your visit to Mr. Wakefield was for anything but the purest of reasons," he stammered, "or that your father is the type of man who would require the services of a, well, never mind. Please accept my sincerest apologies if I said anything to offend you, and if there's anything you need, do not hesitate to ring me. Please enjoy your evening."

Kerrie stepped inside the waiting elevator and was glad the doors closed immediately because she was finding it difficult to keep a straight face. On the one hand, she felt bad lying to the guy, but at the same time, didn't want him thinking she actually was a well-dressed call girl.

CHAPTER 17

When the elevator doors opened into the penthouse's foyer, Andy was standing there beaming with anticipation. He'd been standing there waiting since the front desk called to tell him that Kerrie was on her way up. He couldn't wait to see her again but was a bit puzzled by the amused expression on her face.

"Have I got spinach in my teeth or is my fly undone?" he asked with mock concern, patting himself down to make sure he was properly put together.

"No, you're fine." she said, suddenly forgetting all about the bellman.

They stood there just staring at each other for a very long time, seemingly mesmerized by finally being in each other's company. It wasn't until the elevator doors began to buzz loudly that the spell was broken.

"Do come in and make yourself comfortable." he said, taking her hand and showing her into the living room. "I've taken the liberty of ordering dinner and it should arrive momentarily. Meanwhile, would you care for a drink?" he asked, gesturing towards the bar at the far end of the room.

"A glass of wine would be nice," she said, finally finding her voice.

While Andy prepared the drinks, Kerrie walked over to the other side of the room and stared out the wall of windows. The sun was going down, the city lights were twinkling in the distance, and even though she was thrilled to finally spend some time with Andy, she was also fighting a bad case of the jitters. Would they actually hit it off or would the evening be peppered with uncomfortable silences in between polite small talk?

Kerrie had decided against mentioning the subject of reincarnation or their past life together. Instead, she hoped their meeting would stir something in Andy's subconscious that might lead him to bring it up instead, but was now second guessing herself. She was so deep in thought, she didn't hear him walk up behind her.

"I made sure the room had a western exposure because I do love a beautiful sunset," he said, breaking her train of thought.

Kerrie spun around so quickly, she nearly knocked the glass of wine out of his hand. "I'm so sorry, I didn't hear you coming," she said, clumsily reaching for the sloshing glass. "Did you get any on you?"

"Thankfully, my reflexes are quite good, and not a drop was spilled," he laughed, firmly placing the glass in her hand. "Are you always this jumpy?" he teased.

"Not usually, but I seem to be a nervous wreck at the moment." she admitted, feeling herself start to blush.

"If truth be known," he said, taking her arm and leading her back into the living room, "I've got a slight case of the collywobbles myself."

"A case of the what?" she wondered.

"Collywobbles. A slang term for a nervous stomach," he explained. "*A Bad Case of the Collywobbles* also happens to be the title of the movie I'm currently working on."

"It's a funny little word, but I kind of like it," she said, glad that the conversation was beginning to flow comfortably. "It almost sounds made up, like something from The Jabberwocky."

Being the consummate actor and not being able to resist temptation, Andy began to recite the famous poem.

"'Twas brillig, and the slithy toves did gyre and gimble in the wabe," he said with Shakespearean flair. "All mimsy were the borogoves, and the mome raths outgrabe."

By the second verse, she couldn't help but join in. "Beware the Jabberwock, my son! The jaws that bite, the claws that catch! Beware the Jubjub bird, and shun the frumious Bandersnatch!"

"Well done!" he applauded. "I'm glad to be in the company of a fellow Lewis Carroll fan.

"You've gotta love that Jubjub bird," she laughed. Then seeing Andy walk over to the sofa and sit down, she took a seat at the other end of the couch. There was a brief moment of silence before either of them spoke up, but when they did, it was simultaneous.

"So how are you feeling?" she asked at the same time he asked, "How's the new book coming?"

They tried to politely allow the other a chance to answer, but neither responded immediately and another moment of silence was upon them until they both saw the humor in the situation and burst out laughing.

"Ladies first." he offered.

For the next few minutes, she talked about the book she was currently working on, the good time she had while in London and how glad she was to be out of the limelight for the time being. While he hoped she would also say something about the ugly scene with James at the after party, which would have given him an opening to warn her about him, she didn't bring it up.

When it was his turn to speak, Andy said he was feeling a great deal better, was thankful to be alive, and voiced his concerns that the perpetrator had not yet been identified. "That's why we're keeping the filming so secretive. According to Scotland Yard, that madman could very well be stalking me, so the less everyone knows about my whereabouts, the better."

Kerrie was just about to ask if he had any ideas about who it was that tried to kill him when their conversation was interrupted by the arrival of their dinner. "Room service, Mr. Wakefield," said the porter, pushing the food trolley through the elevator doors.

Any talk of the attack was put aside during dinner in favor of the usual "let's get to know each other better" line of questioning. The rest of the evening went by in a blur but both Kerrie and Andy felt a definite attraction to one another. Neither wanted to spoil the moment by actually bringing up the thoughts that were foremost in their minds and by midnight, Kerrie felt she really should be leaving.

"Thank you so much for accepting my dinner invitation," she said, letting him help her on with her coat. "I'm so glad we finally got to meet again."

"I can't tell you how very glad I was that you contacted me, because after I read your book I wanted to call and congratulate you, but didn't have any of your contact numbers."

"Why didn't you just get in touch with my publisher? They're very good about passing along messages."

"As a matter of fact, I did call them, but when I didn't hear back from you, I assumed you weren't interested in hearing from me."

"Are you kidding? I would have been thrilled, but I never got your message, but we must have been destined to meet again because fate stepped in and made up for the miscommunication."

Even though she said this in a lighthearted tone, she hoped he would somehow pick up on her hint.

Kerrie had just given him the opening he was looking for, but Andy decided that it was too late to follow through. Instead, he suggested another date. "We begin filming next Monday, and we're scheduled to be in town for about twelve weeks. Perhaps we could get together again?"

It was his intention to see Kerrie as often as possible throughout his stay in Los Angeles and the better he got to know her, the greater chance he'd have of being able to warn her about James.

"I'd like that very much. My schedule is flexible so just give me a call whenever you're free. I'm chained to the computer all day and look forward to any chance I get to get to break free. I usually go out with my best friend Meg," she explained, "but she just moved in with her new boyfriend, so I'm pretty much on my own these days."

"I hadn't planned on doing much socializing while I'm here, except for a couple of nights out with some old friends, but I'd be very happy to spend the rest of my free time with a lonely, overworked writer. "

They stood in silence for a moment, each holding onto an unspoken secret, and then, as the elevator doors opened, Andy put his arms around Kerrie and gave her a long, meaningful hug.

"I'll speak with you soon," he said, finally breaking their embrace, then he gave her a kiss on the forehead. "Be safe."

Kerri was unwilling to look away so she slowly stepped backwards into the elevator and held his gaze until the door closed.

167

Meg was careful not to wake Curt when she climbed out of bed early the next morning to call Kerrie. She was dying to find out how her date with Andy went but didn't want to break her promise to Kerrie about not letting him know Andy was in town.

It was still dark outside, so she shut the bedroom door behind her then carefully tiptoed into the living room and made the call.

"I want to know everything that happened last night down to the last detail," she whispered, knowing she had dragged her friend out of bed to answer the phone.

"What time is it?" Kerrie mumbled, trying to focus her eyes on the clock next to the bed.

"It's six o'clock and I know it's early but I wanted to call you before Curt got up."

"I'd rather not talk about it over the phone," yawned Kerrie, who, in addition to wanting to get back to sleep was also worried about Curt waking up. "Why don't we meet for lunch instead?"

"Okay," Meg was a bit disappointed at having to wait. "You can at least tease me with one little detail to tide me over. It's not every day that you get invited to Andy Dickinson's private penthouse for dinner."

"You're making it sound like a clandestine rendezvous, which it wasn't. We had a nice meal, watched the sunset, talked for a bit and then I came home."

"I'm sure there was more to it than that, but since you're going to make me wait to hear the real story, I'll meet you at The Cat and the Fiddle at noon."

"Great. I'll see you then."

Kerrie had trouble going back to sleep and because she didn't want Meg to get the impression that this was just a one-night stand, she decided that it was finally time tell her friend the whole story about her connection to Andy.

Meg didn't think that Curt would be wide awake when she tiptoed back into the bedroom but he was a light sleeper and woke up the moment she got out of bed to make the call. He couldn't make out most of what she was saying because she was speaking in a whisper, but he thought he heard her say Andy's name.

"Who were you calling this early?" he asked, pulling himself into a sitting position.

She was surprised to see that he wasn't asleep, and hoped he didn't hear any of her phone conversation. "I just wanted to give Kerrie a call before it got too late. We made plans to have lunch today and I wanted to make sure it was still on."

"At six o'clock in the morning?"

"Well, sometimes she gets up early and goes for a run," she fibbed, "so I wanted to catch her before she left."

"So, what does Andy Dickinson have to do with your lunch date?" he asked, letting her know that he'd heard the name mentioned. "Surely, you're not flying to London to have lunch with him, are you?"

Meg started to panic, and tried to come up with a convincing explanation. "You must have heard wrong because I didn't say anything about Andy Dickinson," she began. "Kerrie mentioned picking up some produce at the Farmer's Market after lunch and maybe you heard *Andy* when I was talking about *candy*. They've got some sinfully good homemade chocolates at one of the stands."

He didn't believe her for a minute. "Really? Well, is this a private lunch or can I come along? I'm quite fond of homemade chocolates, you know."

"Wow, that's a switch. Up until now, you've never been able to get together with us before, but sorry Babe, today isn't going to be the day. It's kind of a girl lunch thing, if you know what I mean, but thanks for offering."

"I just thought it would be a good opportunity to prove to your friend that I really do exist, but don't worry about it. I've got a few errands to run anyway, so I'll meet you back here later this afternoon."

Meg was so relieved that he hadn't insisted on tagging along, she made a mental note to bring home a big bag of chocolates as a peace offering, then climbed back into bed for a cuddle. "That's what I love about you. You're so understanding."

Once she decided to tell Meg about her and Andy, Kerrie got up and made herself a cup of coffee. She really wanted to call Ted and tell him that she and Andy had dinner together, but talked herself out of it because she was afraid of what he might say since he had already warned her against it. Her instincts were right because when Andy called Ted later that morning, the psychic was furious.

"I can't believe you went against my advice." Ted fumed, after hearing what the actor had to say.

Andy was ready with a comeback because he knew Ted would be upset by the news. "I didn't go against your advice because you told me not to get in touch with Kerrie, and I didn't. She called me, and what could I say? 'I'm sorry, Kerrie, I can't get together with you because my psychic advised against it?'

"That's all well and good," said Ted "but I told her not to try and contact you either. I hope to God you didn't mention anything about James."

"No, and she didn't bring up the past either," he admitted. "We just had a nice, quiet, dinner, but I must admit I was tempted to say something. I just can't bear the thought that James is out there somewhere and that she's in danger. I feel so protective of her I just want to take her in my arms and never let go."

"Just keep those arms to yourself, Andy," said Ted, "and now that you've seen each other, I hope that's the end of it."

He didn't want to let Ted know that they'd made plans to get together again, so Andy denied knowledge of any further contact, but Ted sensed there was more to it. "Don't ever try to lie to your psychic."

"Well, we haven't made any specific plans yet." he said sheepishly. "I just said I'd call her in a couple of days."

Ted was frustrated, but knew there wasn't a whole lot he could do about it. "Look, you know I can't stop the two of you, but remember, you're playing a dangerous game. We both know it was James who tried to kill you in London, and I'm sure he flew back to the States shortly thereafter. It would be bad enough if he found out you are here, but I don't even want to think of what might happen if he were to learn that you've seen Kerrie."

"Look, Ted, I can't promise you that I won't see Kerrie again, because I really think I'm falling for her...again," he chuckled, referring to their love affair in 1862, "and I still think she needs to be told about James, but I'll give the whole situation careful consideration before I decide what to do about it, okay?"

"I've said all I can," sighed the psychic, "so now I leave it to God."

CHAPTER 10

Meg was sitting at an outdoor table at the Cat and the Fiddle and sipping her second glass of wine by the time Kerrie arrived for their lunch date. "Sorry I'm late." she apologized. "Andy called as I was walking out the door. We're going to try and get together over the weekend."

"So, I'm guessing things went well last night?" she asked, hoping to coax a full confession out of her friend. Before Kerrie could answer, the waitress came by to take their orders, but by the time their food arrived, Meg was pretty much filled in about the dinner date with Andy.

"I hope you're not falling too hard too fast," warned Meg, hoping that her friend wasn't setting herself up for a big disappointment. "That fluffy white cloud you're floating on might not be as sturdy as you think."

Kerrie shifted uncomfortably in her seat. She wasn't sure how Meg was going to react when she heard about the past life regression with Ted and the link between her and Andy Dickinson, but she had to be told. "There's a little more to all this than you know, so I want you to hear me out, and don't interrupt, no matter how strange any of it may sound."

Meg agreed. She was clearly puzzled by her friend's cryptic request but listened quietly as Kerrie explained it all. She was horrified to hear about Rachel's murder, but at the same time fascinated to learn that Kerrie and Andy were once Adam and Rachel, and didn't doubt the validity of the story. She believed in reincarnation herself and was glad to finally be able to understand the curious bond between her friend and the actor.

"Why did it take you so long to tell me? I thought you were having some sort of fatal attraction to Andy and was really starting to worry."

"I know I should have told you right away, but I didn't want to say anything until I saw Andy in person. Now that we finally were able to spend some time together, I know for sure that Andy is Adam, but I'm afraid to say anything to him about it. What if he thinks I'm crazy? I feel like there's a strong attraction between us, but I don't know what he's thinking, so it would be risky to bring it up until I'm sure how he feels."

"Maybe you and Andy should have dinner with Ted, and let him do the explaining for you."

"No, that won't work," sighed Kerrie. Ted warned me about trying to contact Andy. He said I shouldn't interfere with fate and he'd be furious if he knew we got together last night."

"Surely he must already know. I mean, he is psychic," laughed Meg, who was so intrigued by the whole story, she was absentmindedly spooning way too much sugar in her coffee.

Kerrie reached over and pulled the sugar bowl away. "In the first place, I don't think he goes around remote viewing what his friends are up to, and secondly, he hasn't called to yell at me about it, so I'm assuming he's still blissfully unaware.

"But don't you think it's a long shot to expect Andy to recognize you as Rachel on his own?" asked Meg, who was now reaching for the water glass because she'd just taken a sip of her coffee and almost choked on how sweet it was.

"If he's meant to remember me, he will. If not, we're just two strangers who happened to meet and we'll see what happens from there. Either way, I have to find out."

While Meg understood Kerrie's logic, all this talk about reincarnation reminded her that sometimes history does repeat itself and voiced her concerns about Rachel's murderer maybe being around as well.

"I wouldn't worry too much about that," said Kerrie, with a dismissive wave of her hand. "A bad soul like that doesn't deserve another life."

"Are you forgetting about Karma?" asked Meg. She was horrified that Kerrie could dismiss the possibility so easily.

"Personally, I don't buy into the theory that a criminal goes straight to Hell and stays there for all eternity after one rotten life. From what I've read on the subject, a soul is given the opportunity to reincarnate as many times as it takes to make things right. Whether that soul chooses to exercise that option is a personal decision."

"Ted didn't say anything about him being around, so I have to assume he's not, and after what I went through in my past life, I'm pretty sure I'm safe from deranged murderers this time around," said Kerrie, trying to sound braver than she actually felt. She couldn't ignore Meg's warning, but at the same time hoped her own theory about being safe during this lifetime was correct.

Curt wasn't lying when he told Meg he had a few errands to run that day. He was planning on getting the oil changed in her car that morning, but after finding out she was going out to lunch with Kerrie, he decided to make another stop along the way and had a GPS device installed so he'd be able to track her every move.

As soon as he handed Meg the car keys and watched her drive off, he quickly installed the GPS software into his phone and was pleased to find that it worked perfectly. Ordinarily, he would have been content just to know where his girlfriend was, but because she had gone to meet Kerrie, he had an overpowering urge to drive over to the restaurant. He hadn't been anywhere near Kerrie since that night at her apartment, and just had to see her again.

The friends were just starting on their dessert when Curt slowly drove past the Cat and Fiddle and was pleased to see that they were sitting out on the patio in plain view and luckily, he found a parking spot nearby. Even though the authorities hadn't been able to find him to serve the restraining order, he knew a police report had been made and thought it best to keep a safe distance away.

But being in such close proximity to Kerrie only reinforced his feelings for her and seeing her sitting there at the table brought back the memory of that day they'd spent sightseeing in London when they'd stopped to have lunch at the Cornish pasty restaurant. He felt a pang of jealousy that Meg was enjoying Kerrie's company today and not him.

He watched as the waitress came by to bring them their bill and saw Kerrie dig in her purse for a credit card while Meg apparently ran off to the ladies' room. Kerrie got a phone call while waiting for her friend to return, and judging by her flirtatious behavior to whoever was on the other end of the line, Curt couldn't help but wonder whether she was talking to Andy and wished he could read lips.

Kerrie was done with her call when Meg returned, and the two of them sat and chatted for another few minutes before leaving the restaurant. He expected their cars pull out of the parking lot and go off in different directions, so Curt was surprised to see them both heading for the same place and decided to follow.

He followed them to The Meadow, a new, upscale shopping center and drove into the parking structure a few car lengths behind. They both found parking spaces on Level 3, so James proceeded up to Level 4. The parking structure overlooked the mall, so he waited upstairs until he saw them get off the escalator then took a nearby elevator down to the mall.

He stayed far enough away so he could blend into the crowd, and watched as Meg and Kerrie strolled past the numerous window displays. It looked as though they had a great deal to say to each other, and he couldn't wait to get home and ask Meg all about it.

When they walked into a nearby shoe store, he thought this would be a great opportunity to get a little bit closer. He knew that shoes shopping was Meg's weakness and reasoned they'd be in there quite a while, so he walked over to the store window and peered in. Sure enough, there was Meg, sitting near the back of the store with a big pile of shoeboxes at her feet. Kerrie was patiently watching her friend try them all on.

He was stuck to the window like a Peeping Tom, and didn't notice a group of teenagers sneaking towards him armed with a couple of Super Soakers, those large squirt guns that can easily drench a person with a single squirt. The kids had been terrorizing shoppers all afternoon and seeing that he was totally distracted, they decided he was a prime target and let the jets of water fly.

It was a hot afternoon and the cold spray felt like a barrage of ice water hitting the back of his shirt. He spun around just in time to see the laughing teens running away.

"Hey! What the hell do you think you're doing?" he hollered, causing people on the street to stop and stare. He thought about running after them, but knew he'd never be able to catch up. When he turned back around, a large number of shoppers had stopped to see what all the commotion was about. "What's the matter with you? He yelled. "Isn't anyone going to try and stop them?"

A few people just shrugged while several others tried to stifle their amusement. As the crowd slowly dispersed, a little old lady dug into her purse and offered him a flimsy handkerchief which he rudely refused.

When he turned his attention back to the shoe store, he was shocked to see Kerrie standing in the doorway just a few feet away, staring back at him. The look of stunned recognition on her face was all he needed to see. He turned and ran off towards the parking structure.

Kerrie panicked when she saw him and hurried back into the store. "Let's go!" she yelled, grabbing Meg by the arm, yanking her out of the chair.

Meg hadn't paid any attention to all the commotion outside and couldn't figure out what was going on. "What's the matter with you? she asked, trying to steady herself because she had one shoe off and one shoe on. "I'm not done shopping yet."

"I don't care. We've got to go!" Kerrie demanded. "I just saw James peeking at me through the window."

Meg was reluctant to leave without buying at least one pair of shoes, and tried to stall for time. "Are you sure it wasn't someone who looked like James?

"No, it was James, and when we made eye contact, he looked like a deer caught in the headlights and ran away."

"Then what's the problem?" asked Meg, sitting back down on and reaching for the other shoe. "Even if it was him, he's gone now, so just relax. You can't expect to go through life without running into people every once in a while."

Kerrie couldn't believe Meg just said that. "What's the matter with you? This isn't some weird stranger we're talking about. It was James, and he's stalking me," she said angrily. "I'm going to go outside and call the police and let them know he's around. According to them, he's vanished off the face of the earth, but if he's hanging out at the mall, at least they'll know he's in town."

"I'll be out in a minute." said Meg, who tried to sound sympathetic, but choosing between two pairs of open toed sandals was foremost on her mind. By the time Kerrie came back, Meg still hadn't decided which pair to choose.

"Look," said Kerrie, feeling a bit better that she'd made the call, "there's no need to spoil your day, so take your time and finish shopping, but I'm going home. It gives me the creeps knowing that James is around here somewhere."

Meg saw how upset Kerrie was and chose friendship over shoes and walked with Kerrie back to the parking structure. "What did the police say?"

"They just asked for the report number, said they'd make a notation that James had been seen at the mall and thanked me for calling."

"How civil of them," said Meg with a touch of sarcasm. "Do you want me to follow you home?"

"No thanks, I'll be fine," she said, putting her key in the ignition. "I don't think James is stupid enough to stick around."

Meg wasn't quite so sure. "If he was stupid enough to follow you here, then why wouldn't he be idiot enough to follow you home?"

"I'm not too worried because like you said, I don't know for sure if he ran into me on purpose or if he was just there by coincidence but in any case, if it was on purpose, he's long gone by now because he's got to know I'd call the police immediately."

Meg looked over her shoulder to make sure he wasn't still lurking somewhere in the parking garage. "That's true, but promise me that you'll drive straight home and call me as soon as you get there, okay?"

"I will, but you'd better watch your back, too, because James knows you're my best friend, and he might try to use you to get to me."

"He'd better not try because Curt will mop the floor with him if he does."

James knew that Kerrie and Meg would no doubt be leaving the mall after their accidental encounter, so he raced home, threw off his wet clothes and jumped into the shower. He was just drying off when he Meg come in.

"Did you have a nice time?" he asked, ignoring the worried look on her face.

"It started out just fine, but we went to the mall after lunch and who do we run into but that James creep," she said, tossing her purse on the bed and kicking off her shoes. "He was peeping into the window of one of the shops were in, and I hope I'm wrong, but I get the feeling he was stalking Kerrie. She was so upset she immediately called the police and then we left right away.

He didn't think a quick glimpse merited a call to the police, but was curious to find out what they had to say and could tell that Meg wasn't too happy about the outcome.

"All they did was humor Kerrie by writing a note about the sighting on her case file. Big deal."

He was both amused and relieved. "What did she expect them to do? Send out the SWAT team or something?"

"Of course not," she said, thinking Curt was being insensitive. She was just about to finish her thought when the phone rang. "That's probably Kerrie." she explained. "I told her to call me when she got home."

By the time she came back down the hall a few minutes later, Curt was lying on the bed, his towel in a heap on the floor.

"I thought you might want a little diversion to clear your head," he suggested, patting the empty space next to him.

"Thanks, but not now," she said distractedly. "I'm really not in the mood."

Instead of being understanding, Curt flew into a rage. "If hanging out with Kerrie is going to upset you like this, maybe you should stay away from her for a while," he yelled. "So what if she saw this James guy at the mall? It's a free country and he should be allowed the freedom to go where he damn well pleases. He didn't try to harm her, did he?"

"No, but he frightened her," she said, taking a defensive step back. She'd never seen Curt blow up like this before.

"And then she frightened you, and now we're standing here arguing over a whole lot of nothing," he ranted. He jumped out of bed, stormed into the bathroom and slammed the door behind him.

"She is my best friend, and I worry about her!" she yelled back.

He was not liking that Meg was putting Kerrie's needs before his, so he ran back into the bedroom and stood nose to nose with Meg. "What about worrying about me for a change? You're

177

driving a wedge between us with all of Kerrie's crap and I've had just about enough. Tell your friend to get a life and stay the hell out of ours."

Taken aback by his mean-spirited reply, Meg took a deep breath then tried to explain that Kerrie was indeed getting her life together, was planning to go out a lot more and would no doubt be too busy from now on to get together very often anyway.

"Why do you say that?" he asked, changing his tone from angry to inquisitive. "Has she met someone?" he wondered, not pleased with the idea that Kerrie might be spending time with another man.

"Something like that." snapped Meg.

"What the hell is that supposed to mean?" he demanded. "Is she or isn't she?"

"I really don't understand you sometimes. A minute ago, you were telling me to stay away from Kerrie and now you're itching to find out what's going on in her life. Yes, she is seeing someone, but I promised not to say more than that, so just be happy that Kerrie will probably be too busy to get in your way and leave it at that."

"Good!" he lied. Even though he didn't like the thought of Kerrie getting involved with any man, at least she wouldn't have the time to chase down Andy Dickinson now that she'd met someone else. "And hopefully this new guy will be able to take her mind off that idiot actor once and for all."

As much as Meg wanted so badly to tell Curt that Kerrie's new guy was that idiot actor, she just couldn't. "I'm not sure that will happen," she said, trying to keep a straight face. "I think she found someone just like him."

"That's impossible," he snorted. "From what little I know about Andy Dickinson, there couldn't possibly be more than one."

"Maybe not." she said, still trying hard not to smile.

CHAPTER 19

James had been so preoccupied worrying about Kerrie's obsession with Andy, he had completely discounted the possibility that she might get involved with anyone else, and was surprised to find out that his jealousy knew no bounds. He was also annoyed that Meg was so tight lipped about Kerrie's new boyfriend.

"You don't even know Kerrie, so why do you care who she's dating?" she asked at breakfast the next morning after he made yet another failed attempt to pry more information out of her.

"I just want to make sure she's getting involved with the right sort of person. You know, someone she can proudly introduce to her friends and not some guy she has to keep out of sight for fear we'll all think badly of him."

Meg had to laugh at the irony, because Curt had never given her the opportunity to proudly show him off.

"Some people might think you're not the right sort of person for me to be dating because nobody has met you yet, and we've been living together for nearly a month."

"It's not like you're hiding me, for God's sake. It's just a case of bad timing, is all."

"And Kerrie's not hiding her new boyfriend, either," she lied. "She's only been out with the guy once and doesn't want to bring him around quite yet in case things don't work out. Personally, I think that's rather sensible."

He thought he might be making some progress in getting Meg to divulge a secret or two, so Curt put down his fork and gave her his undivided attention. "Where did she meet him? I thought she was so busy with the new book she didn't have time for socializing."

Meg decided it wouldn't hurt to give him a little bit of information, and explained that Kerrie first met him in London during her book tour.

"A fellow tourist?" he asked.

"No, actually, he's a Brit," she said before realizing she'd probably said too much.

Curt was still not thinking it was Andy Dickinson and continued his questioning. "Did she say where she met him? And if he's British, what's he doing here in Los Angeles?"

"He's here on business, I don't recall where she said she met him, and will you please stop drilling me. She hasn't told me much about him, but she's happy and that's all I care about because after all the crap that sick, horrible James has put her through, she needs someone in her life right now who cares about her."

Hearing himself referred to as depraved, James felt the need to defend himself. "You're just going on the information Kerrie told you about that James guy. I'd like to hear his side of the story before coming to any conclusions. I mean, maybe she's just not used to having anyone take such a keen interest in her and she might have misjudged him. It doesn't sound to me like she's had very many serious relationships."

Clearly, her ploy to end the conversation wasn't working.

"It's not in Kerrie's nature to exaggerate, but even if she had misinterpreted James' intentions in London, there's no getting around the fact that he attacked her in her apartment. And could you please explain to me why it is that guys always stick up for each other no matter what?"

"I'm not sticking up for anyone," he said, angry that Kerrie had managed to brainwash Meg. "I'm just saying there's a possibility that James might have come on a little too strong in London, and she took it the wrong way. As for the incident in her apartment, I think she just panicked. It sounds to me like the guy really likes her and was probably a bit too forward in trying to tell her so, but I can't believe he meant her any real harm."

Meg didn't want to get into another argument about Kerrie and James, so she got up from the table and carried her dishes to the sink. "Look, I've got to go jump in the shower and get ready for work. And since you've asked me to stay out of Kerrie's life, let's just agree to disagree on this one and leave it at that, okay?"

By the time she left for the fitness center an hour later, he had plenty of time to rehash the conversation in his mind. Who was this mysterious Brit Kerrie was seeing? How long was he going to be in town, and how serious were they? If Andy wasn't still recuperating in London, he would have thought that Kerrie and the actor had somehow managed to hook up, but as long as this new guy wasn't Andy, he could be easily taken care of.

When Andy called Kerrie that evening, he could tell that something was wrong. It took a little bit of coaxing before she told him about her encounter with James, then went on to explain about the attack in her apartment. Andy was livid, but listened quietly, not wanting to let on that he knew anything about James other than the little she had said over dinner at the hotel.

He had hoped James would back off after the incident at her apartment, but it now seemed as though he was stalking Kerrie, and Andy feared for the worst. He did his best to console her, then suggested they have a late dinner together at his hotel that evening. "I know we weren't planning to get together until the weekend, but I think it would do you good to get away from the apartment for a while and I won't take no for an answer. I'll send a car for you at around eight."

As soon as she stepped out of the elevator that evening and saw his smiling face, all of Kerrie's troubles were temporarily forgotten. There was something about being in Andy's company that made her feel safe. Dinner was delicious and the conversation between them flowed easily. They talked a little bit about Andy's new movie, and knowing that he was playing the part of a wizard gave Kerrie an opening to question him about his belief in the occult. If he admitted to having an interest in such things, she might be able to steer the conversation towards the subject of reincarnation.

"Did you do any kind of research to prepare for the role?"

He was intrigued by her question, but didn't actually think it was anything other than a polite query, so his answer was rather non-committal. "If you're asking me whether or not I believe in the metaphysical world, I'd have to say I'm open to the possibility, but I didn't run out and sign up for a crash course in witchcraft," he joked. "I've learned a great deal about it just by reading the script. It's a fascinating subject, don't you agree?" he asked, hoping she'd take the bait and perhaps give him an opening to bring up the subject of past lives.

"I never gave it much thought until after I'd read the book, and then I did read a lot of other books on the subject and am especially intrigued with Karma and reincarnation," she admitted. "I hope you don't think this is too off the wall, but I often wonder about my past lives."

"I don't think it's odd at all," said Andy. "As a matter of fact, I'm very fond of the theory that people share many lives together over time, which explains why some people naturally gravitate to one another."

"Like the two of us?" she blurted out.

As much as Andy wanted to admit that he knew all about their past life together, he remembered Ted's warning, and decided against it for the time being. Keeping her safe from James in this lifetime was more of a concern.

"I know it's really none of my business, but I'm worried about you and I want you to know that I will do everything I can to see that James doesn't bother you again," he began. "I know a few people in town who can easily track him down and furnish the police with his address, then once they are able to serve him with the restraining order, if he puts so much as a toe out of line, they will lock him up. Meanwhile," he continued, "my car and personal bodyguard are at your disposal should you need to venture out alone, and I've arranged for certain security measures to be set up throughout your apartment."

Kerrie was clearly disappointed that he'd changed the subject from past lives to security, but was surprised to hear that he was going out of his way to protect her. "I appreciate the thought, but I don't think all that is necessary. Especially the car and the bodyguard. You're not exactly safe yourself these days."

"The studio has too much invested in this picture to allow anything to happen to me. At the present time, I'm worth quite a bit more to them alive than dead," he chuckled. "I'm under contract for three more pictures if Collywobbles does as well as expected, so don't worry about my safety. I want you to remain unharmed until we can track James down, okay?"

While all of Andy's plans sounded good in theory, they hadn't gone into effect soon enough because when Kerrie's limo pulled up to the hotel earlier that evening, James' car was right behind it.

As soon as Meg left for work, James drove to Kerrie's apartment in the hopes of catching a glimpse of her new suitor. Instead, he arrived just in time to see her climb into the limo and drive off. He trailed the car to the hotel, followed her into the lobby and watched as she got into the elevator. He had been to the hotel several times before and knew it was one that lead up to the penthouses and went directly to the front desk to see if he could find out who she was visiting in the pricey suite.

"I'm sorry, sir. The identity of our guests is strictly confidential." said the clerk, whose name badge identified him as Scott Peoples.

"Surely you can make an exception in this case, Scott," he said, leaning in a bit closer. "You see, my wife and I are having marital problems, and I think she's seeing someone else," he said in a conspiratorial whisper. "I'm ashamed to admit it, but I followed her to the hotel this evening, and seeing her going up to one of your penthouse suites leads me to believe my suspicions are true. If that's the case," he continued, "I'm going to be filing for divorce immediately, but I really do need to know for sure. So if you could just tell me who is up there," he said, reaching into his pocket for a hundred dollar bill, "I'd really appreciate it."

The temptation was great because Scott really needed the money, but knew things would be far worse if he lost his job over a bribe. "I'm sorry, sir," he sighed, "but it's against hotel policy."

James wasn't about to give up that easily and hoped that a little gentle persuasion and another hundred-dollar bill would buy him the information he wanted, but before he could proceed, their discussion was suddenly interrupted by a ringing phone. Glad for the distraction, Scott excused himself for a moment to answer the call.

With the clerk's attention elsewhere, James peered over at the phone console on the front desk. The lights on the phone were marked in code, but the call also came up on the computer screen and showed that the caller was someone in Penthouse 2.

"Yes, Mr. Wakefield. Of course, sir," said Scott to the caller. "I'll send it right up."

In his haste to be accommodating, Scott neglected to realize that he had spoken the actor's registered name out loud; a mistake that did not go unnoticed by James.

Then, hanging up the phone, the clerk turned back to James. "I'll be with you as soon as I make sure this dinner order is on its way. It's for a very important guest who doesn't like to be kept waiting."

"Take your time," said James, thankful he had a moment or two to try and figure out another way to wheedle more information out of the hapless clerk.

As soon as Scott finished his call to the kitchen, James was ready to resume his quest. "I suppose you deal with a lot of VIPs like this Mr. Wakefield every day."

"Well, of course I do." said Scott, puffing up with self-importance. "After all, this is a five-star hotel."

"And I'm sure you're privy to a lot of dirty little secrets." goaded James, with a sly wink.

Scott was happy to be the center of attention, and leaned over the counter towards James. "I could write a book," he whispered. "You wouldn't believe all the truly scandalous goings on in this place."

That gave James an idea. "Well, if you should ever decide to write that book, give me a call," he said, reaching into his pocket and producing a business card. "I work for Barton Publishing House, and the company is always looking for a good tell all book."

"Wow. That's terrific." said Scott, cradling the card as though it were made of gold. "People that write those kind of books make a lot of money, don't they?"

The conversation was going exactly the way James hoped it would.

"A book like that could set you up for life," he assured the gullible clerk. "In fact, several of our first-time authors are now comfortably living a life of luxury, and all because they came up with one good idea. It's like winning the lottery, but with much better odds."

While such occurrences were rare in the publishing world, James knew he was talking a good game, and could feel Scott letting down his guard, so he stepped in for the kill.

184

"Well, I'm sorry to have troubled you, and seeing as how you are unable to assist me any further about who my wife is visiting, I'd better let you get back to work."

"Oh, it was no trouble," said Scott, who really didn't want the conversation to end quite yet. "In fact, it's more like a lucky break. I always did want to write a book, and now you've opened my eyes to the possibility of actually doing it."

"Call me anytime and I'll be glad to discuss it with you further," said James, who was now ready to reel him in. "I'm sure you've got some great stories to tell, and Barton Publishing is a very prestigious house. We also offer our authors quite a large advance. So large, in fact, you could quit this menial job and devote all your time to writing."

Scott couldn't believe his good fortune. "Really? That sounds like a dream come true, but wouldn't I get in trouble tattling on all those famous people? Isn't that libelous?" he asked.

"It all depends on how you go about it," said James. "I'm quite sure many of your guests register under a pseudonym, don't they? Like that guy, Wakefield, was it? The one you were just speaking to? I'm sure that wasn't his real name, but I could tell by the way you were speaking to him, he must be someone very important."

"Oh, he is, and you're right. Mr. Wakefield isn't his real name, and he is quite famous. You'd know him right away if he walked across the lobby."

Thankful that Scott was so gullible, James proceeded with his line of questioning.

"That famous, is he?" he mused. "I wonder what line of work he's in? A philanthropist, perhaps? A politician? A famous author? My wife knows a lot of them. But, never mind. I know it's all very hush-hush," he said, acting as though it really didn't matter, "but there is one question that you can answer without giving too much away: If Mr. Wakefield did happen to walk across the lobby right now, would my wife be walking with him?"

Scott wasn't sure how to respond and got very fidgety. He knew the answer was yes, but was afraid he'd say too much and struggled to come up with an appropriate response. He needn't have tried so hard because James got all the information he needed by the pained look on the clerk's face.

"Don't sweat it, Scott. I'm not going to stand down here all night and wait to confront them, but thanks for the information," he said, giving Scott a pat on the back. "And give me a call when you decide to write that book. The first chapter could be titled, 'Penthouse Rendezvous.' Has a nice ring to it, don't you think?"

CHAPTER 20

Kerrie was appreciative of Andy's efforts to keep her safe, but being under the watchful eye of bodyguards, even though they were to remain well out of sight, made her uncomfortable and the fact that she couldn't even tell anyone about the arrangements, not even Meg, was also a burden.

By the time Kerrie got home that night, everyone was discreetly in place. She thought there might be big, burly men with pit bulls pacing back and forth in front of her house but everyone was well out of sight. The limo driver, seeing the puzzled look on her face, explained that the guards were carefully positioned around the neighborhood, not on her doorstep. "We've also installed audio sensors in every room, so in the unlikely event your stalker happens to get past any of us and into the house, just yell for assistance and we'll be able hear you." he added.

That bit of news concerned Kerrie because now she was more concerned about her personal privacy than a break-in, but when the driver explained that the sensors were programmed only to pick up loud noises, not the usual day to day sounds, she felt a little better.

"Oh, by the way, since you've already made a police report against Mr. Goldman, Mr. Dickinson has arranged with the phone company to put a tap on your telephone. They won't be listening in on your conversations, but will be able to trace the origin of all incoming calls. That way, if James tries to contact you from a land line, we'll be able to find out where he's calling from."

All this was quite overwhelming and at the same time slightly amusing because of all the fuss. "Is there anything else I need to look out for, like bomb sniffing dogs, men wielding poison darts, trip wires or land mines?" she teased.

"No, I think that about covers it, except for the activated GPS device on your cell phone. Leave it on at all times, and make sure you take it with you whenever you leave the house, okay?"

"Sure. But don't you think all this is going a bit too far? I mean, you've all gone to an awful lot of trouble to protect me from just one crazy guy."

The driver, who looked like a cross between the Incredible Hulk and Ali Baba leaned over to her and whispered, "I shouldn't be telling you this but we have reason to believe that James Goldman is far more dangerous than he appears to be, so all these precautions really are quite necessary."

Kerrie didn't like the sound of that., but at the same time, it was like a light bulb went off in her head and she knew exactly what he was referring to. "This has something to do with the assassination attempt on Andy, doesn't it? Is James a suspect?"

"I'm sorry, I can't go into any further details, but just know that Mr. Dickinson has good reason for taking all these precautions." Then, seeing the knowing look on Kerrie's face, he added, "Let me just say that you and Sherlock Holmes share the same gift of deduction. And now if you'll excuse me," he said, indicating that their discussion was officially over, "I must get back to the hotel. Have a pleasant evening."

She felt like a character in a James Bond movie as she watched the limo pulled away then walked into her house and locked the door behind her. In just a matter of hours, everything had changed, not because of her armed guard, but because Andy was finally back in her life.

When Meg called the next morning to see how things went on the date, Kerrie had to be careful not to say too much, but didn't think it would be breaking a promise by mentioning her suspicions about James having something to do with Andy's *accident.*

"I was wondering about that myself," said Meg. "It's not like James didn't have a motive in wanting to see Andy dead, but have you said anything to the police about it If not, maybe you should call Scotland Yard and tell them, too."

She didn't want to tell Meg about last night's conversation with her driver, but she just said that she had the feeling that it had already been done because Andy told her that a few days before the accident, James confronted him in a coffee shop and warned him to stay away from her. That was shortly after James attacked her in her apartment, which lead her to believe that he got scared and flew back to London right after that and that's why the police weren't able to find him to serve him with the restraining order.

"That was about the same time Curt was away, wasn't it? asked Meg. "Wouldn't it be a creepy coincidence if he and James flew back to L.A. on the same plane?"

Once again, Meg managed to bring her boyfriend into the conversation. "But Curt was coming back from Paris, wasn't he?"

"Well, yes, but he said something about stopping over in London on his way back, so it's possible they could have taken the same flight home."

Kerrie was tired of hearing about Curt and she tried to end the conversation. "I guess that will have to remain one of life's little mysteries because Curt and James don't know each other, so we'll never know, will we?"

Meg wasn't about to let it go and was starting to get herself all worked up. "I just hate to think that poor Curt could have been crossing the Atlantic with a lunatic on board the plane. James could have flipped out at 10,000 feet, done something stupid and everyone could have been killed."

"With an imagination like that, you should be the writer." laughed Kerrie, thinking that Meg's mind needed an Off switch. "Look, Curt came back all in one piece, so quit thinking about what might have been. He's fine, you're fine, and unfortunately, James seems to be fine, too."

"And how fine is Andy?" teased Meg, hoping that things were getting a little more serious between them.

"I'm sorry to disappoint you, but you're a little premature with that line of questioning," she said. "All I know so far is that he's a great hugger, and hopefully things will progress from there as time goes on."

Later that evening, Meg as Curt was unloading the dishwasher, she was thinking about her discussion with Kerrie and wanted to make sure that Curt had, in fact, stopped over in London on his way back from Paris. "You didn't happen to be sitting next to a deranged-looking man on your plane ride back from London, did you?"

"No, but I wish I had, because I got stuck between a man who apparently hadn't bathed in weeks, and a crazy religious fanatic who said her savior was an armadillo named Chester who spent his days patrolling the universe on a moonbeam to rid our world of some evil beings called Crinkies. Why do you ask?"

"No reason, really," she said, wiping the tears of laughter from her eyes. "Kerrie and I were just talking about things, and figured out that you and James came back from overseas about the same time and I thought there was a possibility that the two of you might have come back on the same flight."

"With dozens of planes flying out of Heathrow every day, it would be a long shot if we had." he said, wondering what else Kerrie had to say. "And besides, what would James have been doing in London?"

Meg didn't want to let him know that she knew about the confrontation between James and Andy in the coffee shop, so she tried to steer the conversation in a different direction. "I dunno. I guess James is on her mind lately and she was just thinking out loud. She's still very upset about seeing him at the mall yesterday."

Being reminded of his bungled attempt to see Kerrie the previous day was still a sore spot. "Did she happen to say anything about Andy and her intentions to get together with him or was James the topic du jour?" he wondered.

"I guess she's preoccupied with her new boyfriend." she explained. "She's been seeing him every day."

"Really?" he said, thinking it might be a good idea to start hanging around the hotel in the hopes of catching them going in or out. Surely, they had to leave the suite once in a while. "Where's he staying?"

"I really don't know," she lied, "but I'm assuming he's somewhere close by. She said he's here on business, and even though he'll be here for several weeks, he didn't want to rent one of those tacky corporate apartments."

"He must work for a big company for them to put him up for an extended stay like that. What did you say he does for a living?"

"Um, I don't think Kerrie ever said—or at least I don't remember if she did." said Meg, hoping that she sounded convincing. "All I know is that he makes a good living and travels around quite a bit. If things work out between them, Kerrie might be doing a lot of traveling herself in the future."

'There's no way I'm going to let that happen.' James thought to himself.

"Wouldn't it be romantic to travel the world with someone you love?" she sighed, thinking about their upcoming honeymoon in Paris.

"You mean she told you she loves him?" he asked, feeling his face flush with anger.

"She didn't have to tell me. I can hear it in her voice. And speaking of love," she said, putting her arms around his neck, "I hope you realize how much I love you."

Ordinarily, hearing those words would have prompted him to take her by the hand and lead her into the bedroom, but the thought of Kerrie being in love with someone else was completely distracting. He pulled away from Meg and said he needed to make a quick trip to his office to check the mail.

"Can't it wait until tomorrow?" she asked, clearly disappointed by his sudden change of mood.

"I won't be long," he promised, giving her a quick peck on the cheek.

James drove straight to the hotel, hoping Scott, the desk clerk was on duty that night but when he walked into the lobby, he was disappointed to find a rather matronly woman standing in behind the desk instead.

He didn't feel like going to all the trouble of trying to charm her out of any information about the mysterious Mr. Wakefield, so James ordered a drink from the bar in the lobby then sat down on a sofa facing the penthouse elevators. By the time he'd finished his second scotch and soda nobody had either come or gone from the penthouse so he decided to take matters into his own hands. There was a bank of house phones at the far end of the lobby, so James walked over to make a call upstairs. He had to find out who Kerrie was visiting. "Mr. Wakefield's suite, please," he told the operator.

Andy and Kerrie had been watching a movie and he'd just put the DVD on pause and walked into the bathroom when the phone rang.

"I'm not expecting any calls, so would you mind telling whoever it is that I'm busy and ask them to leave a message?" he yelled through the bathroom door.

She felt a bit uncomfortable about answering someone else's phone, but picked up the receiver and offered a timid, "Hello?"

After a moment of silence on the other end, she realized that whoever was calling was probably expecting to hear Andy's voice and might have thought they had the wrong room. "This is Mr. Dickin--, er, Mr. Wakefield's suite," she said, quickly reminding herself of his made-up identity. "Is there anybody there?" she asked the seemingly dead line.

James felt as though a lightning bolt shot through the phone line. That slight slip of her tongue was all he needed to hear. She had intended to say,'Mr. Dickinson's suite,' then caught herself. He was almost certain it was Kerrie who answered, but had to make sure. "Excuse me, who is this?"

"Who are you calling?" she countered, thinking it was no doubt a wrong number.

Before James had the chance to answer, Andy walked out of the bathroom. "Who is it, Kerrie?"

Even though Kerrie and Andy were still in the dark about who was calling, those four simple words told James not only who he was talking to, but who she was with. The actor's voice was unmistakable, and James was furious that Andy not only managed to slip into the country unannounced, but was able to hook up with Kerrie so quickly. He threw the receiver against the wall in anger and fought hard against the urge to force his way up to the penthouse suite and confront them. He stormed out of the hotel instead because he need time to think about what to do next.

"That's funny," said Kerrie, handing the receiver to Andy.

"Whoever it was seems to have walked away without hanging up. It sounded like he dropped the phone or something."

"Hello. Who's there? Hello?"

All he could hear were footsteps on an uncarpeted floor, indiscernible chatter and a live band playing somewhere in the distance. Andy immediately reached for his cell phone and dialed a preprogrammed number. When the phone was picked up on the other end, Andy could hear the same background music that he'd just heard on the other line. "Hi, Tim, it's me. You haven't seen our stalker anywhere around there, have you?

"No sir, I haven't" said the bodyguard.

"Okay, then do me a favor and have a quick look around for a pay phone that might be off the hook. I'll hang on."

Kerrie was beginning to get nervous, because when she tried to ask Andy what was going on, he put up his hand as if to signal that he was busy.

After a couple of minutes of anxious waiting, Tim finally came back on the line.

"Yes, I'm here," said Andy. "Okay, hang on."

Kerrie watched as Andy picked up the other phone and held it to his ear. "Tim? Is that you? Yes, I'm thinking the same thing. All right, then, do what you can. No, I don't think there will be any need for that. She's better off staying here tonight. Right. Okay, let me know if you hear anything. Thanks."

"What's going on?" she asked, after he'd hung up both phones. From the tone of the conversation, she pretty much guessed that it had been James who rang the room and he was somewhere nearby."

"I think it's best you stay here tonight. We think it was James on the phone. He is probably long gone by now, but even if I post more men around your house, I don't think it's wise for you to be there alone."

She had always dreamt about what it would be like to spend the night with Andy, but not under these circumstances. The other thing that troubled her was that she was supposed to leave early in the morning to attend a two-day book fair in Palm Springs. She had been asked to be a featured speaker on the first day, then do a book signing on the second. She and Andy had already made arrangements for him to meet her there on the second day and they would drive back home together.

"I'm sure I'll be fine if I go home tonight." she protested. "I really need to pack and get ready for tomorrow."

"Just make a list of the things you'll need and where you keep your overnight bag. I'll have Tim go over to your apartment and pack for you. He can bring your bag here later on. If he happens to forget anything, I'm sure we can find what you need in the hotel shops but I don't want you going back home tonight, nor will you be driving yourself to Palm Springs."

Andy was so insistent, she knew there was no other choice but to agree, but thought she'd better call Meg and remind her that she'd be out of town for a couple of days. When Meg picked up the phone, she sounded quite angry.

"Hi, it's me. What's wrong?"

"Oh, sorry. I thought you were Curt," said Meg. "He said he was going to his office to pick up some mail and promised to be right back, but that was three hours ago and I hate the way he seems to always lose track of time."

"Listen," Kerrie began, ignoring what her friend had just said. "I'm going to be staying with *my friend* tonight, and want to remind you that I'll be leaving for the book fair in Palm Springs in the morning."

"Oh yeah, I forgot all about that. Thanks for letting me know." The part about Kerrie spending the night with Andy hadn't yet sunk in. "Are you driving all that way by yourself?"

"No, I've decided to take the Amtrak," she fibbed. "I'll take a cab to the station, and have made arrangements for someone to pick me up and take me to the hotel when I get there."

"Okay.," she said cheerfully. "Give me a call when you get back and let me know how it went. Imagine, my best friend a featured speaker!" she teased. Then, hearing a man cough in the background, Meg suddenly remembered that Kerrie said something about spending the night with Andy.

"Was that him, and are you really spending the night at the hotel?" she giggled.

"Um, yes, but it's not what you think and I really can't go into it right now," she whispered, mindful that Andy was close by. Then, returning to her normal voice she said, "I'm sure I'll have a lot to tell you when I get back on Sunday. Meanwhile, don't be mad at Curt. You know how guys are. Send them out on a short errand and they come back three hours later having completely forgotten what they went for in the first place. It must have something to do with excessively high testosterone levels, so make the most of it when he gets back."

"I will," said Meg, "and I hope you get to do the same."

"The bedroom is set up with two queen sized beds, so I'm sure you'll be comfortable enough," said Andy, after Kerrie hung up with Meg, "but if I snore too loudly, wake me up and I'll go sleep on the couch."

During their past couple of nights together, Andy had treated Kerrie like a little sister and seemed to show no romantic interest in her at all. This bothered her, in a way, but at the same time, she was glad that he had decided to take it slow.

A few minutes later, Tim was at the door with Kerrie's bag and after suggesting she take it into the bedroom and make sure everything she needed was there, he and Andy went off to the living room to talk.

As she peeked at what was in the suitcase, Kerrie decided that Tim must be married because he hadn't left anything out and even thought to pack some extra goodies like her iPod and her copy of the latest book she was reading which had been sitting on her night stand. By the time Kerrie was done checking her bags and went back into the living room to congratulate him on a job well done, Tim was just leaving.

"I want you to personally drive Kerrie to the desert tomorrow," Andy told him as they stood in the doorway. "Make sure there are enough people there to keep a watchful eye over her and I'll fly up Sunday noon and ride back with you."

"You're sending bodyguards to the book fair?" she asked, after waving goodbye to Tim. "Is that really necessary?"

"Given the fact that James showed up at the mall, then somehow managed to find you here, what's to stop him from following you all the way to Palm Springs?" I'm sure he's keeping a very close eye on your personal appearances as well, so we can't risk you being there without protection."

"You're probably right," she shrugged, "but since he's managed to elude detection up until now, what makes you think anyone will be able to ferret him out at the book fair where there will be huge crowds of people for him to blend into? And it's not like you can have him arrested for just being there even if he does pop up."

Andy suddenly looked worried. "While it's true James hasn't been arrested for doing anything of a criminal nature yet, hearing your voice on the phone in my room a while ago might be all the incentive he needs to cross the line."

"I don't think he heard enough of your voice in the background to know it was you," she said, hoping that she was right.

"He may be crazy, but James is not a stupid man because if he were, he would have been arrested for the attempt on my life by now," said Andy, who had walked back into the living room and was now pouring himself a brandy. "He's been clever enough to allude the authorities on two continents, so I'm quite sure he's been able to figure out that we are together, and every precaution must be taken."

"Then you shouldn't come up to Palm Springs on Sunday in case he sees you there. Why tempt fate?" said Kerrie, suddenly worried about Andy's safety as well. "And if you think he knows I'm coming here to see you it might be a good idea to check out of the hotel and find a room somewhere else."

Andy was pleased by her concern, and assured her he was taking steps to keep them both safe. "In the first place," he said, motioning for her to join him on the sofa, "I do not intend to call attention to myself at the book fair. I'm just coming to pick you up, and will remain in the limo until you're done with your book signing," he explained. "And as far as changing hotels is concerned, that is already on my agenda and I'll see to it just as soon as I get you moved into your new apartment."

Kerrie was a little uneasy that plans were being made behind her back. "What new apartment? You're the one who needs to hide out, not me."

In truth, she had been thinking about moving for a very long time but couldn't afford anything better than what she already had.

"Look, Kerrie, a friend of mine owns a very nice condo in a high-rise complex on the West Side and he's been trying to unload on me for ages. He doesn't need it anymore because he's very rarely in town. It's in a full-amenities building with someone at the front desk at all times and I think it will do nicely."

"It's a wonderful idea in theory, and I appreciate the thought, but I'm going to have to say no. That condo is probably way out of my price range," she said, thinking that would be the end of the discussion.

"You're acting as though you have a choice," he laughed. "Just graciously accept my offer for now and we can work out the details later on, okay? It's not as though I can't afford it, you know."

"I've seen ads in the real estate section for those condos and even Bill Gates would think twice about spending that kind of money."

"Your safety is worth more to me than the cost of a condo and besides, your moving in will end up saving me money in the long run. Do you have any idea how much this penthouse suite is costing me?"

It almost sounded like he was planning to move into the condo with her.

"It would only be a temporary arrangement," he said, as if reading her mind. "Just think of me as a house guest. It's quite a large unit, and since I'll be working very long hours, I doubt you'll even know I'm there unless, of course, we happen to cross paths on the way to the kitchen in the wee hours of the morning," he laughed. "Now enough of this tiresome conversation. Let's order and watch that movie, shall we?

CHAPTER 21

James arrived home in the foulest of moods. He stormed past Meg, walked into the bedroom and slammed the door behind him. He needed to calm down and then come up with a plausible explanation for both his temper and his tardiness.

"Honey, what's wrong?" she asked knocking gently on the door. She had never seen him act like this before and worried that something terrible might have happened.

"I'll be out in a few minutes," he said, trying hard to hide his anger. "It's just some unexpected bad news at work. Nothing to worry about. I just need a little time to myself."

"Is there anything I can do?" she wondered, hoping he'd let her in and tell her all about it. "I'm a great listener."

"No thanks." he said with great difficulty. He needed her to get the hell away from the door and just leave him alone.

Meg walked back into the living room and turned on the television. A few minutes later, Curt came out of the bedroom and sat down next to her and absentmindedly grabbed the remote. He had calmed down somewhat, but she could tell that something was still bothering him.

"Are you hungry? Can I get you anything?" she asked, in an effort to start a conversation.

"No, I'm fine, thanks." he said, angrily flipping through the channels. There was a coldness in his voice that Meg didn't like at all and for the first time in their brief relationship, she felt as though he was a total stranger.

After a few more minutes of uncomfortable silence, he finally turned to her and asked, "So, what's been going on with Kerrie and her new boyfriend?"

That was the last subject she expected to hear him use as an ice breaker, and said so.

"I guess I'm just trying to get my mind off my problems," he said with a sheepish grin, "and since you haven't said much about Kerrie lately, I was wondering how she was doing."

Meg lied once again and said she hadn't heard from Kerrie in a couple of days.

He knew that couldn't possibly be true, but rather than challenging her statement, he decided it would be best to drop it for now and apologize for his bad behavior instead because he was planning on going out again and wanted to leave on a happy note rather than a suspicious one. "Look, I'm sorry about storming in here like an angry bull and shutting you out. I just had a nasty surprise at work and lost my temper because I wasn't sure what to do about it, but after giving it some thought, I think I've got a plan."

"Good." she said, clearly relieved by his admission. "I've never seen that side of you before and you had me worried."

"I didn't mean to upset you, and I know I probably owe you a better explanation of what's going on, but that will have to wait because I need to go back to the office and sort a few things out." "But you just got home," she said, looking at him like he had two heads. "Can't it can wait till morning?"

"I'm afraid not," he said. Meg was sounding more and more like his nagging mother every day. "This is something that needs my immediate attention, and it's probably going to be a long night, so don't wait up." Then, just as he'd done whenever Rose tried to talk him out of something, he was on his feet and out the door before she had the chance to stop him.

Now that he knew that Kerrie and Andy were seeing each other, he needed to find out how serious their relationship had become so he drove to Kerrie's house. Restraining order or not, he had to confront her and find out the truth.

He was infuriated when he didn't see any lights in the window as he drove past her apartment and her car wasn't parked on the street as it normally was. In his mind, the only possible reason

Kerrie wasn't home was because she was still with Andy, so he decided to go back to the hotel.

He parked far enough away so that he had a clear view of the penthouse from his car, then took out his binoculars and peered up at the penthouse windows hoping for a peek inside. The curtains weren't drawn, but because the room was dimly lit, all he could see were two figures huddled on the sofa bathed in the glare of what must have been a television set.

James checked his watch and was shocked to see that it was now two o'clock in the morning and realized, to his horror, that Kerrie must be planning on spending the night. The thought of her sitting on the sofa next to Andy was bad enough, but thinking about what they would probably be doing later on was more than he could stand. If only he'd thought to bring his long range rifle, he could have put a stop to it once and for all.

He kept a night long vigil never taking his eyes off the window even after the room went dark and he watched them walk into the bedroom room an hour or so later. Ugly visions of the two of them in bed together plagued his mind the rest of the night and by the time the sun came up, James was an angry, tortured soul.

Around six thirty, he got out of the car long enough to stretch his legs and relieve himself in a nearby alleyway and got back just in time to see Andy and Kerrie standing near the penthouse elevator door. She was holding onto the handle of a suitcase and as the elevator doors opened, Andy gave her a long embrace.

Now in a great hurry to make sure he wouldn't lose her in traffic, James jumped back into the car and quickly drove around to the front of the hotel to catch her as she drove off but instead of the parking attendants bringing Kerrie her car, he watched with interest as she climbed into the back seat of a limousine.

He was going to follow the limo back to her house before trying to confront her, and was puzzled when the car took off in a different direction and was heading towards a nearby freeway onramp.

So many different scenarios were popping into his head that James barely paid attention to where they were going. He just kept on driving and it wasn't until he saw the "Palm Springs Next 4 Exits" sign that he realized how far they had actually gone. It was now almost nine o'clock, and James thought he'd better call Meg and make up some lie about having to go out on a job so she wouldn't worry.

Meg wasn't at all happy with the news, but her mood lightened when he explained that the new client was in Indian Wells, just a few miles from Palm Springs.

"What a great coincidence. Kerrie is going to be the featured speaker at a book fair in Palm Springs today, so maybe if you get done early enough, you can stop by and introduce yourself. She's been dying to meet you."

"I bet she has," he laughed, wondering what Meg would think if she really knew the truth. "Maybe I 'll just do that."

"Please try," said Meg. "It's about time the two of you finally got to meet." Then as an afterthought she added, "Too bad you won't be staying the weekend, because tomorrow she's doing a book signing and if you were running late today, then you'd have another opportunity to catch up with her then, but since I'd much rather see you tonight, hurry home."

"I will," he promised, thankful that he'd called and found out what this long drive to the desert was all about.

James followed the limo to The Wyndham Hotel driveway and watched Kerrie walk into the lobby, overnight bag in hand. While she was checking in, he parked his car on the street a couple of blocks away and walked back to the hotel. There was an announcement board standing next to the front desk that listed the events of the day and he was pleased to see the Book Fair was on top of the list. Kerrie's speech was scheduled at four o'clock that afternoon, which gave him plenty of time to decide his next move.

The phone was ringing as the bellman unlocked the door to Kerrie's suite and handed her the key. She thanked him, handed him a tip then ran across the room to see who was calling.

"I trust the accommodations are to your liking?" said Andy, glad to hear that she'd made it to the hotel without incident.

"Yes, it's very nice," she said, kicking off her shoes and hopping up on the bed, "but I must admit that I'm starting to get a little bit nervous about getting up in front of all those people this afternoon. What do I know about public speaking?"

Andy couldn't help but chuckle. Even with his long list of movie and television credits, he still got butterflies when he had to get up in front of large crowds of people and just be himself. "You know your subject well and that's all that matters," he assured her. "You'll do just fine."

"I guess so," she sighed, nervously picking at a piece of lint on the bedspread, "but I wish it was over and done with because I'm just not used to being the center of attention and besides, the sooner I give my speech, the closer I'll be to seeing you. It's so beautiful here, and I 've got nobody to share it with."

As much as Andy wished he was there, he was busy with the details of getting Kerrie moved into their new condo.

"Ordinarily I'd offer you my condolences," he explained, sounding just a bit peevish, "but having just spent the last two hours with the realtor, signing an obscene number of documents, disclosures and deeds, I think I'm the one who needs a hug," he said, sounding like he really meant it. "And now, I'm standing in the middle of our new living room waiting for the movers to arrive with your things. The cable company will be here later this afternoon, and after they've gone, I've got to go back to the hotel, pack my bags and then check out. I imagine by the time you're done speaking to the masses, I'll be soaking in our new Jacuzzi tub and patting myself on the back for a job well done."

"I can't believe you're doing all the work yourself," she said. "I'm feeling a twinge of guilt. Don't famous movie stars usually hire people to handle all the details?" she teased.

"While I appreciate the compliment, I hardly see myself fitting into that esteemed category, especially here in the States," he explained. "To you lot, I'm just another one of those British blokes with the funny accent who pops up every now and then."

"You mean when you popped up at the Oscars, The Golden Globes, The Emmys and countless other award ceremonies and walked off with the big prize, nobody knew who you were?" she reminded him, "Quit selling yourself short."

"I'm not," he said in all seriousness. "I was just saying that so you wouldn't think all this notoriety has gone to my head," he laughed, "and I quite expect to be seen at next years' Oscar ceremonies, with you on my arm, of course, because I get the feeling that Collywobbles is going to do very well at the box office."

"I hope I do as well this afternoon, but I'm still feeling bad that you're running around getting all this stuff done for me, and I'm not around to help."

"I'm not doing all this for you, Kerrie," he said softly. "I'm doing it for us."

The comment caught her off guard and for a moment she was speechless. Rachel and Adam were an "us" back in 1862, but she didn't dare think of herself and Andy as a couple until just now.

Her prolonged silence gave Andy a moment of concern. "Kerrie? What's wrong? Are you still there?"

"Oh, sorry," she apologized, not wanting to admit that he had just made her wildest dreams come true. "I guess my mind was wandering."

Just then she heard a doorbell ring in the background. "It sounds like the movers have arrived, so I'd better let them in. Good luck this afternoon, and I'll call you later on to see how it went."

Kerrie couldn't wait to tell Meg about the move and what Andy had said, but thinking a long hot shower would help steady her nerves, she decided to make the call a little later.

Since Curt was going to be gone all day, Meg decided to try and rearrange the bedroom closet so they'd both have more room. He had brought so much stuff with him, she thought it would be a good idea to get some of her things out of the house and into storage until they moved to a bigger place.

When she carelessly yanked a pair of roller blades that she hadn't used in ages off the top shelf, Meg accidentally knocked one of Curt's storage boxes to the floor and its contents went flying in all directions. She bent down to scoop the pile of papers back into the box when a large newspaper clipping caught her eye. Down at the bottom of the page were side by side photos of Kerrie and Andy Dickinson. The headline above his photo read, "Dickinson Catching A Bad Case Of The Collywobbles," and above Kerrie's it said, "American Author In Town To Promote Best Selling Book."

Wondering why Curt would be saving this page of the London tabloid, or how he even got it in the first place, Meg began rummaging through the rest of the pile to see if there was anything else of interest. By the time she was done, Meg had gathered together nearly every article ever written about Kerrie and her book as well as a few odd clippings about Andy Dickinson. She couldn't understand why Curt was saving old newspaper articles about Kerrie and Andy and wondered whether or not she should ask him about it when he got home, but then immediately decided against it for the time being because she didn't want him to think she was digging through his personal belongings.

She had just put everything back in the box and was attempting to hoist it back up onto the shelf when the phone rang. After giving it one final shove into place, she ran for the phone and was happy to hear Kerrie's voice.

"I thought I'd better fill you in," she began, obviously in a very good mood. "Andy decided my apartment wasn't safe and he's moving me into a large, spacious, two-bedroom high rise condo on the West Side."

Meg was more surprised than she wanted to let on. "You're kidding! When did all this happen?"

"Last night, actually, right after I called you," said Kerrie. "It's a long story, but here's the condensed version: Apparently James followed me to the hotel and I don't know how he knew Andy was staying in the penthouse, but he called upstairs from the lobby," she explained. "Andy was in the bathroom and asked me to answer the phone, but when I picked it up James didn't say anything. A few seconds later, Andy called out my name and asked me who it was and it sounded like James dropped the phone, so we're guessing he's figured out that we're seeing each other so Andy decided to buy this condo on the Westside from a friend of his, kind of a safe haven for the both of us, and had all my things moved over there this morning."

Meg was glad that Andy stepped up to do something about keeping Kerrie safe, but wondered how she was going to afford a place like that.

"Well, we've still got to work that out, but Andy was very insistent, and since he'll be staying there whenever he's in town, it's a good deal for him, too. As a matter of fact, he's checking out of the hotel this afternoon and moving in tonight."

"I do feel better knowing that you'll be hiding out from James," said Meg, "but you and Andy hardly know each other and now you're suddenly living together? Are you sure that's wise?"

Even though she had to admit that Meg's concerns made sense, the thought of moving in with Andy overruled any logical arguments against it. "We'll be just fine and if it doesn't work out, I can always camp out on your sofa for a while and play house with you and Curt, can't I?" she joked.

For a split second, she was tempted to tell Kerrie about finding the articles Curt was saving, but quickly decided against it. "Of course, you can, but I'm sure it won't come to that," she chirped. "So when will you be coming back from the desert?"

"Andy's coming to pick me up tomorrow after the book signing, so I'm guessing I'll be back in town around seven and I can't wait to see the condo. It sounds so luxurious!" she gushed. "I'll call you Monday morning to give you my new address, and since Andy's going to be busy at the studio all week, you'll have to come by and check it out."

"I can't wait to see it," said Meg, "but what are we going to sit on? Surely, he's not going to move all the rickety stuff of yours to the new house, is he?"

"I didn't even think about that." mused Kerrie. "I guess my stuff would to look pretty shabby in a place like that so I might have to go out and buy some new furniture. Want to come along?" As much as Meg loved shopping, she didn't think she should be the one to help Kerrie decorate the condo. "Don't you think Andy should go with you instead?"

"And risk being seen together in public?" she asked. "I can only imagine what the headline in next week's the National Enquirer would be. "Actor and Writer At Odds Over Love Nest Decor" with an accompanying photo of us bickering about which pattern of silverware to buy?" she laughed. "Besides, you're the only one who knows that Andy and I are going to be sharing the same address and we need to keep it that way because if James found out, he'd blow up the building or something. It's bad enough that he caught me in Andy's hotel room. And speaking of upset boyfriends, how did things work out with you and Curt last night?"

"We're fine, I guess." she said. "He stayed at the office and worked all night, then called early this morning to say he had a client in the desert that needed to be taken care of immediately, so he took off for Palm Springs. I told him you'd be there for the book fair and he said he'd try and stop by and introduce himself if he had the time."

Ordinarily, Kerrie would have looked forward to finally meeting Curt, but she had her doubts that he'd show up. "It was nice of him to offer, but given his way of always finding an excuse not to meet me, I won't hold my breath."

"Never say never," warned Meg. "He seemed very interested in the book fair."

"We'll see," said Kerrie, still not convinced that he'd show up.

After she got off the phone, Meg decided to finish cleaning out the closet and while she was hoisting another of Curt's boxes back up to the top shelf, she noticed two other newspaper clippings taped to the bottom of the box. The first one was a newspaper article about Andy's assassination attempt in London. Someone had scribbled "R.I.P." across the top in big, bold letters. The second clipping looked as though it had been ripped in two then taped back together again. It was captioned, "Is Andy Randy Again?" and showed the actor standing in front of a bookshop staring at a display of Kerrie's books.

What was Curt doing with all this stuff about Kerrie and Andy?

Meg needed some answers so she called Ted Stephens. Although she had never met Ted before, she was sure that once she explained who she was, he'd be happy to talk to her and maybe be able to tell her something about the clippings why Curt was keeping them. She also thought Ted should know that Andy and Kerrie were seeing each other despite his warning against it.

CHAPTER 22

Meg was expecting to have to explain herself to Ted's secretary, and was very surprised when the psychic answered his own phone with a friendly, "This is Ted. How can I help you?"

After introducing herself as Kerrie's friend, Meg explained her reason for the call. She started out by telling him about the newspaper clippings then snuck in the part about Andy and Kerrie spending the night together in the hotel and their decision to move in together. Ted was less than pleased to hear the news.

"I warned them to stay away from each other!" he shouted, which was unusual for Ted because he rarely raised his voice. "Don't either of them have half a brain between them?"

"That's why I called." she sighed. "Ever since Kerrie told me James followed her to the hotel last night and called upstairs to Andy's room, I've been worried sick."

"He did what?" asked Ted, sounding even more agitated.

After Meg was done telling the psychic about James following Kerrie to the hotel, calling up to Andy's room to see who answered the phone and Andy's decision about buying the condo, Ted insisted she bring the newspaper clippings to him immediately. He was getting an ominous feeling about the whole thing and needed to find out why.

Half an hour later, Meg was sitting quietly in Ted's living room while the psychic used psychometry, a method of reading objects by touch, to see if he could get any information from the clippings. "It is a way to interpret the psychic vibrations contained in objects." he explained. "It gives me the ability to read an object's history or the history of those who may have handled it."

She watched as Ted's expression quickly changed from a benign look of concentration to one of bewilderment. "How are Curt and James connected?" he asked, confused by the information he was receiving.

"They're not." she said, thinking that perhaps Ted was not as great a psychic as most people thought.

"I'm afraid you're mistaken," he explained, putting the clippings down on the table, then rubbing his hands on his trousers as though he was trying to get dirt off them. "Either James and Curt are identical twins, or they are the same person."

"That's impossible," she argued. "Curt is an only child."

"I learned a long time ago that nothing is impossible, Meg, but in order to fully verify the information I'm getting, I need to have something that belongs to James or something he has touched."

"I remember Kerrie saying something about finding a tie clip on her living room floor the night James attacked her," she said after a moment's thought, "but I don't know what she did with it."

"You need to call her right away and find out," he said, handing her his cell phone.

Meg looked at her watch and saw that it was now a quarter to four. "She's out of town at the Palm Springs Book Fair giving a speech, but I'll try."

After trying several times to reach Kerrie, Meg finally left a message on her voicemail. "She's probably going to be tied up all afternoon," she said, finally handing the phone back to Ted. "I'm sure she'll call me back this evening."

"That may be too late," said Ted. If his suspicions were correct, both Kerrie and Meg were in danger. "Do you have a key to her apartment?" he asked, thinking they could go and do a little investigating on their own.

"Yes, but it won't do us much good because when I talked to Kerrie a couple of hours ago, she said that Andy was having her things moved over to the condo this afternoon. They're probably done already," she said, looking back at her watch.

Ted closed his eyes and looked as though he was thinking very hard about something, then asked, "Where is Curt right now?"

Meg wasn't sure what Curt's whereabouts had to do with anything, but she was concerned about the worried look on Ted's face. "When he called me this morning, he said he was on his way to Indian Wells to see a new client."

Ted suddenly jumped up off the couch and grabbed Meg's hand. "Come on! We've got to try and find that tie clip. Hopefully the movers aren't done packing yet."

They ran out the door to Ted's car and he drove like a madman to Kerrie's apartment but by the time they got there, the moving van was just pulling away from the curb and speeding off in the opposite direction.

"Did she give you her new address?" he asked, looking in the rear-view mirror to make sure he didn't lose sight of the van.

"No, all I know is that it's somewhere on the West Side in a high-rise building," she said, trying to steady herself as the psychic made a sharp U-turn in hot pursuit.

Neither of them had much to say during the short trek across town, and when the van finally pulled into the driveway of Kerrie's new building, Ted parked right behind the truck and jumped out. The driver had just gotten out of the van and was heading towards the front door of the building to see if he could locate the service elevator. "What apartment are you taking this load up to?" shouted Ted.

"1717," said the mover without even bothering to turn around to see who was asking.

Without so much as a thank you, Ted ran past him into the lobby with Meg not far behind. He headed towards the elevators, but because this was a security building, the man at the front desk tried to stop him.

"Excuse me, sir, just a minute!" he shouted. "You cannot visit any of our residents without checking in with me first. I will need to call upstairs and find out if they are expecting you."

"We need to get into Kerrie Sherman's condo. Unit 1717," he said, impatiently punching the up button.

"Let me see." said the clerk, casually thumbing through the building roster. "I'm sorry, but we have no resident by that name."

"She's moving her belongings into unit 1717 today and the movers are already here," he said, pointing out the large glass doors to the driveway.

"You must be mistaken." said the clerk, thumbing through some paperwork on the desk. "That unit has just recently been purchased by someone else. I'm afraid we have no Kerrie Sherman on record. Are you sure you're in the right building?" he asked, tossing the roster to one side and going back to his crossword puzzle.

"Oh, for God's sake," Ted sputtered, still hammering at the elevator button. "The unit is probably in Andy Dickinson's name, but those are Kerrie's belongings that the movers are unloading and we need to get upstairs, so would you please put that puzzle aside long enough to ring the unit and tell whoever is up there that we are coming up? It's urgent!"

The clerk had chatted briefly with Andy earlier in the day, but had no idea that the famous actor would be sharing his love nest, and was much more interested in the juicy details than in picking up the house phone to make the call.

"You mean to tell me that Andy Dickinson and *this* Kerrie Sherman are shacking up together?" he asked, pulling a copy of her book out from under the counter and studying the back cover photo. "Isn't he a little too old for her?" he chuckled. "I mean, she's so young and pretty, I thought she'd be hooked up with some hot young guy, not someone old enough to be her father."

"That's none of your business, so would you please just make the call?" urged Ted, who was now very close to losing his temper. "All right, fine!" said the clerk, putting the book down and grabbing the phone in a huff. "Who shall I say is calling on Mr. Dickinson?"

"Tell him it's Ted Stephens and Kerrie's friend, Meg," said Ted, relieved to hear that Andy was upstairs.

After a moment of whispering into the phone, the clerk hung up and said, "While Mr. Dickinson *said* he'd be delighted to see you, he sounded rather annoyed, if you ask me."

Ignoring the clerk's cheek, Ted and Meg piled into the elevator and pushed the button for the seventeenth floor.

"If Andy's already annoyed at our just being here, he's not going to be pleased to hear why we're here, either," mumbled Ted as they made their way upstairs.

Andy was walking down the hall towards them as the elevator door opened. Although he was smiling, Meg could see a flicker of annoyance in his eyes. He greeted them with as much false enthusiasm as he could muster. "Ted! What a pleasant surprise.

And you must be Meg," he said, offering her his hand. "Kerrie's told me a great deal about you, but I must admit I'm rather surprised to see you both here, especially since nobody, not even Kerrie, knows our new address."

Looking past Andy, Ted could see the movers hauling Kerrie's belongings into the condo from the freight elevator at the end of the hall. "There's no time for lengthy explanations, Andy, but I think Kerrie is in trouble," he said, pushing the actor out of the way and running towards 1717.

Kerrie's speech went well, as did the long Q&A that followed, but not used to being the center of attention, she was looking forward to a long soak in the bathtub, a nice meal, and an evening of doing absolutely nothing before having to face the crowds once again tomorrow at the book signing. Once she got back to her room, she called down to room service and ordered dinner then decided to take a relaxing bath while waiting for her meal to arrive.

As she lay in the tub, Kerrie remembered her promise to call Meg but decided that it would wait until later. Since Curt hadn't bothered to show up and introduce himself to her, Kerrie thought he'd probably gone straight back to L.A. and knew that if he was home, Meg wouldn't miss not hearing from her.

The jacuzzi jets were so soothing, Kerrie was just starting to nod off when a loud knock on the door brought her back to her senses. The bathroom door was not shut completely, and thinking room service had arrived early, she yelled for them to come in.

"Just set the tray down on the coffee table," she instructed, hoping she wouldn't need to get out of the tub to sign the receipt. When there was no reply, she assumed it was all taken care of and leaned back, closed her eyes again, and promised herself she'd go eat in a moment or two. Kerrie felt so relaxed, she started to doze off again but was jarred awake when a familiar voice interrupted her tranquility.

"That was quite an impressive speech you gave this afternoon, Kerrie," he said.

At first, she thought she was dreaming, but when she opened her eyes and to her horror, saw James standing at the foot of the tub with a smirk on his face, she realized this was more than a figment of her imagination.

"And you managed to get through the entire afternoon without even a mention of your new boyfriend," he sneered, glaring down at her.

Kerrie's first thought was to try and gently coax him out of the bathroom so that she could put some clothes on, but when she spoke, all her pent-up anger towards him came flooding out instead. "I don't know how you found out I was in Palm Springs, or how you managed to get past my bodyguards, but I'm going to have to ask you to leave before I--"

"Before you what?" he asked, walking menacingly close and then taking a seat at the foot of the tub. He let his hand dangle menacingly in the water before answering. "I thought you'd be glad to hear a glowing critique of your performance." he purred.

Meg didn't immediately follow Ted down the hall to the apartment because she wanted to fill Andy in on why they were there, and let him know about the psychic's impression that Curt and James were somehow connected.

Andy was visibly unnerved after hearing what she had to say, and rushed back to the apartment. The trio tore into each box as the movers brought them in, searching for the elusive tie clip, but it was nowhere to be found.

"Isn't there any other way to go about this?" groused Andy. "I feel as though I'm looking for a bloody needle in a haystack."

Just as Ted was about to answer, something shiny in the bottom of a box he was about to toss aside caught his eye. He reached in and grabbed at the object and the moment he closed his hand around it, his expression immediately changed from merely curious to decidedly unsettled.

"Meg, do you have anything on you that Curt has given you recently, like a ring or a bracelet?" he asked.

"This is his watch." she said, holding out her arm. "I found it in one of his boxes this morning and was going to go out and buy a new battery for it."

"Let me see it." said Ted, snatching the timepiece off her wrist.

It looked as though he was concentrating very hard for a moment, then he opened his eyes and placed both the watch and the tie clip on the floor in front of him and placed one hand on each object. It didn't take long for Ted to get the answer he was looking for and tried to choose his words carefully before speaking. Unfortunately, there was no easy way to break the shocking news to Andy and Meg so he took a deep breath and just blurted it out, "There's no doubt in my mind that Curt and James are the same person."

CHAPTER 23

Kerrie was trying to sound in control but she felt extremely vulnerable lying there in the tub with only a thin barrier of bubbles between them. "Get out of my room, James. NOW!"

He continued to stare, his hand menacingly swirling around in the bubbles. "What's the matter?" he asked innocently, watching her legs pull back whenever his hand got too close. "Is Andy the only one you will allow to get near you these days?"

"I don't know what you're talking about." she lied. "I haven't seen Andy since we were in London."

James suddenly grabbed her ankle and yanked it so hard that Kerrie's legs came up out of the water and the top half of her body was pulled down underneath. Thinking that James was trying to drown her, Kerrie struggled to get a firm grip on the bathtub to try and pull herself up, but her hands were too slippery to do any good. Thankfully, James let go almost immediately and she was able to use her legs for leverage to push herself back up.

"Don't ever lie to me again!" he warned, watching as she reached for a towel to wipe the soap out of her eyes. "Do you think I'm some kind of idiot?" he shouted. "I know all about you and Andy. He's in L.A. and you've been playing house in his hotel room, haven't you?"

"That's none of your business and you're an idiot for following me here, because I didn't come alone. I've got bodyguards looking out for me." she said, hoping to warn him off.

Instead of being concerned by the news, James just laughed. "Considering the fact that I'm sitting here in your bathroom, they're not very good at their job, are they?

While Kerrie wouldn't admit it, she was thinking the same thing.

"Look," she said, trying to reason with James, "if you'd please step out of the bathroom for a just moment, I'd like to get out of the tub and put on some clothes. Then we can talk about what's bothering you, okay?" There was a phone next to the vanity, and once she got him out of the room, she'd be able to call for help.

"You've got three minutes," he said, looking down at his watch. Then he got up and casually strolled over to the phone and yanked it out of the wall. "Three minutes" he reminded her as he walked out the door.

There was a change of clothes lying on the vanity, so Kerrie quickly got out of the tub, dried herself off and attempted to get dressed. Her whole body was shaking so badly as she clumsily tried to zip up her jeans then button her blouse, she seriously doubted her ability to walk out there on her own but when she heard James shout, "Time's up!" she managed to stumble out of the bathroom.

James was standing next to a high back chair near the window, looking as though he was deep in thought. "Don't do anything stupid," he warned, still staring out the window. "I'm not here to hurt you. We just need to talk."

Meg and Andy were stunned by Ted's declaration that Curt and James were the same person, but while Meg had her doubts about the validity of the statement, Andy knew the psychic well enough to believe him without question.

"We've got to warn Kerrie." said Andy. "She's staying at the Wyndham, so why don't you try and get her on the phone," he told Ted, "and I'll call her driver and make sure everything is okay."

When neither the Kerrie, the driver or any of the other bodyguards answered their phones, Andy went into panic mode. "I'm going to call the police." he said, reaching for the phone once more, but before he could pick it up, his phone began to ring. He was relieved to see Kerrie's number show up on the caller ID, but it wasn't Kerrie who made the call.

"Hello, Andy," said the voice on the other end. "Long time, no see."

Recognizing James' voice immediately, Andy felt a combination of rage and fear at the same time.

"I just asked Kerrie if she wanted to say goodbye to you."

The realization that Kerrie and James were together was unnerving and Andy had to make sure that Kerrie was okay. "Let me speak to her right now," he roared. Then, taking a moment to contemplate what James has just said, he added, "What do you mean by 'goodbye'?"

"Oh, that's right. You Brits don't speak American, do you?" chuckled James. "Let me explain myself more clearly. "You see, according to Webster, goodbye is an interjection meaning farewell."

"Don't get cute with me," warned Andy, "and put Kerrie on the phone. I need to know that she's all right."

"Don't get your knickers in a knot, Andy. Why wouldn't she be?" he asked innocently. "And by the way, congratulations are in order because you seem to have recovered quite nicely from your unfortunate freeway accident, haven't you?"

"No thanks to you." Andy snapped back.

"Well, never mind. That's all in the past, and I'm actually glad to see you up and around. In fact, I'm thrilled that I didn't manage to kill you in London," said James, finally confessing to the crime. "Of course, I wasn't too happy at first," he explained, now chatting as though he and Andy were long lost friends, "but in retrospect, it would have been a shame for you to have died and missed all the fun."

Andy had just about enough. "What in the bloody hell do you want from me?"

"You must have figured that out by now, my friend., so don't play stupid." sneered James. "All I've ever wanted is Kerrie, and it seems as though I've finally got my wish." he said, sounding like he'd just found the pot of gold at the end of the rainbow. "And just so you know, I have no intention of harming her so I strongly suggest you not call the police and just gracefully walk away."

"I have no intention of calling the authorities," he lied. "but what about you and Meg? he asked, hoping to get James' mind off Kerrie for the moment. "Don't you think she needs to hear the truth?"

"Well, congratulations again on solving the other part of the puzzle. I'm very impressed, but, no, there's no reason for me to speak to her. As far as I'm concerned, Meg has served her purpose, so why don't we agree to change partners?" he suggested. "Now that I'm done with Meg and you can't have Kerrie, it might be a good idea for you to console yourself with her best friend."

Andy couldn't take the taunting any longer. "Are you so crazy that you actually believe Kerrie would choose you over me?"

When he heard the word *crazy*, something in James' mind snapped. "Oops, I'm sorry. Wrong answer." he chirped, sounding like a lunatic game show host. "Crazy is not the word I was looking for, so you've just lost your final opportunity to speak to Kerrie. Enjoy your consolation prize. Goodbye."

Ted and Meg heard enough of the conversation to understand what was going on and feared the worst, but before either of them could say anything, Andy took off running towards the door. "I'm going to Palm Springs, and I'll call you as soon as I find anything out." he yelled over his shoulder.

Without hesitation, Meg got up and ran after him with Ted not far behind.

Andy ran to the freight elevator which was standing open at the end of the hall, shoved the movers aside, and pounded on the down button as the other two piled in.

"I don't think Kerrie is in any immediate danger," said Ted, panting hard after the short sprint. "But what the hell are you going to do once we get there? Surely, he's not going to stay at the hotel like a sitting duck."

"Meg, keep trying to get Kerrie's bodyguards on the phone," said Andy, ignoring Ted's question. "Ted, call upon your spirit posse to keep a watchful eye over Kerrie," he instructed as the elevator doors opened at the lobby. "I know what it feels like to lose her and I cannot let it happen again!"

The desk clerk, alerted by the commotion of three people scrambling out of the elevator and racing to the front door, looked up briefly, then went back to his crossword puzzle as the trio climbed into Andy's car and sped off for the desert.

As soon as he hung up on Andy, James threw the phone on the bed and turned his attention to Kerrie, who was standing in the doorway, still shaking uncontrollably.

"Are you angry that I suggested your boyfriend take up with Meg?" James asked sweetly. "Surely you wouldn't begrudge him a sympathetic shoulder to cry on, would you?"

217

Only having heard one side of the conversation, Kerrie didn't know anything about the Curt-James connection. "He won't need anyone's shoulder to cry on, because I'll always be there for him. And what does Meg have to do with all this, anyway? She already has a boyfriend."

"Oh, didn't I tell you?" he laughed. "Curt has gone away, and it's probably a good thing because now that Meg knows all about him, I doubt she'd be interested in ever seeing him again."

"Why? What did he do?" she asked suspiciously.

"You might say that Curt was leading a double life." he said, pulling out his wallet and showing her a driver's license with Curt's name but James' picture. "You see, Curt is just an alias I created to be able to get friendly with Meg so that I could keep an eye on you." he explained.

"You, stupid son of a bitch!" she screamed, knocking the wallet out of his hand, before making a mad run towards the door. James didn't chase after her because he had jimmied the lock so that she wouldn't be able to get it open.

Once she realized that she couldn't get out, Kerrie turned around and ran at James in a fury. When she got within reach, she swung her fist in anger hoping to knock him out but his quick reflexes allowed him to back away just in time. Then he grabbed her arm and twisted it hard behind her back knocking her off balance. As she fell to the floor, he let her go. "I really don't want to hurt you so I suggest you learn to control your temper, and we'll get along just fine," he warned.

Kerrie nearly fell flat on her face, but immediately tried get back on her feet, but because she fell hard, she couldn't manage it. "You're really sick, you know that, don't you?" she cried. "So, what are you planning to do? Keep me locked in this hotel room forever?"

"That's no way to treat a lady." he chided, gallantly offering her his hand. "As a matter of fact, I've planned a rather nice forever for the both of us, but of course, that all depends on you."

Normally, the drive to the desert only took a couple of hours, but Andy was stuck in rush hour traffic and his blood pressure was rising as the car crept along at an incredibly slow pace. "How do you people ever get anywhere in this bloody town?" he raged, banging his fist on the steering wheel. "It's insane!"

218

"Relax, Andy," said Ted, trying to calm him down. "We don't even know for sure whether James actually has Kerrie or not. He might have been bluffing to lure you into some kind of a trap. It's you he wants dead, not Kerrie."

The psychic's logic did make sense, but Andy knew that James was not thinking logically. He was certain Kerrie was with James and all he could think about was getting her away from him.

"Shouldn't we call the police or something?" asked Meg, thinking that the authorities could at least go to the hotel and see that her friend was all right.

"No, not yet." said Andy, remembering James' warning. "I'm sure Ted is right. It's me he wants to harm, not Kerrie."

James was in the process of helping Kerrie up from the floor when there was a knock at the door followed by a loud, "Room service!"

James grabbed Kerrie by the arm and stood her up and pushed her through the bathroom door. "Get in there and don't say a word or I'll have to kill the server, do you understand?" he hissed angrily. The room service guy appeared to be getting impatient because he knocked loudly again.

"I'll be right there," James called out cheerfully, as though nothing was wrong.

Taking a look over his shoulder to make sure Kerrie had shut the door behind her, James walked over and opened the front door.

"Just leave the cart over there by the window," he instructed, handing the guy a $20 bill as he walked by.

The porter was a young man of college age who looked as though he could really use the money and was obviously pleased by the generous tip.

"Thank you very much, sir. Enjoy your meal," he said with a big grin. James didn't like the fact that he was looking around the room expectantly, and not making a move to leave. "Is there something I can help you with?" he asked, trying to mask his annoyance.

"I was under the impression that this was Miss Sherman's room and I was hoping to tell her how much I enjoyed her book," he explained, pulling the newly released paperback version out of his jacket pocket. "I even brought my own copy to see if she would autograph it for me."

"Miss Sherman just stepped out for a few minutes, but if you leave the book with me, I'll see that she signs it." said James, plucking the book from his hand. "You can pick it up when you come back for the cart. Who should she make the autograph out to?"

"Jake Elliot," said the porter, grateful for the generous offer. "And you are?"

"I'm James Goldman, Miss Sherman's publicist," he said proudly. "I accompany her on all of her public appearances."

While most people would have had enough sense to give out a fake name under the circumstances. James had such a large ego, he felt it necessary to let the porter know that he was an important person in Kerrie's life.

"So, I guess you know her pretty well then?" asked Jake, eager to hear some juicy gossip.

"Yes, we're very close," he bragged, trying to give the impression that there was more to their relationship than there actually was. He was so wrapped up in trying to milk his five minutes of fame, he actually forgot that Kerrie was in the bathroom.

"You're a lucky man, Mr. Goldman," said the porter, picking up on not-so-subtle hint that James was the man in her life, "and I guess I should know better to believe everything I read."

The comment caught James off guard. "What are you talking about?"

Jake was thrilled to think that he had some "inside information." "Well, the story only came out today, and since you've been so busy downstairs, you probably haven't had the chance to read about it yet."

"Read what?" James demanded.

"It's about Miss Sherman and Andy Dickinson, of course. It's in all the papers." he whispered, as though he was passing on classified information. "They're saying that Andy secretly snuck into town a few days ago, and was staying at the Roosevelt Hotel, but checked out this morning and has moved into some swanky apartment on the West Side."

"Why should I care what Andy Dickinson does?" asked James, thinking that Jake was just chatting away as an excuse not to leave. "And what has all this to do with Kerrie?"

"Well," he began, feeling like a fisherman that just hooked a very big fish, "a reporter for one of the tabloids happened to see a moving van load up all of Miss Sherman's belongings and take them over to a condo that Andy apparently just bought. He said it looked as though they're moving in together."

"They most certainly are not!" yelled James, whose sudden outburst startled the porter.

"I guess you would know." shrugged Jake, looking at James as though he were some sort of loose cannon. "Well, I'd better get going now," he said, turning quickly towards the door. "I'll be back for the cart and my book in an hour or so."

As soon as James was out the door, James raced for the bathroom where he found Kerrie sitting on the edge of the tub, crying.

"I'm sure you overheard our little conversation," he said, looking very angry. "Is it true? Were you planning on playing house with Andy?"

When Kerrie didn't answer, James grabbed her by the arm, dragged her out of the bathroom and threw her on the bed.

"Answer me!" he demanded. "Were you planning on moving in with Andy Dickinson or not?"

When she still didn't answer, James took hold of both her shoulders and tried to shake the truth out of her.

"Stop it!" she shouted, finally finding her voice. "I was only moving into the condo to get the hell away from you."

James was so startled by her outburst, he let go and took a step back before responding. "So, Sir Fucking Galahad comes charging in on his white steed to rescue the poor damsel in distress. How very British of him."

"At least he's concerned about my happiness, which is more than I can say for you," she shot back.

"What? You don't think I'm not concerned about you?" he answered in mock disbelief. "I think you've got it all wrong, Kerrie. I'm here to protect you from him," he said, changing his tone. "Taking up with Andy Dickinson is a very big mistake, because he'll end up hurting you. He's a trophy collector, Kerrie, and you're this week's prize. Don't you understand that?"

Kerrie had to laugh. "In case you hadn't noticed, he's not the one holding me hostage."

"Don't be ridiculous. I'm doing no such thing," said James, truly believing that he was there for her own good.

"Then what do you call breaking into my hotel room, locking me in and then trying to drown me in the bathtub? she asked.

Obviously hurt by the allegation, James tried to explain his actions. "I didn't try and drown you," he said defensively. "I accidentally knocked your leg to the side and you lost your balance and slipped down into the water. I'd hardly call that attempted murder."

Kerrie didn't believe a word of it. "If you've got my best interests at heart and truly care about me, then prove it by walking out that door."

"I'm afraid it's too late for that," he sighed, "If I know Andy, he's probably on his way to the desert right now to come and save you. That's why we've got to get going," he explained.

Kerrie knew James was probably right and had no intention of leaving. "I'm not going anywhere with you," she said defiantly. "I'm going to wait right here until Andy arrives, and trust me, he won't be coming alone so I suggest you get out of here before he has you arrested...not just for kidnapping me, but for attempted murder on him."

James bent down so that he and Kerrie were nose to nose. "One way or the other, we'll be gone long before he gets here because there is no way I'm going to willingly step back and allow you and Andy to ever be together again. I love you and we were meant to be together, and if I can't have you, nobody will. Do I make myself clear?"

Those words sounded eerily familiar, but Kerrie couldn't imagine why.

CHAPTER 24

"Bloody hell!" groused Andy. Traffic had been moving slowly for a few minutes and he actually felt like they'd made some progress but once again they were at a standstill. Still 70 miles out of Palm Springs, he was beginning to panic because he'd still not been able to reach Tim or any of the other bodyguards by phone. What Andy didn't know was that once the conference was over, Kerrie suggested that since she was planning to stay in her room all night, she told them all to take the evening off.

At first Tim was hesitant to accept her offer, but struck a compromise when she suggested that they all at least go out and have a long, leisurely dinner, and check in on her when they got back.

Neither Ted nor Meg had much to say during the long drive. Meg was still in shocked to find out that James had tricked her into believing that he was actually Curt, and she blamed herself for not realizing it sooner. Ted, on the other hand, had placed himself in a light trance and was concentrating on keeping his psychic channels open.

"What's the game plan when we get there?" asked Meg once the traffic began to move again.

Andy had been so busy fussing about being stuck in traffic, he really didn't know what the plan was once they got there and took a moment to think things out before answering. "The first thing we need to do is locate Tim and find out how James managed to get past the guards and into Kerrie's room. Then I think it would be a good idea to make sure they are both still up there before deciding how to proceed. We've got to be careful, though, because James is obviously quite unstable."

Because Kerrie was stubbornly refusing to leave the hotel room, James needed time to figure out a way to get her out of there, but since he was almost certain that Andy was on his way, and had no doubt called the police as well, time was not a luxury he could afford. He was pacing back and forth in front of the bed when a loud knock on the door broke the silence.

"Room service!" called the cheerful voice.

Grabbing Kerrie's arm and yanking her off the chair, James dragged her towards the bathroom and shoved her through the door. "I don't want to hear a sound out of you," he warned, before shutting her in. "Not a peep."

Afraid of what he might do if she dared try and make herself known to Jake, Kerrie sat down on the edge of the tub and listened as James let the porter in, then explained how she had come back to the room long enough to eat dinner and sign his book, but had decided to spend the evening at a nearby casino and wasn't due back for several hours.

Clearly disappointed at having missed her, Jake took the book from James and set it aside, not bothering to look for the autograph. Then he began to pile the dinner dishes back onto the cart. Had he taken a moment to look under the silver lids covering the plates, he would have seen that Kerrie's dinner had not been touched but he was in too much of a hurry to notice. "I'm sorry I didn't get to meet her, but please thank Kerrie for the autograph," he said, holding his hand out of James. "I can't wait to show this to my boss," he explained, nodding towards the book. "She said Miss Sherman had half a dozen bodyguards and they'd probably throw me out if I even asked."

James was in such a hurry to get rid of Jake, he shook his hand then put his arm around the porter's shoulders and walked him to the door. "I 'll make sure and thank her, and maybe you'll be able to catch up with her tomorrow at the book signing and the two of you can have a little chat."

"I'd love that!" said Jake, clutching his autographed book like it was gold. "Well, have a good night."

Kerrie didn't hear anything after that and assuming the porter had left, she walked over to the sink to throw some cold water on her face. She needed to buy herself some time to try and figure out how she could get away from James. Knowing that he was certifiably insane, she didn't want to do anything to set him off, but at the same time wondered if physically attacking him might not be an option and looked around the bathroom for some kind of weapon. She knew she wouldn't be able to overpower him, but if she could at least disable him long enough to get out of the room, that would be good enough.

What she needed was something hard and heavy to arm herself with, but the only thing that looked remotely dangerous was an incredibly, sharp nail sticking out of the wall next to the vanity. Earlier in the day she heard what sounded like construction work going on in the room next door and thought maybe the carpenter had accidentally missed his mark with the nail gun.

The cold water felt good on her face, but when she groped for the towel, Kerrie's hand accidentally knocked against a bottle of perfume that was already teetering on the edge of the vanity. The delicate bottle hit the faucet then fell into the sink with a loud crash.

"What was that?" asked Jake. Apparently, he hadn't left after all.

James also heard the bottle shatter and was more than a little annoyed by the sudden disturbance.

"It sounded like someone just dropped a glass or something in your bathroom," said the porter, taking a step forward to go and investigate.

"Unless we've got poltergeists in here, I don't think so." laughed James, blocking his way. "It was probably someone in the room next door. You know how thin these adjoining walls are."

"That's true." Jake admitted with a shrug. "I was picking up a cart in room 1701 last night and could actually hear someone blowing their nose in the room next door. But if I were you," he said, still wanting to go have a look for himself, "I'd go check just to make sure."

"I'll do that, but I'm sure it was nothing." James was trying to act as though it really was nothing, but at the same time he was so angry at Kerrie, he was ready to explode. "Now, if you'll excuse me," he said, "I've got a few things I need to do before Kerrie gets back."

"Oh, right." said Jake, turning back towards the door. He wanted to stick around while James checked out the bathroom, but could tell that the publicist wanted him out. "Thanks again for the autograph, and maybe I'll see you tomorrow at the book signing."

James nodded and managed a faint smile, quickly shut the door between them, then stormed into the bathroom.

"What the hell were you trying to do?" he hollered, rushing up to Kerrie and slapping her hard across the face. The force of the blow threw her up against the wall and he was amused by the stunned expression on Kerrie's face. It looked as though she was about to say something when all of a sudden, her expression went blank, her body stiffened up and then she began to shake. Thinking this was merely a sympathy ploy, James just stood and watched as Kerrie's body continued to convulse and then fall to the floor a moment later. He was really impressed that she managed to pull off her wounded sparrow routine so convincingly.

"Okay, enough of the theatrics," he yelled, straddling her crumpled body. "Don't think I'm going to feel sorry for you because I know you're faking it. I barely touched you, so knock it off. We've got to get out of here before Andy and his posse arrives."

Kerrie's eyes were open but she wasn't responding, so James gave her shoulder an impatient nudge with his foot. "Get up, damn you!"

The pressure from James' foot pushed Kerrie's unresponsive body over onto her side, and he saw that there was a little blood on her cheek. Thinking it was only a scratch, James bent down for a closer look and was horrified to see a trail of blood trickling out of her ear. He couldn't understand how that could be since he hadn't hit her hard enough to do any real damage.

As he glanced up to see what she might have bumped up against, James saw a very large, blood-covered nail sticking out of the wall with a few strands of Kerrie's hair clinging to it.

It was then that he realized this was more than a scratch. He knelt down and tried to shake Kerrie awake, but her limp body shook like a rag doll. In a panic, he put his head on her chest to listen for a heartbeat and when he couldn't hear anything, he grabbed at her wrist to feel for a pulse.

226

James didn't need a medical degree to come to the conclusion that Kerrie was dead.

"Noooooo!" he wailed, bending over to take her in his arms. "You can't die!" he cried, hugging her lifeless body. "YOU CAN'T DIE!"

He sat there rocking back and forth, willing her to come back to life, but James' grief soon turned to fear with the realization he would be held accountable for her death if anyone found him in her room.

Reluctantly pulling himself away, he kissed Kerrie gently on the lips, and was just about to slip out the front door when he heard footsteps and loud voices out in the hall. Not knowing what else to do, James ran out of the bathroom, threw open the door to the balcony, climbed over the railing and jumped the two floors to the ground.

At that same moment, Andy burst through the door and frantically began looking around the room for Kerrie. A moment later Meg, Tim and Jake, who was just down the hall, heard Andy's mournful scream. They ran in after him to see what was wrong.

Seeing Andy kneeling next to the lifeless body on the floor, they knew there was nothing anyone could do to help her. Jake immediately called down to the hotel manager while the others tried to gently convince Andy that he must step away so as not to disturb the crime scene.

"Get out of here and leave us alone," he roared, obviously overcome with grief, "and shut the bloody door behind you."

He sat alone with Kerrie even after the police arrived to conduct their investigation, and was only persuaded to let go of her when the coroner arrived to take her body to the morgue.

After the police questioning, an all-points bulletin was issued for James, and Andy, Ted and Meg tearfully headed back to Los Angeles to make the necessary funeral arrangements. Andy was so overcome with grief he couldn't drive so Ted took the wheel on the journey home.

"If I had just gone with her, none of this would have happened!" cried Andy.

"If it's any consolation," sighed Ted, looking back at them in the rear-view mirror, "I'm quite sure he had no intention of killing her. I think it was just a horrible accident."

"How in the hell is that supposed to make me feel any better?" yelled Andy. "Accident or not, it is still that bastard's fault that she's dead and I'm going to make sure that he pays dearly for what he's done."

Strangely enough, James was thinking the same thing about Andy. He was standing in line at the airport waiting to board the next plane to Puerto Valletta, Mexico and could think of nothing else but seeking revenge on the actor for Kerrie's death. "If he'd only died in London," he thought, "none of this would ever have happened."

******

They tried to make her funeral a private event, but in the week since her body had been found at the hotel, accounts of Kerrie's death were splashed across the front page of newspapers from Palm Springs to London and the cemetery was overrun by the media. All eyes were on Andy, who wore a sorrowful expression throughout the short graveside service. Because he refused to talk to the press, speculation was running rampant about both his reason for attending the funeral and the fact that he was so visibly grief-stricken. Nobody could figure out his connection to the young author but the tabloids had a field day reporting all sorts of possibilities. Was Kerrie Sherman actually Andy Dickinson's love child? Was she perhaps carrying *his* love child? Only one astute source came anywhere near the truth when they speculated that Kerrie's murder could possibly have had something to do with a love triangle, but they had wrongly shifted the blame to Andy, suggesting that perhaps he was responsible for her death because he caught her with a younger man.

The police would only say that an investigation was underway and there were no suspects. In truth, the authorities were hot on the trail of James Goldman because his fingerprints were found at the scene and the testimony from Andy, Meg and Ted pointed to him as the prime suspect. The problem was, James was nowhere to be found.

228

Work on the Collywobbles movie was suspended for several weeks at considerable expense to the production company, but the savvy studio heads knew that the tragic murder mystery surrounding their lead actor would bring in big revenue once the movie was released and that would more than compensate for the delay.

After the funeral, Andy remained locked away in his hotel room. He couldn't bear going back to the condo, and had Tim arrange to have Kerrie's belongings moved to a storage facility for the time being. The only people he had any contact with were Ted, Meg, and the police, who were still at a loss to explain James' disappearance.

When the authorities called to give him the results of the autopsy a few days later, Andy listened carefully to the coroner's report then became physically sick. Kerrie had died as the result of a long, sharp foreign body entering her ear canal, "causing a deep puncture wound to the vital centers of the brain with evidence of intracranial cerebral hemorrhage." The only positive finding, if one could call it that, was that she had died instantly.

Ted spent a great deal of time counseling the actor through his grief. He reassured Andy that Kerrie was fine, but needed time to make the full transition to the other side.

"You need to understand that Kerrie is not gone forever," the psychic explained. "She has merely taken on another form of existence, just as you both have done many times in the past, and the longer you grieve, the longer you hold her here on the Earth plane, so you must think about letting go. Tell her that it's okay to cross over and once she adjusts to life on the other side, she will come back to visit from time to time, but for now, you must allow her to rest."

That night as he lay in bed, clinging tightly to a small moonstone ring he'd removed from her finger before the coroner took her body away, Andy said his final goodbye.

"Kerrie, I love you with all my heart and always will, but it's selfish of me to keep you here," he began. "Once you've completed the transition, please come back and let me know that you are all right, but for now, you must go."

Given the magnitude of his grief, he could well have been imagining it, but as soon as he let her know it was all right to leave, Andy was sure he heard her whisper, "I love you, too."

Meg was sitting in front of the television absentmindedly flipping through the channels when the six o'clock news finally came on. Due to the circumstances of Kerrie's tragic murder, and because someone supposedly in the know leaked the information that Andy and Kerrie had been very much in love, stories following the police's progress, or lack of it, in trying to solve the case were being reported on a daily basis and she was curious to see what far-fetched theory would be the headline of the day. While the authorities had still not publicly named James Goldman as a suspect, they did finally admit to the press that they had a very good idea of who Kerrie's murderer was and were doing everything possible to bring him to justice.

"The frantic search for Kerrie Sherman's killer continues," said the reporter with animated sincerity. "Authorities now have reason to believe that a man resembling the suspect's description boarded a flight from Palm Springs International Airport to an undisclosed location just hours after Miss Sherman's body was discovered in her hotel room. The young, best-selling author was in town to deliver a speech and attend a book signing at the Palm Springs Book Fair. A source close to the investigation admits that the police are outraged that their prime suspect has manage to elude authorities, but say they are doing everything possible to make sure this dangerous criminal is apprehended. When asked about the circumstances surrounding the tragedy, a spokesman for the fair was quoted as saying, "Truth is stranger than fiction."

In a related story, Andy Dickinson, the distraught boyfriend of Miss Sherman will be returning to England early next week to shoot the final scenes of his upcoming fantasy, *A Bad Case of The Collywobbles*, in which he plays the role of Thomas Wakefield, headmaster of a prestigious wizarding school outside of London. If you've read the best-selling book, you know that the Wakefield character has suffered his own tragic loss, so Andy, with the tremendous amount of grief he's been living with these past few weeks, will be playing this angst-ridden role from the heart. Maybe all you amateur seers out there should consult your crystal balls to find out whether an Oscar nomination is predicted in Dickinson's future. In other show business news..."

Meg switched off the sound. This was old news to her because the detective in charge of the case had already admitted to Andy that James very likely did slip past airport security that night and a full investigation of how he was able to get away so easily was now underway.

CHAPTER 25

After he finally returned to work and completed the remainder of the L.A. shoot, Andy spent his last night in Los Angeles with Meg and Ted. Leaving Kerrie behind, despite the fact that Ted assured him she would always be with him in spirit, made him feel as though he were abandoning her, and the grim reminder of how he ignored Ted's fateful warning about history repeating itself if he didn't stay away from Kerrie made him feel completely responsible for her death. It would be the penance he would have to pay for the rest of his life.

He couldn't understand how Meg could even look him in the eye, much less invite him for a final meal, but was grateful for the invitation. At the end of the evening, he tried to apologize to both of them for Kerrie's death but Meg stopped him before he could even get started.

"You've got to stop beating yourself up over this understand that nobody is pointing a finger at you." she began. "James is the only one accountable and I know that Kerrie would be really angry at you for trying to take the blame.

When he opened his mouth to disagree, Meg wouldn't let him interrupt.

"I don't think you can even begin to imagine how happy you made her during your brief time together, and I know for a fact that she would have chosen a short life knowing that you loved her rather than living to be a bitter old woman and never having had the chance to find out. "

After listening to what Meg had to say, Andy still wasn't convinced. "I thank you for trying to make me feel better, but there is nothing you can say that will take away this terrible guilt."

"Maybe this will help." she said, pulling a small, sealed envelope out of her pocket. "It's addressed to you."

He recognized Kerrie's handwriting immediately. "Where did you get this?" he asked, grabbing the letter from Meg.

"I found it in her purse after the coroner released her personal effects. I got one as well.

He was anxious to find out what Kerrie had written and as if reading his mind, Meg got up from the table and said, "I've got a stack of dishes soaking in the sink and Ted offered to dry, we'll I'll leave you to it."

Grateful for the opportunity to read Kerrie's letter alone, he carefully removed the handwritten note from the envelope.

Dear Andy,

It's a long drive to the desert, so I thought I'd use the time constructively. I'm not sure where to begin, but after some not-so gentle prodding, Ted told me yesterday that the secret I've been keeping from you all this time is the same one we both share. Rachel and Adam are finally together again, and while we never had the opportunity to live happily ever after in 1862, I'm looking forward to many happy years in this lifetime and for many more to come. I am so thankful we've been able to finally find each other and it wouldn't matter if the world came to an end tomorrow, because the love I feel for you will last an eternity.

Ted tells me there's one other thing you know that I don't, but said he thought it would be better if I heard it from you, so I can't wait for you to read this and then you can tell me all about it. See you soon!

Love always,

Kerrie."

Andy was furious that Ted told Kerrie everything else, but didn't say anything to warn her about James and stormed into the kitchen to confront him.

"Why didn't you tell her the whole truth?" he demanded, snatching the dish towel out of Ted's hand to get his undivided attention. "Why didn't you tell her about James instead of leaving it to me? If you had bothered to mention that her ex-publicist was the raving, murderous lunatic who killed her the last time, she might not be dead!"

Ted seemed unruffled by the actor's outburst. "I thought it would be best for her to hear it from you, and even if she knew about James, she wouldn't have been able to do anything about it," he explained. "It's like I told you in the car a few weeks ago, James had no intention of murdering Kerrie. It was you he wanted dead, but destiny had other plans and claimed its rightful victim. That leaves you and James to pick up the pieces and live out your own destinies."

"To hell with destiny! James' fate is in my hands now."

Ted just smiled. "Do what you think you must to make yourself feel better, but things will ultimately turn out as they were intended to, no matter what."

"You know, Ted, I'm beginning to wonder whose side you're on," said Andy accusingly.

"There are no sides to be taken. This isn't a football match, for God's sake. This is life and it's up to you to make your own choices while you are here, but sometimes they don't always play out the way we hope they would," the psychic explained. "I'd like nothing more than to see James burn in Hell, but it's not up to me, and I don't want to see you place yourself in peril while you seek to right his wrong. Don't forget, he's still out there, and he's already tried to kill you once."

"There's no reason for him to come gunning for me now," reasoned the actor. "Kerrie's dead and I'm sure he's blaming me somehow and hoping I'll stay alive for many years to suffer some tragic Karmic fate."

"Ah, but you're assuming he believes in such things. Not everybody does, you know."

"I'll take my chances," he said gruffly. "Meanwhile, it's getting late and I've got an early flight in the morning, so I'd better get back to the hotel and finish packing."

"I'll walk you to the door," said Meg, taking the towel away from Andy and drying her hands. She had listened quietly throughout the heated exchange, and felt sorry that there was nothing she could do to make Andy feel any better.

"Please apologize to Ted for me," he said after giving her a hug and kiss goodbye. "I think he knows me well enough not to take offense at my outburst, but if the fence needs mending, give it a quick patch, okay?"

"I will, Andy, and please stay in close touch. With James still out there somewhere, I can't help but worry about you."

While James might have been far away, he wanted to make sure that he was not forgotten...a least as far as Meg and Andy were concerned, and over the next few weeks, made sure to remind them that he was still around.

His first communication to Meg came in the form of a telephone call. When she answered the phone, she heard Elvis Presley croon, *"Are you lonesome tonight? Do you miss me tonight? Are you sorry we drifted apart?"* and then the caller hung up.

A barrage of other messages followed, including snippets of "Lonely Nights," "What Becomes of the Broken Hearted," and "It's Too Late." The songs were edited in such a way that James was easily able to convey his thoughts without having to say a word.

Andy was getting similar phone calls, but of a slightly different nature. While Meg's were just plain cruel, Andy's calls were melodious threats in the form of titles like, "Straight Shooter, "Going, Going, Gone," and "Don't Fear The Reaper."

The authorities were notified and both their phone lines were tapped in the hopes of tracking James down, but he soon tired of the game and changed tactics.

Meg opened her mailbox one afternoon to find a copy of the book *How To Survive the Loss of A Love* and Andy was sent *Affairs in Order: A Complete Resource Guide for Death and Dying*. Both books were sent as gifts from an online bookstore with only the purchaser's name for reference.

While all of his little mind games were somewhat effective in upsetting Meg and Andy, they both viewed James' efforts as childish yet harmless attempts at drawing attention to himself because even though he was in hiding, it was quite apparent that he couldn't stand being out of the limelight and needed to act out. His antics continued over the next few weeks by email, which linked Andy to websites such as findadeath.com, murderersontherun.com and unspeakableacts.com. All of Meg's correspondences sent her to dating services like match.com, but James soon tired of those as well, and all communications from him stopped completely.

Both Andy and Meg had gone back to work and were trying to lead normal, productive lives but they both understood that the chronic pain of losing Kerrie would never go away.

For Andy, the final days of shooting the movie were bittersweet. On the one hand, he was sorry to see it end because work afforded him the opportunity to think about something other than Kerrie, but at the same time he was glad to be able to have some time alone and was looking forward to returning to the Isle of Sark for a much-needed rest. It was the only place on earth where he could completely relax. He had hoped to one day share the island treasure with Kerrie but knew that since she would always be with him in spirit, he would never be going there alone.

The wrap party was pleasant enough, but Andy stayed only long enough to thank everyone involved because he was anxious to get home and pack. His plane was leaving at noon the following day and he was expected at his manager's office in the morning and take care of some unfinished business.

Andy was a few minutes early for their meeting, so he took a seat in the outer office and picked up a magazine to pass the time. When she stepped out of her office to greet him, her first comment was, "You look a fright."

Peering over the top of the magazine, he said, "In case you've just crawled out from under a rock and missed all the excitement, I've had a few problems to sort out recently."

After a few minutes of chit chat over a cup of tea, they got down to business. "It looks like you're free and clear for the next few weeks," she said, checking his itinerary, "but don't forget that you've promised to make an appearance at that charity event in

Chelsea on the 23rd, and at Kew Gardens on the 30th to unveil the Kerrie Sherman rose."

The speckled yellow and powder blue rose was a hybrid that a local nursery had been experimenting with, and when they heard about Kerrie's murder, it was decided to name the flower in her memory. Andydidn't have much interest in plants, but when he saw a photograph of the Kerrie Sherman, he was taken by the fact that the haphazard splashes of blue were the exact color of her eyes.

"Yes, yes. I'll be back in plenty of time," he said, impatiently checking his watch. He wanted to get to the airport a little early, so he got up from the desk and walked over to the window to make sure his limo was still parked outside and that the driver was still in it. Knowing how impatient some drivers could be, he hoped this one hadn't been cheeky enough to stroll across the street for a cup of coffee and keep him waiting.

Satisfied that both the car and driver were in place, Andy turned back to his manager with a final request. "Please don't take this personally, but unless you have it on good authority that the world is coming to an end, I'd prefer not hearing from anyone, including you, while I'm away," he said. "And now, if we're all done here, I'll be off."

He was just getting into the limo when an upstairs window flew open and he heard his manager call out, "Andy, wait! I forgot to give you something," she yelled, waving a thick manila envelope.

"Oh, for God's sake, woman, now what?" he moaned.

"Just hang on a minute and I'll bring it down," she said, then slammed the window shut before he had the chance to answer back.

Tapping his foot and checking his watch every ten seconds, Andy was glad to finally see her rushing out the front door. "What's so important that it couldn't wait until I got back?"

"This," she said, handing him the oversized envelope.

Andy took the parcel from her and gave it a quick glance. The thick envelope was blank except for his name written in small letters on the front and without giving it a second look, he tried to hand it back to her. "I'm not taking any scripts with me no matter

237

how fabulous you may think this one is," he said. "I'm sure it can wait until I get back.

"No, it can't." she said cautiously, handing it back to him. "I'm not saying you have to read it immediately, but I think you should take it with you and look it over at your leisure."

Usually, she wasn't this pushy and Andy was getting annoyed. "You know I'm not a voracious reader, so what makes you think I'd be interested in this?"

"The author."

Searching the envelope once again for clues as to who the mysterious scribe might be, Andy's eyes were once again drawn to the handwriting in which his name was written. Taking a closer look, he recognized it as Kerrie's.

"The package arrived at my office a few days after her murder but I thought it best to wait a while before giving it to you," she explained. "Take it with you and if you're up to it, have a look, but if you think it will be too painful, at least read the note she attached to the cover. Maybe it will give you some idea what the book is about."

There were very few things in this world that could render Andy Dickinson speechless, but this was one of them. Fighting back tears, he nodded and got into the limo. As much as he wanted to tear the envelope open and see what Kerrie had written, it was too soon, so he unzipped one of his suitcases and put the manuscript inside. Then he placed a call to Meg to ask if she knew anything about Kerrie's new book.

It was four o'clock in the morning in Los Angeles and Meg sounded groggy when she picked up the phone but after hearing why Andy was calling, she told him what she knew. "Kerrie mentioned that she was done with the book and was planning to send you a copy when you got back to England. I think it would have made her nervous to have you read it in front of her." she explained. "She was pretty secretive about the plot and storyline, and all she would say was that it was a very personal work and knew that you'd understand."

"I don't think I'm up to reading it just yet," he admitted.

"I'm not sure I'd be able to read it either," she sighed. "I'm having a hard enough time believing she's really gone. Every time the phone rings, I keep expecting it to be her."

"Meg, I know this may not be the right time to bring this up, but I'm concerned about you. Losing one's best friend is horrible enough, but you're also having to deal with the burden of James' betrayal and I hope to God you're not also trying to shoulder some of the blame for Kerrie's death."

"I did at first," she admitted, "but I've been talking to Ted quite a bit lately and he's made me realize that this was something nobody could have done anything to stop. He said it was James' karma to have Kerrie taken away from him by his own hands because he murdered her in 1862, and because he wasn't the least bit repentant, he was destined to repeat the murder as punishment."

"It's just too bad the rest of us were punished as well," he said bitterly, as the limo pulled up to the British Airways terminal. "Listen, I don't mean to cut you off, but I'm on my way to the Isle of Sark and I've just arrived at the airport. Go back to sleep and I'll give you a call in a couple of days. You have my cell number if you need me, right?"

"Yeah, I do."

"Right, then. And the next time you speak to Ted, let him know where I am, and tell him I'll be in touch."

CHAPTER 26

Even though he was a celebrity, Andy still had to go through the rigid airport security checkpoints like everyone else before he was allowed access to the boarding area. The lines were long and it took him well over an hour to finally be cleared. Once he checked his luggage and obtained his boarding pass, he strolled over to the gift shop to pick up something to read then headed back towards the VIP lounge to wait for his flight.

Andy was a people watcher and always amused to see how different people dealt with everyday life. He particularly enjoyed the airport's lively atmosphere, which brought out their best and their worst. There were tears of sadness when a loved one said goodbye and tears of joy when they returned. There were angry passengers who missed a connecting flight and had no other option but to sit around and wait several hours for the next one, and others peacefully taking a nap while waiting for their boarding call.

Just as he was about to enter the VIP lounge, Andy saw something out of the corner of his eye that made his blood run cold. A man who looked exactly like James Goldman was furtively walking across the concourse at a rapid pace. Without hesitation, Andy dropped his carryon bag and took off after him. The man was a long way off so Andy ran as fast as he could to catch up. It probably wasn't the wisest thing to do because for all he knew, James might have somehow slipped a gun past the security checkpoints, but he didn't care. All he knew was that he had to stop him from getting away. The man somehow seemed to sense that he was being pursued, because he, too, picked up the pace and started to run as well. Andy was weaving in and out of the crowd like a madman, shoving people out of his way as he went.

Having a famous actor running amok in the airport did not go unnoticed and Andy, very much out of character because he was not known as an action hero, was beginning to draw a crowd. Several adoring fans stopped to cheer him on.

"Stop that man!" he yelled, pointing in the direction of the fleeing suspect. "The man in the tan jacket, over there! Stop him."

Having no other reason to get involved other than the fact that Andy Dickinson told them to, several of the more athletic young men in the crowd joined in the pursuit. Much faster than even Andy or his quarry, they managed to close in on the man, tackle him to the ground and pile on top of him to make sure he didn't get away. When the man underneath the pile struggled to break away, his captors proceeded to take justice into their own hands and pummel him into submission. By the time Andy arrived with the airport police in tow, six burly guys were perched on top of the now silent figure.

"What in the bloody hell is going on here?" yelled one of the officers. "Get off of him before you smother the bloke to death!"

Andy was hovering over the pile, anxiously waiting to look James in the eye and then stomp on his face.

"What is the meaning of this?" asked another one of the officers, pulling Andy back.

"That's James Goldman." said Andy. He could barely get the words out because he was so short of breath from running so hard. "He's a fugitive from justice and wanted for the murder of Kerrie Sherman back in the States."

Hearing they had a felon on their hands, the officers drew their guns and pointed them at the suspect as the young men began to pile off. As the last man stood up and walked away, everyone stared down at the dazed, but conscious man who was lying on his stomach and trying to pull himself up with great difficulty.

The moment he finally managed to sit up and turn around, Andy was horrified to realize that he made a terrible mistake. While the man could have easily been James Goldman's brother, he clearly wasn't the murderer.

"Are you all right?" he asked, pulling away from the policeman to try and minister to the man. "Do you need an ambulance?"

The man looked up at Andy, and after recognizing the actor wondered aloud if he hadn't somehow been pranked on some hidden camera television show.

Andy was glad that the poor guy wasn't screaming for his lawyer and helped him up, explained the case of mistaken identity and apologized profusely for the grievous error.

"No harm done, I suppose," said the man, dusting himself off. "If it had been my girlfriend that had been brutally murdered like yours was, I'd have done the same ...or worse."

After the victim assured both Andy and the police that he had no intention of pressing charges for the assault, the crowd slowly disbursed and Andy walked back to the VIP lounge just in time to hear the boarding call for his flight. He was ashamed at having caused an innocent man such a fright, but thankful that the guy wasn't seriously hurt.

The tension of the past few weeks having finally caught up with Andy, who slept most of the way to Sark. Once the plane landed, all Andy wanted to do was check into his room and have a long soak in the tub. The hotel had sent someone to meet him and as he handed the driver his baggage claim check, he thought that both Ted and Meg would have a good laugh at his expense when he told them about the incident at the airport.

His thoughts were interrupted when the driver came back with only one of Andy's suitcases. "It seems that your other bag has been lost in transit," he said apologetically, "but I've already arranged for the airlines to put a tracer on it, and hopefully it will turn up in a day or two."

Since both his suitcases looked alike, Andy wasn't sure which bag he was missing and at first it wasn't any big deal. He'd had bags lost before and they were always found and returned in a reasonable amount of time, but when he remembered that Kerrie's manuscript was in one of the bags, he dug around in his pocket for the suitcase key and when he opened the suitcase, it was not the one containing the precious envelope.

"We must find the missing bag as quickly as possible because there is something in it that is irreplaceable," he said, trying to keep calm. "I don't care if they have to send trained monkeys into the baggage compartments of every plane that took off from Heathrow in the past 12 hours. I must have that bag!"

Andy was a basket case by the time he arrived at the hotel and called Meg right away to tell her what happened. Then he asked her to call Ted and see if he could somehow figure out where his bag might be found.

"It's not that big a deal, Andy," said Meg, sensing he was way more upset than he needed to be. "That wasn't the only copy of the book, you know. All I have to do is go to the storage facility and look through the boxes and find her computer. She always kept her master copy on the hard drive, and she was very good about backing up her work, so I'm sure I'll find a copy on disk as well."

"It's not the bloody book I'm worried about. There was a personal note attached to the manuscript, and I'm sure she didn't save that on the hard drive."

"Okay, I'll call Ted right now," she promised, "and I'll let you know if he comes up with anything. One way or the other, I'm sure your bag will be found so try and take it easy, and we'll talk soon."

Andy's peaceful holiday was starting out badly. First there was the case of mistaken identity at the airport, then the airlines lost his bag. He hoped that would be the end of it, but was superstitious enough to believe that bad things come in threes and wondered what the final insult might be. He prayed that whatever was to come wouldn't be anything major because with his already-frayed nerves he felt certain he wouldn't be up to the challenge.

Meg finally got in touch with Ted, he told her the lost bag would be located and delivered to Andy within a couple of days, but from his tone of voice, Meg got the impression that something wasn't quite right.

"I'm just a little on edge today," the psychic explained when she asked what was wrong, but didn't go into any detail.

Meg knew exactly how he felt because most of her days were still unbearable. When she wasn't overcome with grief at the loss of her best friend, she was beating herself up for falling in love with a man whose only intention was to use her to get to Kerrie. Why hadn't she been able to see through him? Had she been so desperate for someone to love that she blinded herself to all the signs that something was not quite right? And despite what Ted said about the murder not being her fault, she couldn't help but think that it was.

"Maybe you need to follow Andy's lead and get away yourself." he suggested. "It's doing you no good at all moping around the house, and if I were you, I'd think along the lines of a remote, uncrowded island somewhere in the Atlantic perhaps."

"You mean somewhere like Sark?" she asked, thinking Ted's idea did have its merits.

"Why not Sark?" he urged.

"Well for one thing, I don't want to intrude on Andy's holiday." she explained. "He needs this time to himself to sort things out."

"I'm sure he does," said Ted, "but if he's so intent on being cut off from everyone, why does he keep calling you?"

"Because I'm his only link to Kerrie, I suppose, but I can't go barging in on him without an invitation. It wouldn't be right." she argued.

"You must go," he said without further explanation. It sounded more like an order than a suggestion, but Meg knew better than to question Ted. "I'll make all the arrangements and get back to you later this afternoon. Is your passport in order?"

"Yes, but--"

"Look, Meg," he interrupted, "spirit is telling me that you need to leave for Sark immediately. Andy needs you."

By noon the next day, Meg was on the plane to England. The long flight gave her the opportunity to reflect on recent events and she was looking forward to seeing Andy again. Although she knew there could never be anything more between them than friendship, she genuinely liked Andy and hoped that a few days together would help them both begin to recover.

After landing in London, Meg made her way to another terminal for her connecting flight to Sark only to find that her flight was canceled because of bad weather and the next plane out wasn't scheduled until noon the next day. Rather than hang around the airport, she saw this as a good opportunity to explore a bit of London then find an inexpensive hotel in which to spend the night. She thought about calling Andy to warn him that she was on the way, but decided to surprise him instead.

A call from the hotel manager woke Andy up early the next morning.

"Your bag has been located, Mr. Dickinson and I've got it here at the front desk." he said. "It seems that another passenger picked it up by mistake and didn't realize it wasn't his until he checked into his hotel room in Belfast." he chuckled. "Shall I have someone bring it to your room?"

Andy was relieved and very happy to hear some good news for a change. "Yes, thank you. I'm just going to hop in the shower, so I'll leave the door unlocked and they can just set it down anywhere."

As soon as he hung up with Andy, the manager rang for one of the bellman. "Brian, would you mind delivering this bag to Mr. Dickinson? He's in room 201."

"I'd be happy to, sir." said Brian. This was his first day on the job and he was eager to please. He had arrived at the hotel two days before and while the manager thought it odd that the well-dressed American was looking for such a menial job, he was currently shorthanded, so he was hired on the spot.

"Mr. Dickinson will be in the shower, so please don't disturb him," he warned. "Knock first, and if he doesn't answer just leave the bag on the bed and lock the door on your way out. "You may not know who he is," he continued, not sure whether Andy's notoriety had crossed the Atlantic, "but Mr. Dickinson is one of the U.K.'s most beloved actors and a regular customer, so we do all we can to ensure he has a pleasant stay."

"Yes, I'm familiar with his work, and there has been a great deal written about him in the American press because of his relationship with that writer that was killed a few weeks ago." said Brian, as he bent down to pick up the suitcase.

"Yes. A tragedy indeed." he sighed, then quickly changed the subject. "Don't dawdle, because Mrs. Jenkins in room 307 is requesting assistance with a stuck dresser drawer."

Brian was relieved that Andy didn't answer his knock and let himself into the room. Going against the hotel manager's orders of dropping the suitcase off and leaving, he took the liberty of having a look around instead. There wasn't anything of interest until he happened to glance over at the actor's unmade bed and noticed a small gold ring suspended from a long gold chain lying next to the pillow. Brian quickly walked over and picked up the chain to have a closer look. He held it tightly in his palm and closed his eyes as though trying to take some of the essence from it, but was interrupted a few seconds later when he heard the shower being turned off.

Reluctantly tossing the chain back on the pillow, he made a grab for the suitcase and hoisted it up to the foot of the bed then hurried out the door. Seeing that ring again brought back a flood of memories. She was wearing it in the hotel room the night of the accident and he wanted to take it off her finger then, but didn't have time. It enraged him to see that it was Andy who was now holding it dear and wondered what else of hers he might have kept.

Andy saw the suitcase laying on the bed when he walked out of the bathroom and reached into his jacket pocket for the key and opened it up to make sure the manuscript was still inside. He was relieved that it was, and decided to take it down to the beach with him and see if he could manage to get through any of it. At the very least, he planned on reading the note she'd attached to the cover.

Putting on his swimming trunks and then grabbing a beach towel, Andy headed towards his favorite sunbathing spot, a remote cove that he happened upon on during one of his previous visits.

At about the same time Andy was settling in at the beach, Meg was checking into the hotel.

"Could you please tell me what room Mr. Dickinson is staying in?" she asked after signing the register.

"Are you a friend of Mr. Dickinson or just a devoted fan?" he asked suspiciously. It was hotel policy not to give out any information about any guest, especially the famous ones.

Anticipating the third degree, Meg reached for her cell phone and showed the manager the list of her most recent incoming calls. They were all from Andy.

"Yes, of course." he said, handing her back the phone. "Mr. Dickinson is in room 201, but if I'm not mistaken, he's gone down to the beach. Poor man has been through so much lately, a little fresh air and sunshine will do him good. He looked so pale and haggard when he checked in I hardly recognized him."

"Yes, well thank you for the information," she sighed, "and since I'm a bit weary myself could you have someone show me to my room?"

"Brian? Front desk please." he called into the intercom.

A moment or two later when Brian hadn't responded, the manager walked out from behind the desk and escorted Meg to her room himself. "You would think he'd be a little more attentive on his first day of work," he mumbled as he led her to the elevator. "I should have hired a local lad."

"Yes, well, here we are," he said, after opening the door to Meg's room. "I'm sure you'll be quite comfortable here. Shall I send someone to tell Mr. Dickinson that you've arrived?"

"No thank you. That won't be necessary. I'd like to surprise him."

"I'm sure a pretty lass like yourself will be a sight for sore eyes." he said with a wink. "And if there's anything you need, please don't hesitate to call."

She needed a quick shower to revive herself, so Meg got undressed and walked into the bathroom. While she was standing underneath the refreshing flow of water, she thought it would be a good idea to stop and pick up a picnic lunch and a bottle of wine and take it down to Andy. So, after her shower she called down to the front desk to see if they could fill the order. Pleased to hear that they could, she put on her bathing suit and robe then headed down to the front desk.

"Mr. Dickinson can usually be found about a quarter of a mile from here in that direction," the manager said, pointing to his left. "I'm sure you won't have any trouble finding him, but if you'd like, I can have someone accompany you."

"I should be fine, but even if I did get lost, I don't think I'd mind very much because the island is beautiful," she laughed, taking the picnic basket off the counter and heading for the door.

Brian didn't have any trouble finding Andy, either, because as soon as the actor left the hotel, the bellman followed him at a safe distance until they reached the cove. Then he waited impatiently for the right moment to make an appearance, and it didn't take long for the window of opportunity to open up.

As Andy laid out a beach towel and settled in, Brian saw him pick up the envelope containing the manuscript and carefully tear open the flap. He then pulled off the note attached to the front cover and began to read it. A moment later, he set the note down and wiped his eyes, giving Brian just enough time to sneak up behind him.

Suddenly, Andy felt something cold and hard touching the back of his head and heard the familiar voice. "Hello, Andy. Doing a little light reading?"

The actor quickly straightened up and turned around only to find he was staring into the barrel of a gun. A bellman-clad James had his finger on the trigger. Strangely, Andy's demeanor remained calm despite the implied threat.

"Starting a new career, are we?" he asked with a wry smile, alluding to the uniform. "My, my. How the mighty have fallen."

James held the gun steady. "You seem to be awfully brave for a man who could be about to die, but then again, you've always been a brilliant actor."

Ignoring the threat and James' snide remark, Andy just laughed. "While I appreciate your assessment of my talents, I much prefer my own company, so I'd appreciate it if you would please state your business and then leave me alone. In case you hadn't noticed, I'm a bit preoccupied at the moment."

Looking down at the blank manuscript cover, James first thought Andy was preparing to read a script until he saw the handwritten note in the actor's hand. He quickly snatched it away and was horrified to see that it was from Kerrie. It read:

Dear Andy,

I've just finished my second book and wanted you to be the first to read it. Of course, if my suspicions are correct, you may very well be the only one who ever reads it. This dark thought could just be my wild writer's imagination working overtime, but somewhere in the back of my mind, I'm worried that history might repeat itself. In any case, I want you to know that writing this book was a labor of love because it is based on our story and I dedicate it to you. You were my inspiration and will always be my muse. This book affirms that we were always meant to be together, and by the time you're done reading it, I hope you will realize that nobody will ever be able to tear us apart.

With all my love, and I hope to see you soon,
Kerrie

James' facial expression changed from merely curious to absolutely livid by the time he finished reading Kerrie's note to Andy. "Is there no end to this?" he yelled, crushing the paper in his hand and throwing it to the ground. "Kerrie is dead and she's still managed to contact you!" Then looking down at the manuscript he asked, "What did she mean when she said the book was *your* story?"

"I don't know," shrugged Andy. While he knew that James had murdered Kerrie once before, he was quite sure that she didn't have a clue and was curious to find out what she had written, especially because of her cryptic reference to her suspicions. "I was just getting ready to find out when you interrupted me."

"Maybe we should find out together." said James, pointing to the manuscript with the barrel of the gun. You're the actor, so read it to me," he demanded.

Andy felt very calm as he picked up the book, then opened it to the front page and began to read the prologue out loud.

"Adam Morgan stood silently at the foot of the grave staring down at the coffin. The tearful funeral service was over and the heavy-hearted mourners were now filing out of the cemetery leaving him to say his final goodbye in private. He felt like screaming, but had no voice. He wanted to cry, but there were no tears left. This was the day he was supposed to marry Rachel, not bury her."

Tears welled up in Andy's eyes. That single paragraph explained a great deal. He now fully understood what Kerrie's was referring to in her note. She had figured out on her own that it was James who killed her those many years ago and knew he would try and do it again. Yet despite the threat, she risked it all, tempted fate and willingly put her life in danger to be with the man she loved.

"Go on," shouted James, impatient with the delay. He clearly didn't have a clue what was going on.

"There's no need to continue." said Andy, closing the cover. "I know what she was trying to convey and doubt very much that you'd understand."

"Try me." said James, releasing the gun's safety with a loud click.

"If it is your intention to kill me, just be quick about it. I have no fear of death," said Andy, still appearing to be quite calm. "On the contrary, knowing what I know now, I'm rather looking forward to it."

At first, Andy's comment caught James off guard. How could anyone in their right mind want to die? But after giving the matter a moment's thought, he began to understand what Andy meant.

"I don't believe in any of that afterlife reincarnation crap," said James, lowering the pistol, "but I'm not stupid enough to discount the possibility, so on the off chance there really is something to it, I'm not going to be the one to deliver you to Kerrie"

"Then I'll have to do it myself, won't I?" said Andy, suddenly reaching for the gun.

"You're bluffing." yelled James, pulling his hand away.

"Am I?" asked Andy, still eyeing the gun. "If you thought for one minute there was the slightest chance you could reunite with Kerrie on the other side, you'd kill yourself right now, wouldn't you?"

"Of course, I would," said James. Then, looking as though he was thinking it over for a moment, he added, "but there is no other side. There is no heaven, no hell, no God and Kerrie is dead. I DIDN'T MEAN TO DO IT BUT I KILLED HER AND SHE'S DEAD!" he wailed, collapsing to the ground into a fetal position and muttering incoherently to himself.

Andy could easily see that James had finally snapped and in his current state of mind, James could be of no harm to anyone but himself.

As he rocked back and forth in the sand repeating Kerrie's name over and over again, Andy gingerly reached out and was able to take hold of the gun with no resistance, but just as he was about pull it away, James' other hand clamped down on his wrist like a vice.

"No, I won't let you go see Kerrie," he said, sounding like a petulant child. "It's me she wants, not you. She told me so last night. I bet you didn't know she talks to me every night, did you?

She comes to me when I go to bed, kisses me on the forehead and tells me she loves me."

Knowing it was useless to allow James to continue to ramble, Andy yanked his wrist out of James' grip. The gun fell to the ground and both men rolled in the sand struggling for possession. Suddenly several shots rang out.

Meg was on her way to surprise Andy when she heard the gunshots. Fearing the worst, she dropped the picnic basket, she ran towards the sound. As she got closer to the scene, she could just make out what looked like two bodies lying motionless side by side.

Her first instinct was to run and get help but it was a long way back to the hotel and there was no time lose because she knew in her heart that one of those men on the beach was Andy.

She felt as though she was running in quicksand as she rushed towards them, and ran straight to Andy. He was lying on his stomach with no visible wounds but it didn't look like he was breathing. She was afraid to roll him over, so she reached for his wrist to try and take his pulse. At first it was very faint, and then it stopped completely, but not before he managed to open his eyes. He looked straight at Meg and began to whisper something. She couldn't hear him so she put her ear down to his mouth. A moment later, she was in tears as she pulled herself away. Andy was gone.

Cradling his lifeless body in her arms, Meg was so overcome with grief that she didn't even bother to look over at James and was startled when she heard him call out to her.

"I bet you didn't shed any tears for me when I walked out on you," he taunted. "And he's not really dead, you know. It's all playacting because he wants to scare me into thinking that he's with Kerrie now, but I know better," he snickered. "No, Andy The Great is not dead, but I will soon be," he said, putting the gun to his head. "He can spend the rest of his life eating his heart out knowing she'll be with me instead."

Meg was hearing words come out of James' mouth but didn't understand anything he was saying. All she knew was that she couldn't allow James to kill himself because she wanted him to stand trial for Kerrie and Andy's murders. She lunged for the gun, but James was too fast and she watched helplessly as he gleefully

251

pulled the trigger, but instead of a shot ringing out, all she heard was a dull click.

Thinking the gun misfired, James pulled the trigger again and again, but the gun was empty.

"Well, never mind," he said calmly, acting as though he didn't have a care in the world. "As long as Andy is still alive, that's all that matters."

Meg looked up at James and smiled. "Oh, but he's not," she said in an equally unruffled voice. "See for yourself." She backed away from Andy's lifeless body.

As he crawled over to investigate, Meg was able to see that James had also been shot. Blood was oozing from his right shoulder, and his right arm just above the elbow. He appeared to be losing a great deal of blood, but wasn't acting as though his wounds were serious as he rolled Andy onto his back and put his ear to the actor's chest to listen for a heartbeat.

"Now do you believe me?" she asked defiantly. "Andy's with Kerrie and there's nothing you can do about it. What's more, you made it happen."

"You think so, do you?" he said, grinning from ear to ear. "I've got plenty of ammunition left and it won't be long before I join them."

"I don't think so," said a loud voice behind him. Meg had seen the police officer break out of the crowd that had gathered nearby once the shots rang out. "It's going to be a long time before you see anyone, lad," the man continued. "It looks to me like you're going to jail for a very long time."

"I didn't kill him!" yelled James as the officer grabbed him by the arm and pulled him to his feet. "It was self-defense."

"And was it also self-defense when you murdered Kerrie Sherman?" screamed Meg, as the police officer handcuffed James.

"Kerrie Sherman?" the officer asked, doing a double take. "Is this the bloke that murdered that poor young woman in the States not long ago?"

"Yes, it is, and he's the one who attempted to kill Andy Dickinson several months ago in that freeway shooting, and now he's finally succeeded killing Andy," said Meg, pointing to Andy's lifeless body.

"Blimey! That is Andy Dickinson, ain't it?" he asked, walking over to get a closer look. "Lord have mercy on his soul."

"Judging by what he said to me with his last few breaths, I'm sure he already has," said Meg as she looked down at the serene expression on Andy's face.

What he had whispered in her ear just before he passed, was, "Read my will. Please honor my request."

A few days later, Andy was laid to rest in a private service.

He was the one who had paid for Kerrie's burial, but nobody, other than the cemetery, knew that he had actually bought a double plot so that when the time came, he could be buried next to Kerrie. Aside from their names and their dates of birth and death on the tombstone, the inscription was simple:

In life after life, age after age. Forever.

ABOUT THE AUTHOR

Marla Brooks is an author and a practicing witch. She is the creator of The Witch's Oracle Deck, and several books including The Ghosts of Hollywood Series, and two spell books. She is also the host of "Stirring The Cauldron" on the Para X Radio Network.

Other titles from Haunted Road Media:

Almost everyone has a ghost story. Real people. Real stories.

In this third volume, read about more haunted houses, supernatural creatures, messages from pets from the other side, haunted history, experiences during paranormal investigations, psychic experiences, and more, including a dedicated section to the historic Mineral Springs Hotel. ENCOUNTERS WITH THE PARANORMAL: VOLUME 3 reveals more personal stories of the supernatural and paranormal, continuing to explore the realm beyond the veil through its contributors.

For more information visit:
www.hauntedroadmedia.com

www.ingramcontent.com/pod-product-compliance
Lightning Source LLC
Chambersburg PA
CBHW070343260626
47160CB00003B/1129